EVERYBODY SHRUGGED

EVERYBODY SHRUGGED

Walt Pilcher

First Published 2017 by Fantastic Books Publishing

Cover design by Christian Bentulan

ISBN (eBook): 978-1-912053-56-8
ISBN (paperback): 978-1-912053-57-5

PRAISE FOR *EVERYBODY SHRUGGED*

Everybody Shrugged is a high concept comic novel in a style reminiscent of the best of James Thurber, Dave Barry and early Woody Allen, with a touch of Saturday Night Live, Monty Python and the spirit of a multitude of *New Yorker* cartoons thrown in for good measure. What more can we say? It's pretty good.

Bupkis Reviews

In a deft and entertaining finessing of a classic macroeconomic conundrum, *Everybody Shrugged* describes the perfect national government policy: one that deprives us of both guns *and* butter.

Harmful Substance World

Pilcher triumphs in a prescient display of objective socio-political analysis. Glad we're not living in such a time.

Craig and Angie Lister

Learn how to perform a simple home rat test for harmful substances and how to protect yourself from dangerous everyday chemicals and ultraviolet rays with no more than galoshes, a muumuu, cheap sunglasses, and a wide-brimmed hat.

Durango Falcone

Close, but not exactly what Rachel Carson had in mind?

Book City Reviews

Yet another stirring tale written with the pen of a master storyteller, which Mr. Pilcher purchased on eBay from the estate of a famous author.

Winnovation Magazine

Pretty much exactly what Ayn Rand had in mind?

Book Country Reviews

Everybody Shrugged heralds new life for old landfills.

Lisa Condo, CEO,
Al's Superior Oil and Juice Mining Company

No harmful substances were abused in the writing or publishing of this book.

Fantastic Books Publishing

Are you kidding?

The Surgeon General

DEDICATION

This book is dedicated to my once long- but I hope no longer-suffering family – my beautiful, wise and talented wife, Carol, and our equally beautiful, wise, talented and now grown children, Todd Pilcher, Jennifer Schneier and Carolyn McAllister – because of my neglect of all of them during the initial drafting of this book which began some years ago. I don't include our dog, the late Heidi Barker, to whom I would only rarely have paid much attention anyway.

This is not an autobiographical book, so there is no point in asking me, "Do you see yourself or any of your family members in the character of (name a character)?" No, I don't, emphatically. In the first place, as you will see, none of the characters in this book is capable of writing a book (a flawed doctoral thesis maybe in the case of two of them, but not a book), but I believe my family members, all of them, are utterly so capable, whether they ever choose to write one or not.

Carol is an artist, and a darn good one. Todd and Jennifer are lawyers, and darn good ones. Carolyn manages her husband's dental practice, and she does it darn well. Each with his or her brilliant spouse is raising two of our six wonderful grandchildren. So everybody turned out okay in spite of my neglect (assuming you have no problem with lawyers and dentists – and why on earth would you?) but all credit goes to

Carol. In a *New Yorker* cartoon by Robert Weber, a middle-aged man running out the door with golf clubs in tow thanks his harried wife for the wonderful job she did raising the children. That says it well, using golf instead of writing as the irresponsible preoccupation in question. The irony, of course, is that now Carol plays golf when she's not painting, and I usually make my own lunch.

That's fair.

ACKNOWLEDGEMENTS

My thanks to Dan Grubb and his merry band at Fantastic Books Publishing for believing in me, first by publishing a short story and a poem of mine, then publishing my collection of stories and poems called *On Shallowed Ground, including Dr. Barker's Scientific Metamorphical Prostate Health Formula® and other Stories, Poems, Comedy and Dark Matter from the Center of the Universe*, and now by sticking their necks out yet again to publish *Everybody Shrugged*. Not everyone "gets" my stuff, but apparently they do at FBP, and now you have another opportunity to do so as well. For that, I'm very grateful.

Smoke

A mirror on a wall in DC's White House,
the Looking Glass from Oxford's Christ Church hall:
Both see the world around for good and all,
yet comprehend no more than does a church mouse
which scenes reflected there are false or real
or slyly sprung from vain imaginations
going forth to seal the fate of men and nations,
throwing over common sense for guise and feel.
No matter how each episode's rehearsed,
how sleight the hand for mixing fact with fiction,
the mirror tells its tale of contradiction
that's never upside down but is reversed.
Such insight is a warning for us all,
exposing pride that goes before a fall.

Reprinted from *On Shallowed Ground*
Walt Pilcher, Fantastic Books © 2015

PROLOGUE

June 1977, The Pentagon, Arlington, Virginia

Today the old dogs of war would launch the DEATHCOM strategy they had been planning ever since Congress banned all the military's weapons.

Major General Atlee T. Hunsucker rested his heavy attaché case on the dusty concrete floor and cleared his throat to alert the soldier dozing at the guard desk, a copy of *Rolling Stone* open upside down on his chest.

"Oh, it's you," said the soldier sleepily. He put down the magazine and shuffled over to unlock the security gate.

"Thank you, young man." Hunsucker picked up the attaché case, shifting an unlit cigar from one corner of his mouth to the other.

"No problemo."

With a weary sigh, the old man stepped through and made his way down an empty corridor to the familiar door to the secret sub-basement Pentagon conference room.

He pulled a plastic card from his wallet and looked furtively up and down the corridor. Then he slipped the card into a slot next to the door and stepped back. The door swung open. Cigar smoke billowed out. He retrieved the card, stared at it for a second, shrugged, and put it back in his wallet. He

1

stepped into the room, and the heavy door swung shut behind him.

"Good morning, Atlee," said a deep voice. "On time as usual."

"Morning, gentlemen."

Hunsucker wasn't sure who had spoken. As his eyes adjusted, he could see the long conference table and the brown leather chairs around it, empty except for two. These were occupied by Lieutenant General Victor Gotham and his twin brother, Lieutenant General Oscar Gotham. Their identical cigars, similar corpulence, and shared wrinkles of advanced age made it difficult to tell them apart. In the smoke-filled room it was impossible unless one knew, as Hunsucker did, that Victor always sat at Oscar's right, the military position of honor. Although Oscar was the elder twin, having been born thirteen minutes ahead of his brother, Victor was the senior officer by date of rank, having received his third star one day before Oscar, a situation Oscar had never fully accepted.

Hunsucker took a seat to Oscar Gotham's left and lit his own cigar. There was a loud pounding on the door, followed by shouting.

"Can you hear me in there? Hey!" More pounding. "I can't get in!"

Hunsucker went back to the door. "Is that you, Homer?" he shouted.

"Yeah! Listen, I forgot my stupid ID card. Can you let me in?"

"The time lock won't let the door open from the inside until the meeting is scheduled to be over!"

"That's just great. Now what am I supposed to do?"

"Hold on a minute." Hunsucker pulled out his MasterCard and slid it under the door. "Here, try this!"

"What in the Sam Hill is this?"

"Just try it."

After a moment, the door swung open, revealing the tall but wizened figure of Brigadier General Homer Vandall. He entered without removing his aviator-style sunglasses, handed Hunsucker the card with a slight shrug, nodded to the Gotham brothers, and took a seat near the foot of the table. He lit a large cigar.

Hunsucker took his own seat again and turned his eyes toward Victor Gotham, who was ready to begin.

Gotham stood up slowly and began to speak, heedless of the brown tobacco juice dribbling from his lips on to his green Class A uniform jacket.

"Did you all receive your copies of the plan?"

"Yes," said Oscar Gotham.

"Yes," said Vandall.

"I didn't get mine yet, sir," said Hunsucker.

"Crap!" said Victor. "I even typed it and ran the copies myself, to keep it confidential, and I hand-carried it to your office."

"Then I'm sure it's there, but since my secretary only comes on Tuesdays, she probably hasn't gotten to it yet. If you like, I could go look for it. No, wait, the door is locked."

"Never mind. I was planning to read it aloud anyway. It's just that I was sort of proud of the way it turned out."

"It was excellent," said Oscar, "although there are one or two little things I might have expressed differently."

"Yes, it was quite good," said Vandall.

"Thank you, gentlemen, thank you. Now, let's go through it. Atlee, why don't you look on with Homer there?"

"No need," said Vandall. "I've committed it to memory." He took the plan out of his breast pocket and shoved it across the table to Hunsucker.

"It's got coffee stains on it, Homer."

"I wouldn't complain. That's a luxury we're not going to have much longer. Or these cigars either."

With that, Lieutenant General Victor Gotham read the first page of the summary.

TOP SECRET   TOP SECRET

MISSION PLAN, SUMMARY OF, AND ORDER

Debilitations Extreme and Afflictions Tenacious and Hopeless

Command (DEATHCOM), The Pentagon, Washington, DC

SITUATION ESTIMATE

Under environmentalist pressures, Congress is funding private sector groups to augment the Environmental Protection Agency's massive efforts to identify all possible harmful substances and recommend legislation to restrict or tax their use. A broad range of common substances are now deemed hazardous to health, including tobacco, caffeine, butterfat, many chemical food additives, marijuana, hexachlorophene, most cosmetics, exhaust emissions, and fluorocarbons. Many more will be added.

The Defense budget has been cut and the Military stripped of weapons because war is characterized by harmful substances. While the Enemy continues to stockpile, America is selling its nuclear inventories to countries like Honduras and Peru to "spread the burden of hemisphere defense." The manufacture of conventional weapons is prohibited. Training is curtailed, and soldiers have almost nothing to do.

"You might have added one thing," said Vandall. "We can't even *look* military anymore since they say the starch in our fatigue uniforms causes cancer in rats. Droopy, wrinkled fatigues … very bad for morale."

Gotham turned the page and continued.

DEATHCOM MISSION, THE

We, the officers of DEATHCOM, accept our sworn duty to national defense regardless of limitations imposed by Congress. We will support, at any cost, the Mutually Assured Destruction (MAD) doctrine because a strong arsenal known to the Enemy is the best deterrent to aggression.

STRATEGY

Using substances Congress deems harmful, DEATHCOM will create chemical and biological weapons of types designed to skirt existing international bans and will stockpile them in sufficient quantity for a "first strike" capability to blanket any or all aggressors with said harmful substances and with enough in reserve for a potential counter-retaliatory strike.

The said arsenal will be prepared in secret, to be revealed to the Enemy only when necessary as a last resort to prevent war. It will be kept secret even from the Commander-in-Chief, the President of the United States, in order that his position not be compromised (plausible deniability) during the preparation phases.

By covert manipulation of computers handling Army administrative tasks, DEATHCOM will create the clandestine Mundane Ammunition Dump Command (MADCOM), taking control of geographically dispersed abandoned Army ammunition dumps where the weaponizing will be conducted and the weapons then stockpiled underground. MADCOM will be headquartered at Camp Robert Horatio Shafto near Omaha, Nebraska.

Oscar Gotham listened spellbound to his brother's words, neither of them noticing that the long ash from Victor's cigar had fallen on to Oscar's head. When Victor paused again to catch his breath and turn the page, Oscar rose, the ash toppling unnoticed to the seat of his chair.

"Would you like me to read the rest of it for you, Victor?"

"Yes, thank you," said Victor, slumping back into his chair. "My eyes aren't what they used to be."

"Not to mention all the smoke in here," said Vandall.

"We may be old," said Hunsucker gruffly, "but we're not ready to fade away!" Every time he remembered that officially all of them were retired and no longer had any actual authority, it made him angry. It wasn't right.

When Congress cut defense spending, hundreds of thousands of military jobs were eliminated, and most military posts were closed. The Pentagon itself, once the symbol of the Free World's military might, was now practically deserted, with many windows broken and boarded up, burned out light bulbs not replaced, and only a skeleton crew of security, maintenance, and clerical personnel to support what little official business had to be conducted. Most of the highest-ranking officers had been summarily retired, but some, like this group, had been allowed to keep their offices while they looked for jobs in consulting or real estate or otherwise tried to figure out how to start lonely new lives after thirty or forty years of commanding divisions of troops and millions of dollars in equipment.

Retirement so younger officers could carry on the mission of national defense was one thing. Abandoning the mission entirely was clearly another and completely out of the question.

But this could be prevented, and there could be a return to days of former glory, by men with the courage, fortitude and patriotism necessary to keep on with that mission.

The reading finished, Oscar Gotham sat down, grinding the still unnoticed ash into the fabric of his trousers.

"Well, gentlemen, what do you think?"

"It's exactly what we agreed to, Victor," said Hunsucker.

"Yes, it is," said Vandall. "I just wish we could speed up the timetable and let the Commies know we mean business."

"Let's get on with it then. The plan is approved."

"May I have the honor of signing first, Victor?" asked Oscar. There were signature blocks for Victor as commander and for each of the other generals in turn.

"Well, all right, but we'll use my pen."

The document made its way around the table. As each general signed, the others applauded solemnly. Then they all lit fresh cigars.

They sat puffing contentedly for a moment before Victor Gotham spoke again.

"The next order of business is the selection of a commanding officer for MADCOM. Atlee, you've been going over the computer printouts. What do you have for us?"

General Hunsucker opened his attaché case and took out a thick manila envelope. He extracted a photograph and set it before the group.

"His name is Farina," said Hunsucker, "Second Lieutenant Henry

Anthony Farina. His friends call him Tony. He's currently assigned to Fort Lewis, Washington, as Club Officer. I think he's our man."

The face in the picture was a handsome one, dark and mature looking in spite of its youthfulness. It was one of those faces that is intensely attractive to women but at the same time immediately commands respect from most men.

Though not Vandall who said, "He's just a kid."

"Yes, but he has potential," said Oscar Gotham.

"He does look a bit lean and hungry, doesn't he?" said Victor Gotham. "But you can't tell much from a picture. What do we know about him, Atlee?"

"Quite a lot. We have his military records, of course, along with the background information he provided when he enlisted. Plus, after the computer singled him out I talked the CIA into doing a special investigation for me."

"How did you get them to do that?" asked Oscar Gotham.

"I simply told them I thought he might be planning to write a book exposing the CIA. They were very thorough."

Hunsucker took out some more papers.

"Let's see here … early years … yes, here we are. Born and raised near Disneyland in California. Father abandoned the family when little Tony was five. Personality profile: aggressive, impulsive, impatient; live life for the fun of it, and do it your own way. Above average intelligence, but failed eleventh grade, apparently because there were more interesting things to do. Often truant during hunting season. Once missing for two weeks after somebody blew up the plumbing in the public library by flushing dry ice down a toilet, but nothing ever proven. Uh, let's see ... at age 15 hitchhiked here to Washington just to see a Fourth of July fireworks display at the Washington Monument."

"Very entertaining," said Vandall. "But what about his service record?"

"That's where it gets more interesting. It says here, 'Life was a lark for Farina until he received his first real scare when he was allegedly involved in a cherry bomb accident in which his girlfriend's parents were killed. Although no charges were filed, he panicked, dropped out of college, left town, and joined the Army.'

"'In Basic Training he demonstrated outstanding proficiency at bayonet drill and grenade throwing. He was assigned to combat duty in Viet Nam.'"

The other generals were listening more attentively now.

"From here on, it gets confusing, and this is where the CIA was very helpful. Let me quote from their confidential report."

Hunsucker picked up another sheet of paper and began to read again.

After only a week in-country, PFC Farina's platoon were dropped near the village of Cao Dung where they were mistakenly ambushed by a squad of ARVN recruits on a training exercise. They were pinned down between hostile friendly fire to the front and a terrified skunk to the rear. The platoon leader was wounded and the radio disabled.

PFC Farina took command and ordered a frontal assault. He fired rifle grenades in the direction of the ARVN troops but hit no one. Disregarding his own safety he fixed his bayonet and singlehandedly attacked in the direction of the friendlies, thinking they were the enemy, not knowing they had fallen back. When it was over, 14 water buffalo, 27 chickens, six pigs, and the skunk lay dead. The Army covered up the incident by calling Farina a hero and promoting him to second lieutenant.

They all puffed in silence for a moment before Victor Gotham spoke up.

"Now that you mention it, I think I do remember reading about The Battle of Cao Dung in *Newsweek*. It pretty much ruined the local economy for a while, but at least the villagers ate quite well for a couple of months first."

"Farina certainly demonstrated courage under fire. He didn't run away," said Oscar Gotham.

"And it looks like he made good use of his training," said Hunsucker.

"The kid sure has a fascination for things that blow up," said Vandall. "Oscar, what would they call that in the world of psychoanalysis?"

"How about 'a fascination for things that blow up'? How on earth should I know?"

"Well I think he's either a loose cannon or he's perfect, I'm not sure which. But maybe we can use him after all," said Vandall.

"He looks good enough, Atlee," said Victor Gotham, effectively ending the debate.

"Thank you, sir. And he's available, too. The Fort Lewis assignment was meant to be a placeholder until they figured something out for him, and he's behaved himself, but he's been there a long time, and since they've closed the Officers' Club he's had nothing to do."

"The war's been over for two years. He must be the oldest second lieutenant in the Army by now," said Vandall.

"Yes, and no doubt restless," answered Hunsucker. "They're just waiting for him to get into trouble, but they can't retire him without creating a public relations problem. What we have will fit his talents perfectly, given the right indoctrination and training."

"All right, Atlee, thank you very much. Oscar, see to it that orders are cut promoting Second Lieutenant Tony Farina to first lieutenant and transferring him to the Pentagon immediately."

"Certainly, Victor. Homer, would you take care of that, please?"

"Right away."

"Excellent," said Victor Gotham. "Gentlemen, I'd say this meeting can be adjourned."

"It won't do us much good," said Hunsucker, glancing at his watch. "That stupid door isn't scheduled to open for another forty-five minutes."

CHAPTER ONE

April 1981, Camp Robert Horatio Shafto, Nebraska.

By 0730 hours the sun had burned away the haze of a foggy dawn, and the soldiers at Camp Shafto, the Army ammunition dump a few miles outside of Omaha, were reporting to their duty stations. Major Tony Farina, the commanding officer, was still in his BOQ, wiping the last traces of shaving cream from his face with an olive drab towel. He glanced through the night messages a second time and tossed them disgustedly back on a desk.

"Nothing but scattered reports," he mused. "A police station bombed in Detroit, a couple of IRS offices ransacked here and there, marchers at the White House … just doesn't add up to much. I wish somebody would analyze this stuff before it's brought to me."

SP4 Jenkins, the major's orderly and driver, stuck his head into the little room.

"Captain Leon is here, sir."

"Good. Send him in."

Captain Leon was the Executive Officer and second in command to Farina. He strode in and headed straight for the messages on the desk.

"Morning, sir. What's the news on this day of days, eh?"

"I wish I knew what to make of it, Iggy. Be right with you."
Major Farina stepped into the latrine and closed the door.

He had dressed only as far as his combat boots, fatigue pants,
and olive drab tee shirt. He combed his shiny black hair and regarded himself in the mirror. The comb slipped out of his hand,
but he caught it between his thigh and the wash basin. Was it
nervousness, or just too much hair tonic? He mused some
more.

"Must be the thrill of the chase, that's all. Can't afford to get
nerves. Plenty of time for a situation estimate before we have to
make any moves."

After almost four years of preparation there was no point in
rushing into a mistake now.

The Pentagon years had been the toughest, but at least he had
gotten three promotions out of the experience, and now he was
a field grade officer with an impressive title: Commanding Officer, Mundane Ammunition Dump Command (MADCOM).

By outward appearances it wasn't such an impressive assignment, but the command was large, with far-flung dumps all over
the country, and Major Farina had enjoyed the time it had taken
to build it. By cultivating the personal loyalty of his officers and
men and putting them through rigorous training, Farina had
managed to enlarge, shape, and develop his command to the
point where it was now almost ready to become the instrument
of its designers in Washington.

Almost, but maybe not quite. How long would it take? A

month? Another year? Major Farina pondered these questions as he slipped the comb into his pocket, strode back to the bedroom, and put on his fatigue shirt.

"Well, Iggy, what do you think?"

"Sure doesn't add up to much right now," said Captain Leon with a shrug. "Since this is the day more of the new harmful substance laws go into effect, I would have expected a lot more trouble. I see most of the incidents took place in industrial areas, but even that isn't much to go on, is it?"

"No, and that's just the point. If that's all the action there's going to be, it'll be pretty risky to make our move when we're ready. On the other hand, if it snowballs it could reach a peak before we're ready. We'll just have to sit tight for a while and see if any kind of a trend seems to be developing."

"Yeah, you're right." Captain Leon had wanted to say the same thing himself but somehow hadn't been able to sense the proper time for interjecting it into the conversation. This only added to the immense respect he already had for his commanding officer.

Farina continued. "Iggy, call a staff meeting for ten hundred hours in my office."

"Okay, I'll pass the word."

"I'll want everyone prepared for a complete review of our situation. Also, I want hourly news reports brought directly to me all day, no matter where I am."

"Got it!"

"Okay, I'll see you at the meeting. Right now, I'm going to have a cup of decaf and a couple of hard boiled eggs here while I make some notes, and then I have to go over to the S-1 shop to give a re-enlistment speech."

Captain Leon saluted his friend with mock formality and left.

After his breakfast, Farina donned a helmet liner and strode outside. SP4 Jenkins, who had been dozing against the side of the building, snapped to attention and saluted smartly. He extended an arm in the direction of a shiny, olive drab bicycle parked at the curb. Attached to the bicycle was a spartan sidecar, and stenciled on each of three narrow fenders was a white, five-pointed star in a circle and the legend, "U.S. ARMY T.P. 40." On the handlebars, next to a generator-operated headlight, was a placard with the familiar white letter "0" on a blue field. An Officer's Bike.

"Where's the jeep?" asked Farina, annoyed, as he returned the salute.

"It's against the law now, sir, like almost everything else with an internal combustion engine, but the Motor Pool's issuing these until the steam jeeps get here."

"Well, nuts!"

One of Major Farina's first orders upon arriving at Camp Shafto was to outlaw the "s" word in honor of his favorite World War II hero, General Anthony McAuliffe who, when his 101st Airborne Division was surrounded by Germans during the Battle of the Bulge, answered the German commander's order to surrender with the single word, "Nuts!" Because he and McAuliffe shared the same first name, Farina liked to think they carried the same fighting spirit as well.

"Nuts is a good four-letter word, and I'm sure you'll have no trouble learning to use it while you're here," Farina was fond of telling the men as often as he needed to. And he tried to practice what he preached.

The two men rode off together on the bike, Jenkins pedaling furiously at first, but slowing down after only about two hundred meters. He lunged and panted pathetically on the little hill going by the Officers Club, until finally Major Farina made him stop.

"I'm okay, sir. Honest. This is only my first day on this thing. I'll be in shape in a week or so . . . Oh jeeze, I think I'm going to throw up."

From their position near the crest of the hill, they could see much of Camp Shafto laid out below them. The official boundary of the military reservation encompassed twenty square miles, providing enough buffer to keep trespassers away. The actual troop and storage area was encircled by two concentric chain link fences topped by electrified barbed wire. The space between the fences was patrolled by sentries carrying old M-1 Garand rifles with contraband ammunition. At the one entrance gate, two MPs were always posted, checking both incoming and outgoing traffic and refusing admittance to those without special clearances or orders from Major Farina. Traffic was light.

All the buildings within the dump were the "temporary" wooden type of World War II vintage except for the combination PX and Post Office, which was of brick. The layout of the camp was simple. Three hundred meters from the gate was a small, square parade ground. East of that was a baseball diamond. To the south were the PX/Post Office, library, Quartermaster Laundry, dispensary, barber shop, canteen, and sundry other concessions. To the north were the quarters of the senior NCOs. (No quarters for wives and families were authorized for MAD installations, and there were no women in the dump at all, nor anywhere in MADCOM for that matter. There would be no hanky-panky on Farina's watch, and nuts to any women's libbers who might have a problem with it.) To the west but facing the sunrise stood the Command Post, or headquarters building, flanked on both sides by smaller buildings housing the various staff sections, or "shops" in Army idiom, for administration, operations, training, intelligence, and supply. A tall flag pole stood in front of headquarters with Old Glory flying from the top.

Next to the flag pole was a Civil War cannon from which, in years past, blank charges had been fired each day during the Retreat ceremony at seventeen hundred hours. The cannon had been donated to Camp Shafto by an American Legion post in Alabama.

One night, shortly before Major Farina arrived to assume command, some young soldiers full of 3.2 beer loaded the old weapon with real grapeshot they had stolen from an antique store near the city. It was oversize, but still they managed to force it deep into the barrel along with a liberal quantity of blasting powder. They wrenched the cannon around to the left and aimed it in the general direction of the Officers' Club before dropping a match into the firing hole and running like crazy. Nothing happened after about a minute and a half, so one of the men who had more of a snoot full than the others crept up to the cannon to investigate. After a few minutes of poking around it in the dark, he staggered back to the barracks to sleep it off.

Later that night, patrolling MPs noticed the cannon had been moved, so they returned it to its original position. When the miscreants awoke the next day they could hardly believe their eyes at the sight of the old cannon, apparently undisturbed. Vastly relieved, they shrugged off the incident as nothing more than an alcoholic hallucination.

That evening, as the honor guard and bugler approached for the Retreat ceremony, the cannon went off with a roar that was heard for ten miles. Not only did the guilty boys wet their pants right then and there, but also the shot demolished a general store on Highway 75, and the cannon itself was heaved backward into the headquarters building, causing heavy damage, but no injuries. Miraculously, the gun itself was unscathed.

A formation of all personnel was called immediately. As

everyone stood at attention, MPs slowly walked up and down between the ranks, arresting anyone whose pants were wet.

When Major Farina took over, he had the cannon plugged permanently. After that, the sounds of Retreat were heard on a loudspeaker operated by a cassette tape player locked in the Adjutant's desk.

Barracks for the enlisted men were lined up in several rows behind the headquarters building. There were accommodations for over 2,000 men, yet in the daytime the camp appeared almost deserted. This was because most of the work was going on underground, and those whose duty hours were at night slept in the daytime. Farina worked the men hard, but kept them imbued with his own intense enthusiasm for the mission. They felt they were accomplishing something important, and morale was sky high in spite of the fact that, as one waggish corporal was fond of remarking, everyone was literally "down in the dumps."

Beyond the barracks was the Motor Pool, and beyond the Motor Pool were several acres of what appeared to be Indian mounds. These were the sunken storage rooms for live ammunition, made of iron and dense concrete and covered with a thick layer of earth. Most were empty and locked tightly, at least officially. Unknown even to Farina, one of the rooms was being used by a cartel of senior NCOs to run a wine making operation which was immensely profitable. They put the stuff up in empty beer bottles they fished out of the Dempster-Dumpsters behind the NCOs' and Officers' Clubs by the caseload. A promising experiment was now underway to make the wine out of sugar beets. Beets were more easily obtainable in the Omaha area than grapes, and they were afraid Major Farina might be getting suspicious of all the grape vines climbing over the inner electrified chain link perimeter fence. Furthermore, harvesting the grapes could be dangerous in wet weather.

In another storage room, an enterprising corporal named Borgia was cultivating mushrooms. Lacking any training in this art, he had borrowed a mushroom and fungus reference book from the post library. Every Saturday he went to a forest a few miles from the post and hunted for wild mushrooms that appeared to match the pictures of edible varieties in the book. Taking samples back to his secret storage room, he nurtured the promising ones until they were ready to be tested. The test was a simple one. Borgia would take a handful of chopped mushrooms to the PX canteen and secretly sprinkle them on some other soldier's pizza. If the test mushrooms were harmless, Borgia's plan was to cultivate more of the same kind, pack them in old jelly jars, and take them out to be sold to tourists at gas stations along Interstate 80 under the mimeographed label: "Borgia's Best Buttons – Native Nebraska Mushrooms at Popular Prices." If not, the soldier got sick, and Borgia knew he had to keep looking. So far, six varieties had been tested, and not one proved acceptable. Meanwhile, the pizza was getting a bad reputation, making the tests difficult to carry out. Corporal

Borgia was considering packing up a few hundred jars of some promising variety without bothering to test, just to get his business off the ground.

Major Farina was aware of this particular clandestine activity, but he took no action except to avoid ordering pizza at the canteen. One way or another, Borgia might yet prove useful.

As at all Army posts, the soil of Camp Shafto was sandy and only sparsely covered with short, wiry grass – the kind of grass for which all drill sergeants develop a deep, personal fondness. Farina not-so-fondly remembered from Basic Training being the victim of an unwritten Army regulation specifying the exact manner in which a drill sergeant must approach a recruit, clench his fists at his sides, stand rigidly pouting, and cry, "That's *my* grass! You stepped on *my* grass!" He thought he had read somewhere that as one of the works programs of the 1930's the Roosevelt Administration had the War Department engage private contractors to haul enormous quantities of sand from eastern North and South Carolina and Georgia to Army posts all over the country. In the military, uniformity has always been important.

There wasn't a single tree in the camp.

Major Farina got out of the sidecar and helped Jenkins push the bike the rest of the way up the little hill. Then they both remounted and coasted the distance to the headquarters area, giving Jenkins a rest.

"I'll get off here, Jenkins. After the re-enlistment speech, I've got a staff meeting in my office, so you can meet me there at chow time."

"Yes, sir," said Jenkins, saluting.

Farina returned the salute, did an about-face, and strode off toward the small building housing the administrative section, or the S-1 in military parlance. At the door there was a full length mirror with a sign saying, "Dress Right, Soldier!" Major Farina paused at the mirror to check his gig line and adjust his helmet liner one more time. It was exactly zero nine hundred hours—time to put aside thoughts of the critical decisions needing to be made and focus on this moment. He strode inside and stood at the door of a small assembly room full of men eager to be inspired by their revered commanding officer.

CHAPTER TWO

April 1981, Leland F. P. Mason Wesley, Jr., University, California

The latest restrictions would go into effect at noon California time, and Dr. Gardiner Mellors Lavager, BS, MS, Ph.D., was pleased. It did mean some inconvenience, but it represented years of dreams and hard work continuing to pay off. Already, all internal combustion engines were outlawed for surface transportation. All tobacco products had been banned, along with anything containing caffeine. Soon monosodium glutamate would be forbidden, as well as bacon and hot dogs. The list was long and, happily, getting longer.

True, the bills to outlaw artificial sweeteners, alcohol, and scratch 'n' sniff ads and requiring everyone to wear hats while out in the sun were still hung up in committee, but they would come, they would come. After all, Lavager recalled with satisfaction, at one time the paper dye bills had also looked doomed. Nevertheless, after today, no nose would be blown nor toilet flushed with anything but white tissue, except maybe by those few diehards who had begun hoarding the bad stuff when it looked like the President would sign the ban into law. High school gyms would be festooned with white crepe paper for every big dance, and cheerleaders would be every bit as vivacious with white pom-poms as they had ever been with the old ones of red, blue, maroon, and every other polluting color under the sun.

Of course, there was always a minority who didn't appreciate what was being done for them, he reflected. A peaceful protest demonstration or two, that was to be expected. And even the bombing of a police station or an IRS office now and then, while deplorable, were just the birth pangs of a better world. It would pass.

Today, the workmen were putting the finishing touches on the new security devices they had installed at Lavager's laboratory. His lab now resembled a large concrete pillbox, while three weeks ago it had looked like any of a score of other buildings on the Southern California campus of Leland F. P. Mason Wesley, Jr., University, where the predominant architectural style was Spanish and ivy, with graceful arches, colonnades of stucco and, everywhere, red tiled roofs.

Students on bicycles pedaled from class to class, to the dorms, Student Union, or liquor store, most of them oblivious to the important work carried out in this one building. It was set well apart from the nearest other structure, in a natural hollow where in fact it couldn't be seen from the Main Campus unless one climbed up the hallowed old Struthers Memorial Bell Tower.

No one went up there much anymore. Not since they installed the heavy, reinforced glass on the observation deck as a deterrent to suicides. That had been, and still was to some extent, controversial. The student suicide rate had become embarrassing, especially with its little spikes on Parents' Weekend. On the other hand, the glass atrociously muffled the bells, making them sound like somebody was mugging the Good Humor Man.

There was no question where Dr. Lavager stood on the issue. "Noise pollution and suicide amount to the same thing in the long run," he had observed in a letter to the editor of the campus newspaper, *The Masonite*. "So it's not a question of solving one problem and creating another with the glass; it's really solving two problems at once." The next morning someone threw a rock through the windshield of his experimental electric automobile with an anonymous note suggesting he do unto himself that which many believed he was doing unto them.

Shortly after that incident, Dr. Baldwin, the university president, began insisting Dr. Lavager have the security of his lab improved. First it was merely burglar alarms, extra locks, and a little brick fence disguised as a garden wall. But one thing had led to another due to the mounting tension over the new laws, most of which had been recommended to Congress by Dr. Lavager himself. Now the lab building had new walls of dense concrete five feet thick and a new bombproof roof. Security cameras scanned the landscape on the other three sides.

At each corner of the building, hidden by dense bushes, was a machine gun emplacement. Two more camouflaged guns would be located on the roof. The guns hadn't arrived yet but were expected any day. None being available locally, they had been ordered from an Army ammunition dump near Omaha.

All guns would be manned by campus police working four-hour shifts. None of these men had ever pulled the trigger of a machine gun before, but Dr. Baldwin had authorized extended practice sessions at the shooting gallery in the amusement arcade in the Trailways bus station downtown. The training theory made good sense: Shooting into riotous mobs with real machine guns requires far less accuracy than trying to hit a skittering wooden duck with a beam of light from a plastic rifle, knowing your time will be up any second.

The garden wall around the building was now six feet high with only one entrance. Broken glass was embedded in the top of the wall, and barbed wire extended its height another two feet. At this moment, the gardener was planting poison ivy vines on both sides.

Inside the lab, still in the protective hi-top galoshes he wore rain or shine, Dr. Lavager sank into an armchair which was almost obscured by piles of books, papers, and overstuffed manila folders. Now with more fruit of his labors about to be borne in just a few hours, he allowed himself a rare moment of relaxation and meditation.

After all, Lavager carried a heavy responsibility as unofficial head of the American Eco-Toxicology Association, recipient of over 75% of the Government's harmful substances research money.

A frequent visitor to Washington as an Association representative, Lavager was recognized by legislators, the EPA, the Surgeon General, the Consumer Product Safety Commission, and professional colleagues alike for his intense dedication to the task of identifying harmful substances, his brilliant research work, the logic and clarity of the restrictive legislation he and his associates drafted, and for his utter disregard for the mounting uneasiness of the public over most of the laws he proposed.

Much publicity was given to his work, but fame was shunned by Lavager himself. He had reluctantly consented to taping an interview for a TV talk show just to please his associates, however, and he was mildly interested in seeing it on the air later this morning.

In private, "Gardy" Lavager wasn't an imposing figure. At 49 and only now approaching the apex of his career, he simply considered himself a late bloomer. Handsome in spite of balding grayish hair, he kept a well-trimmed jet black goatee, enhancing, he felt, his professorial image. Lavager had no vices which might sully his body. For breakfast he ate bran flakes in skim milk. Lunch and dinner were usually frozen free range chicken, potatoes, green vegetables, and filtered or distilled water. No coffee, tea, or carbonated beverages of any kind, except Alka-Seltzer now and then, and nothing fried. He exercised regularly and brushed his teeth with baking soda— no toothpaste with its fluoride or abrasive brighteners—three times a day.

He gazed fondly at his surroundings. The laboratory wasn't

modern looking, but it was one of the best equipped in the country for the kind of research that took place within its walls. It had once been a classroom affording an excellent view of the Bell Tower through an enormous picture window, now filled in with concrete. Opposite the window was a wall-to-wall greenboard. Small sticks of chalk poked out of the yellow dust piled high in the chalk tray, and the greenboard was covered with lists, diagrams, and flow charts. There was no eraser.

Near the middle of the greenboard a doorknob broke the verdant monotony. Via the main corridor, it opened the only door leading to the outside world, the only other door in the lab being the one to the large storage closet behind Dr. Lavager's chair. Lavager had had a toilet and shower installed, moved his cot, a refrigerator, a microwave and a toaster oven from his bachelor apartment in town and had been making the closet—the whole lab, really—his home for the past several months.

Radiant heaters crouched on the floor under the window. In rows facing the greenboard were six large tables, each with a thick, black composition top, gas jets, Bunsen burner, and sink with hot and cold running water. The water faucets would, of course, soon be equipped with the new activated charcoal filters from the IRS.

Two of the tables were covered with racks of test tubes, beakers, hypodermic syringes, notebooks, and other apparatus representing experiments in various stages of completion. Two dozen rat cages were stacked by the window, each with a little bottle of water hanging from the side. On another table was a portable TV, outfitted with the required X-ray filter.

Lavager smiled wryly and slowly got up from the overstuffed chair. The chair sucked air so loudly he barely heard the knocking at the green door.

That will be Letitia, he thought.

Lavager had had a younger brother who was a geologist of some renown. Unfortunately, he and his wife were killed by falling stalactites when a prankster threw cherry bombs into a cavern they were exploring near Knob Lick, Kentucky. The couple were survived by their daughter, Letitia, Dr. Lavager's niece. She was still a minor when her parents died, so Lavager became her guardian.

He opened the door a tiny crack and waited for the usual "Joe sent me" from his niece, their little joke, since it was a green door, if only on the inside. Letitia had planned a small celebration of orange juice and oatmeal cookies in honor of the new laws and to watch the TV interview. She would come early to get things ready. His part-time lab assistant, George Smith, was to show up later.

At the door, silence greeted him. After a puzzled moment, he widened the crack a bit.

"You okay, Doc?"

It was Wong Lee O'Grady.

The little gardener stepped into the room. He carried a vacuum cleaner. Wong Lee stood 5'4" and had a compact build, an almost stereotypical Irish face but with more than a hint of Asian ancestry, and red hair.

"I just come flom stlaighten out you office, Doc. Was a mess."

That was true. The office was a few steps down the corridor, but it was piled so high with papers and just plain junk that the only times Lavager went into it anymore were to answer the telephone or make sure the TV security monitors were working properly. All the records of his research were there, along with files of correspondence with his colleagues in the Association.

"Awso, I find one you elaser ou'side. Now you ret me crean up dis prace a ritto, get leady for big cereblation today, okay?"

"Thanks, Wong Lee. I guess I do tend to let things go a little, don't I?"

Lavager always felt Wong Lee's broken English disguised characteristics that didn't quite fit the Oriental gardener/janitor stereotype. True, Wong Lee was good at his job both outdoors and in, even the more odious tasks such as cleaning out the rat cages from time to time. Beyond that, in the two years since they had met he had seemingly "adopted" Lavager, advising him on little matters of housekeeping, listening as the scientist explored new avenues of thought about potentially harmful substances, and responding with anecdotes about the plants he tended and their reactions to various fertilizers and insecticides. Intelligent as he seemed to be on some occasions, Wong Lee was undoubtedly incapable of understanding the implications of Dr. Lavager's work, so his indulgence of the scientist's ramblings was all that much more appreciated, and the two had become fast friends, though Lavager was ever mindful of the obvious class distinction between them.

Lavager consistently beat Wong Lee at Chinese checkers, while Wong Lee, surprisingly, was a whiz at Scrabble.

"Why don't you stay for the party, too, Wong Lee?"

"Can't stay too wong, Doc. Got to finish pranting poison ivy." He moved around the room with practiced ease, methodically straightening things up. He plugged the vacuum cleaner into an outlet near the greenboard.

"Well, take your time anyway, and stay as long as you like." Lavager ran his finger through the film of dust that had collected on the back of the door and was wiping the finger with his handkerchief when he heard someone else knocking.

"It's me, Uncle Gardy. Joe sent me!" Try as she might, Letitia never could get the hang of giving the password secretively, which would have made it the proper lampoon it was intended to be, but at least she derived some satisfaction out of the joke, and that was the important thing as far as her uncle was concerned.

At 28 and no longer her uncle's official ward, Letitia worked in Dr. Lavager's lab while acting as a surrogate mother/daughter for the celibate scientist, to whom she felt deeply indebted. Letitia was an intelligent and attractive woman but had been traumatized by the death of her parents when she was a teenager. The prankster with the cherry bombs was her boyfriend, frustrated after failing to seduce her in a clump of bushes near the entrance to the cave they were exploring. Embarrassed and upset, she couldn't bring herself to tell the story to the authorities. The boy joined the Army and left town for good, and Letitia withdrew from almost all social activity. Now she doted on her uncle and lived only to assist him in his vital work.

Letitia entered with a bright smile, and she and Lavager embraced lightly.

"Look, Uncle Gardy, I brought orange juice, oatmeal cookies, and plastic cups – 'cause I know you don't like those paper ones with that gooky wax coming off all the time. And here's my portable stereo in case we feel like a little music later on. I brought my Grofé albums and some Buddy Holly and Sha Na Na for George. Oh, this is going to be fun! It'll be good to see you relax for once."

Her favorite musical composition was Ferde Grofé's "Grand Canyon Suite," parts of which she hummed or whistled incessantly. Before the tobacco ban she had chain smoked Philip Morris filters, except when in her uncle's lab. As a substitute for this habit she now went to the local chapter meetings of a women's lib organization faithfully every Wednesday night.

"Oh, Wong Lee," she exclaimed with a giggle, "I didn't see you standing there. I do hope Uncle Gardy has invited you to spend the day with us."

"Yes, Miss Retisha, he did, but I don't know … gotta rotta prants to prant, you know. But you velly kind," said Wong Lee, self-consciously, "so maybe I stay anyway."

"Oh, good," bubbled Letitia. "In fact, I've got something you can help me with."

With that, she picked up a rumpled grocery bag and held it out triumphantly.

"Look, Uncle Gardy, decorations!"

She turned the bag upside down over the armchair, and a half dozen rolls of white crepe paper fell out along with a roll of cellophane tape.

"Come on, Wong Lee, I can hardly wait to put it up!"

"Very thoughtful of you, Letitia," said Dr. Lavager. Then, still holding his handkerchief, he excused himself and went into the storage closet to wash his hands.

Wong Lee and Letitia began hanging the crepe paper. Returning from the closet, Dr. Lavager looked at his watch.

"It's getting late," he murmured. "Say, Letitia, when is George supposed to get here?"

Lavager wasn't particularly interested, but he knew in order to answer, Letitia would have to interrupt her humming for a moment. It wasn't that he didn't like "The Grand Canyon Suite" … he did … but too much of anything was tedious, and quite possibly harmful, though he hadn't yet fully developed that idea into a general hypothesis. Besides, "The Grand Canyon Suite" doesn't sound like much, hummed.

"He should be here any minute now," said Letitia dreamily, hardly missing a beat of the "On the Trail" movement.

Just now, Letitia thought she might be falling in love with

George Smith, but still somehow she couldn't bring herself to let him get too close. Though she had never confided it to anyone, Letitia hadn't even kissed a man since the day her parents died. She didn't plan to have "relations" even when she got married, although she did fully expect to marry someday. To marry someone who would understand. Was it going to be George? Of course, she knew he was attracted to her, but they had never discussed a possible future together.

George was 37. A few years older than Letitia, yes, but she didn't think that was a problem. A child of the 1950's, he had a clean cut All American type outlook, the stuff of nostalgia, and he looked the part as well. The short, flattop haircut with no sideburns was perfect in combination with his light khaki or sometimes black chinos; thin black belt; white, blue or sometimes pink oxford cloth shirt with button down collar; and thin black knit tie. He appeared this way every day, always wearing white socks and either Hush Puppies or Weejuns penny loafers. And the London Fog raincoat he was never without, although it rarely rained in Southern California except in winter, which it currently wasn't.

While those characteristics alone were enough to turn Letitia's head, what she found especially endearing was the sad story he had shared with her over rocky road ice cream sundaes at Baskin-Robbins one evening after a long but productive day in the lab:

George had played basketball in high school. He was tall but not well coordinated, he explained, and the main reason he went out for the team was to move in the company of the popular "jocks" of the school. Of course, he had to admit it wasn't their company that interested him, as he found most to be ego-centered opportunists who could think of nothing cleverer to do than take advantage of girls and kid George about being a "brain." Instead, it was all those cheerleaders who flocked around and who were especially attentive and affectionate at parties after the games.

Mostly he was a bench-warmer, but it was fun for a couple of years, and by the time George was a senior, the coach was even putting him in the game occasionally, when the score was a runaway or one of the first-stringers was sick or had been suspended from school.

But George's career came to an abrupt and tragic end one evening during the annual student-faculty game. Not one, but two first-stringers were absent, and George was off the bench. With four seconds left, he was driving down court on the way to a layup that would tie the game. The screaming crowd was on its feet. The cheerleaders went wild, waving their multi-colored crepe-paper pom-poms hysterically. In the excitement, one of the girls got part of her pom-pom into her mouth during a long, enthusiastic scream. When she inhaled to get her breath back, the crepe paper was drawn into her windpipe, and she choked to death before anyone realized what had happened. Everyone thought she was writhing on the floor, turning blue (one of the school colors), because she was overcome with the emotion of the moment. After the layup, which he missed, George turned and saw the crowd, the coaches, and his teammates gathered around the small, still figure on the floor. When the student rescue squad arrived with their field stretcher, an Army blanket folded between two bamboo poles, George had gotten close enough to recognize the fallen cheerleader as Gloria Gribble, on whom he had had a secret crush since the beginning of the term.

George never played basketball again. For months, he shuffled from class to class like a zombie, earning grades barely high enough to graduate. He went out of his way to avoid further relationships with girls. And in that, Letitia realized, they had something very special in common.

Dr. Lavager wasn't so focused on his work that he couldn't sense the changes in the way his niece looked at George when they were together. Of course, he wanted her to be happy, and George too, for that matter, but he couldn't help being reminded of the distant past and his own star-crossed foray into romance. It began in high school on a blind date with Giselle Montgomery to see "Gone with the Wind." They dated for eight years until his graduation from Columbia University with a Ph.D. and acceptance of his first job, as an assistant science instructor at a small women's college in Pennsylvania. On the night he was going to propose, right after the Cherries Jubilee, as he was about to slip the ring out of his pocket, she announced she was going to marry the son of a North Carolina tobacco millionaire.

There was yet another knock at the door.

"Who's there?" called Dr. Lavager, expecting a humorous salutation from George.

"It's Ted, Gardy. It's okay to let me in; everything's secure on the outside."

"Ted, come in, come in!" said Dr. Lavager, snatching open the door.

The two men shook hands warmly as Dr. Baldwin came in from the dark hallway. A tall, imposing figure belied Dr. Baldwin's 72 years. His distinguished looking gray hair set off the finely chiseled features of a statesman. Indeed, Dr. Baldwin was a former U.S. Ambassador to both Ireland and Formosa and was still occasionally active in party politics behind the scenes.

"Good to see you, Gardy. Hello, Letitia. And Wong Lee! So nice to see you here too."

Dr. Baldwin had once confessed to Lavager that he felt sorry for Wong Lee O'Grady, although he couldn't put his finger on a reason. Maybe it was his unusual appearance and that his accent was an obstacle to making himself understood by strangers. Baldwin had hired him as a gardener two years ago out of compassion, without insisting on references or the usual battery of aptitude and intelligence tests which were standard procedure at the university for all employment candidates. But

Wong Lee had turned out to be an excellent gardener and a dependable worker, except for his insistence on being away from the university on Irish, Chinese and Jewish holidays, some of which even Baldwin couldn't remember having heard of. Baldwin had patted himself on the back for a good executive decision and forgotten about it.

"Look, I really can't stay," said Dr. Baldwin, "but I did want to come over and congratulate you personally on this special day."

"Well, believe me, Ted, it's a welcome intrusion," said Dr. Lavager.

Letitia had stopped humming.

"Of course, all of you are to be congratulated," said Dr. Baldwin expansively, taking in the three others with his gaze. "Not since Pasteur has so much been done by so few in so short a time to make the world safe from harmful substances, my boy. I know today is only the beginning. If the legislation that goes into effect at noon proves itself, as I am certain it will in a very short time, I expect Congress will be even more willing to act favorably upon all future legislation proposed by you and your colleagues of the American Eco-Toxicology Association. As we all realize—and we pray our realization has not come too late— there is no time to lose in this critical area, where the quality of life, not only for those of us here in America today, but for future generations of Americans, is so much at stake. We thank you, Dr. Lavager, we all thank you."

"We are deeply touched by those sentiments, Ted," said Dr. Lavager, "and we are proud to have been able to play a small part in the betterment of our nation. We are thankful for the opportunity to continue to contribute, until our work is finished."

In the drama of the moment, even the rats had become still in their little cages. Wong Lee appeared deeply moved and clutched his cellophane tape dispenser tightly.

"I know there are detractors," Dr. Baldwin continued, "as there always are when there are issues which are difficult to understand or when special interests seem to be threatened. But the role of government is to lead and protect the people when some of them haven't the incentive to do what is best for themselves. So keep up the good work. You have my support."

"Thank you for those encouraging words, Dr. Baldwin," said Dr. Lavager.

Letitia nodded her agreement. "Won't you stay for the TV interview, or at least a little orange juice and some oatmeal cookies before you go?"

"Well, if you promise not to keep an old man away from his mid-morning nap."

Everyone chuckled. Dr. Baldwin sat down in Dr. Lavager's armchair while Letitia plugged in the stereo and selected a Mantovani album. As the music started, Letitia and Wong Lee went back to their decorating, Letitia blessedly not humming. Half the room was already festooned with the white crepe paper, and the place was beginning to take on a festive air, in a sterile sort of way.

"I wonder what could be keeping George," said Letitia.

"Yes, he's usually quite punctual," answered Lavager.

"Now, now, I'm sure there's nothing to worry about, my dear," said Baldwin.

Lavager brought out some stools and folding chairs from the storage closet and set them near his armchair. As Mantovani played a slow waltz, Letitia whistled, but did not hum, the "Painted Desert" movement in a sort of counterpoint. Everyone made small talk.

Stroking his goatee absently, Lavager began to feel quite relaxed in the midst of all this family-like camaraderie. He firmly believed the fate of the world did rest squarely on his shoulders, but he was confident that with a little more time and diligent effort, everything would work out just fine.

CHAPTER THREE

Twenty soldiers were in the assembly room, sitting in rows of wooden chairs bolted to the floor and facing the front where there was a blackboard flanked by the American flag on one side and the U.S. Army flag on the other. Five feet out from the blackboard was a lectern with slots in front for placards proclaiming the identity of the speaker and the subject of his lecture, in case the speaker himself should fail to make that clear.

This morning the placards read: MAJOR FARINA and RE-ENLISTMENT.

Major Farina removed his helmet liner and stepped into the room, considerately letting his boots hit the floor more loudly than normal.

"Ten-Hut!" cried the first man to see him, a mousey-looking little SP4 who had been eagerly waiting for this special moment which gave him the right, no, the obligation, to give an order for twenty men, many of higher rank, to jump up out of their seats. They all hated his guts for it.

Everyone stood, facing the front of the room. Farina strode to the lectern and turned to face the men, head erect and eyes level.

"Take your seats!" he said.

They sat down.

"Good morning, men!"

"Good morning, sir!" It was a practiced roar, leaving no doubt how much they respected their commanding officer, if not the twerp who announced him.

"This morning I'm here to talk about re-enlistment to you men whose hitches are almost up," he began. "But I'm not going to give you the usual speech about God and country, bonuses, retirement benefits, how much money the government has invested in your training, and all that crap. You already know that.

"No, I'm going to get right to the heart of it and remind you of what we're trying to do here in the Mundane Ammunition Dump Command, why it's so important to the country in these troubled times, and what it can mean to you, the individual soldier. I realize you know all that too, but it's not crap, and it's worth repeating."

Some of the men shifted in their seats, or coughed, but all listened attentively to their commander's words.

"The politicians would have us believe this is a time of enlightenment in America. We've got medical research, a shorter work week, pollution control, occupational safety standards, and, of course, the rush to identify harmful substances and pass laws to protect us from them.

"Some people are pretty unhappy about those laws. After all, a lot of them are out of work and can no longer forget their troubles by smoking, drinking, and eating spicy foods," Farina added with a chuckle.

The men nodded and smiled knowingly.

"And, believe me, they have a right to their opinions, but in the long run they'll be better off. They may be losing their jobs as more and more products are banned, but it's good, what the government is doing for the people, and we've got to support it.

"On the other hand," Farina continued, "some of these same politicians want to carry this idea of a pure environment too far. These 'leaders' of ours have reasoned that, since war means lots of harmful substances, defense appropriations should be cut drastically. But, men, the truth is we're not here to make war in the first place. Our mission is peace through defense, and if preparedness for war happens to be the best weapon in our defense, then so be it!"

The men were sitting up straighter in their chairs, hanging on every word ... even those who had heard the speech before when their previous enlistments were drawing to a close.

"Just look what's happening. While the Enemy continues to stockpile weapons, our military has sold our warhead inventories to countries like Peru and Honduras, paid for, of course, in U.S. foreign aid money, to 'spread the burden of hemisphere defense.' Utterly nuts, right?"

The men were close to applause.

"Now it is true," said Farina, his tone now more conciliatory, "that U.S. border defenses have been beefed up, primarily by means of more frequent patrols by Coast Guardsmen, on foot, at least until electric or steam powered vehicles can be supplied.

So, men, if we're attacked by Mexico or Canada, we sure are prepared!"

The room erupted with laughter, and everyone relaxed. He had them in the palm of his hand, and he continued to lay it on.

"You know their rifles aren't even loaded, likely as not."

More laughter.

"The military has been de-emphasized so much that soldiers mostly just sit around waiting for the end of their enlistments, since there isn't even enough functioning equipment available for training purposes. Most of the ammunition has been issued to the civilian police, and for what? Mainly so they can handle disturbances caused by people fed up with the harmful substance laws. So the Army, in droopy, wrinkled fatigues because Washington thinks starch causes causer, sits around playing cards and having a lot of gas mask drills."

The men started grumbling in agreement and trading epithets about do-gooder politicians and stupid civilians. Farina let them carry on for a few seconds, getting themselves worked up, before he reined them in again.

"All right, at ease, men!" he commanded with good natured authority.

Instantly the room was silent, and all eyes were back on Farina.

"Still and all, men, the military is officially charged with the defense of our country, no matter how hard they make it for us to carry out that mission. In Washington there are still high ranking veteran officers who believe the tried and true theory that a strong arsenal—if the Enemy knows we have it—is the best safeguard against aggression. And we know that the last bastion of our nation's defense now can only be chemical and biological warfare"

The men nodded in self-righteous agreement.

"You men all have Top Secret clearances. You know about our espionage teams." He paused to cast his gaze around the room, seeing nods of agreement. His teams were out all over the country in colleges and universities, anywhere that had government grants for toxicology and human ecology work, stealing the research from under their noses.

He chuckled. "Why, we know about some harmful substances even before Congress does!"

The men began to glow with self-satisfaction.

Farina went on to repeat what the men already knew, about how the harmful substances were secretly weaponized and stockpiled in MADCOM's underground factories.

"I don't have to tell you again," Farina continued, "how critical your work here is to the to ensuring peace in the world."

There was scattered applause.

"And if you remain a part of his magnificent undertaking, you'll know you helped defend our great country when others were ready to give her away. Soon now, we'll be ready to reveal our existence to the Enemy, to let him know we're ready for him and anything he might try to throw at us. We'll put an end to his aggression by having a stronger position. We'll let him know we can hurt him in a thousand ways.

"Think of it, men. We can pollute his air with carbon monoxide. We can put caffeine, cyclamates, and hexachlorophene in his water supply. We can cover his cities with tar and nicotine, and monosodium glutamate. We can stunt his growth. We can make his light bulbs give off harmful radiation. We've got stuff to feed his cows and chickens so their milk and eggs will have more cholesterol. We can shower him with artificial ingredients. We can condemn him with condiments. We can stimulate his allergies and give him heart disease. We can break down his ozone layer. In short, we can kill or debilitate his whole population with what we're doing here. What more could any of you ask than to be able to serve your country in this noble way?"

More applause, and cries of "You tell 'em, sir!"

"No, men, you don't want to get out of the Army, at least not this part of the Army, where we're the only ones left really defending America!"

The men were with him all the way now, and Major Farina basked in their admiration of him. Now it was time for the clinchers.

"Stand up, soldier," said Farina gently, indicating a man in the front row.

The man stood up and reported, "Corporal Wilbur Smallet, sir."

"Smallet, how much longer for you?"

"Eight days and a wakeup, sir."

"That's pretty short all right. What're you going to do if you get out?"

"Thought maybe I'd go back and work my dad's farm in Iowa," said Smallet. "He's dead now, and I'd hate to see Mom have to go to one of those old folks homes."

"But farming's no good, Smallet. The bugs just take over everything now that you can't get insecticides unless you're a big enough agri-business conglomerate to have some pull in Washington."

He singled out another soldier. "What about you, Sergeant?"

"Staff Sergeant Rupert Alderson, sir," said the man, rising as a chagrinned Smallet sat down. "I've been thinking I'd cash in my Savings Bonds, buy some stock in a brewery back in Wisconsin, and throw in with them as a salesman."

"Your beer stock won't be worth squat when they outlaw alcohol. You'll have nothing to sell. What about you, Jefferson?"

The soldier stood up, grinning. "Private First Class William Jefferson, sir! I'm heading for Detroit! My big brother Jesse's up there working on those big fancy cars and getting paid so much he can drink all the beer he wants and still have enough left over to pay our Mama's rent. Least 'till they run out of beer, I guess."

Farina pounced. "Well, not any more, Jefferson. They're laying off in Detroit now like crazy. You'll never make it there! That whole city will be bankrupt pretty soon. You stay here, because you're going to be supporting your brother in another year.

"And that's what I'm trying to tell all of you men. You can't make it any more on the outside, not with everything as screwed up as it is. But here, you've got it made. Uncle Sam looks out for you, and your dependents back home if you have any. And at the same time, you're doing something important for America. You sign those papers, men. You won't regret it, not one bit.

"Atten-hut!"

The men jumped to attention. Major Farina strode to the rear of the room and out the door, confident in the effectiveness of his speech. He had meant every word of it, and he knew the men could sense it was genuine. They would respond to that.

He donned his helmet liner and stepped out into the sunshine, feeling happier and much more relaxed than before.

CHAPTER FOUR

At 9:00 a.m. in Southern California, an hour after the start of Major Farina's staff meeting, George Smith burst into Dr. Lavager's laboratory without knocking.

"Hi, folks! Sorry I'm late, but I had to stop off at the gas station to get some air in my tires." George was flushed and breathing hard from pedaling his bicycle the two miles from his off-campus apartment. He doffed his London Fog raincoat, folded it neatly and placed it on one of the tables.

"Come in, George. It's good to see you," said Dr. Baldwin.

"Yes, glad you could make it," said Dr. Lavager.

Letitia smiled warmly at George and tossed him a roll of crepe paper, holding one end of it so that it streamed across the room. He caught it, laughing, as the streamer settled on Dr. Baldwin's head. The old man brushed it off indulgently.

"Do you know those guys charged me a quarter for the air? Boy, are they mad ... just sitting around over at the gas station boozing it up and complaining about the law against internal combustion engines. One of them recognized me and said some pretty nasty things, so I got the heck out of there in a hurry."

Dr. Baldwin felt a certain tension mounting within himself and cast a worried glance at Dr. Lavager. But Lavager seemed not to have heard George's statement and sat with his eyes half closed, in a reverie, tapping a finger on his knee in time to the Mantovani.

George busied himself with the crepe paper, unobtrusively working his way closer to Letitia as he continued to talk. "Those guys said they'd have to go out of business, but, gosh, I thought there was a government subsidy to help retrain people like that. I mentioned it, and they just laughed. Then they made fun of my raincoat. I don't know what's the matter with some people these days, you know? I mean, what do they expect, for Pete's sake?

"And another thing," he continued. "There are beggars and homeless people popping up on street corners everywhere you go. I've never seen anything like it."

"Really, George?" said Letitia. "But, this is California!"

"What can I say? I'm just telling you what I saw. And it looks like some of them are living in their cars."

"Well, that makes sense I guess, if they can't drive them anymore," she said.

With his lackluster high school grades after the shock of Gloria Gribble's tragic death, George had barely made it into Leland F. P. Mason Wesley, Jr., University, but he graduated after four years with a BS in biology. George was still at the university 15 years later, one of those perennial students who somehow never find it within themselves to leave the safe familiarity of the campus environment and make it on their own. Just now, when George wasn't assisting Dr. Lavager, he was "going for his Masters" in botany.

George did leave the campus briefly right after graduation when he went on active duty with the Marine Corps Reserve for six months. He joined the Marines out of patriotism. They made him a typist, and he had gone to weekend drills once a month and two weeks annual summer camp faithfully ever since. He had attained the rank of sergeant, supervising a section of three other typists. Mostly their work consisted of handling the paperwork on Officer Candidate School applications, officer efficiency reports, and discharge cases for hardship, incompetence and homosexuality. The other Marines swore profusely as a matter of professional pride, but George always used polite euphemisms, as he had been brought up to do, which made him something of a freak as far as the other Marines were concerned.

Although George had made a habit of avoiding women, Letitia was somehow different. At once both aloof and inviting, she intrigued him, awakening feelings long repressed. He sensed she was interested in him, for there was communication in her coy glances as they worked together in the lab or shared a milkshake at the Student Union. But in his newfound and still unfamiliar role of would-be suitor, George had never gotten past kissing the back of Letitia's neck, which he did every chance he got. Sometimes it was awkward or even embarrassing, and he often felt he was taking advantage of her, as when he would accost her while her hands were full of rat food. But she seemed to enjoy it and never made a move to discourage him as long as he stopped there.

Finally, the decorations were all hung. Wong Lee finished straightening up, although there hadn't been time to use the vacuum cleaner. Buddy Holly was on the stereo, and George was sneaking his arm around Letitia's waist. She looked at her watch and pranced away to the table where the food had been set out.

"Juice and cookie time!" she announced.

Everyone converged on the table where Letitia poured orange juice into the plastic cups.

"I'm not very good at toasts, so I won't propose one, even on such an auspicious occasion," said Dr. Lavager gravely, "but I want to thank all of you for what we have been able to accomplish so far."

"Here, here," said Dr. Baldwin as everyone nodded in appreciation and sipped. "Say, isn't it about time for your TV show?"

CHAPTER FIVE

Major Farina strode from the S-1 shop over to the main headquarters building and entered after returning a salute from Jenkins who was pumping up one of the tires on the bike.

"Atten-hut!" called one of the soldiers inside. "Good morning, sir."

"Carry on!" said Farina.

Everyone relaxed and resumed working. Farina strode past the message center and through the room where a dozen soldiers worked as typists and clerks. His personal office occupied the whole rear half of the building, and only a small number of trusted officers and enlisted men were admitted unless he was present. The one door to the office was of heavy wood and had a special lock to which he, Captain Leon and Captain Crockett had the only keys.

He unlocked the door and entered his office. It was pitch dark with the overhead lights turned off, but his familiarity with the room allowed him to make his way effortlessly to his desk, where he switched on a fluorescent lamp.

There were no windows. From the outside of the old wooden building, it merely appeared as if the shades had been drawn, but inside pine paneling covered all the walls, including the original windows. To the left of the desk was the door to what Farina considered the most important room on the base, although he rarely entered it himself. It held the secret files containing records of hundreds of harmful substances and the development work the Army had done with them, including what quantities of each substance had been stockpiled, their location, and a production schedule.

The door to Farina's private latrine stood ajar. Hanging next to it was an obligatory red fire extinguisher.

Farina's wooden desk was old but still quite sturdy. On top, along with the lamp, was a sterling silver name plate engraved with MAJ. H. A. FARINA, COMMANDING OFFICER. There were few papers on the desk, but the work table against the wall next to the latrine was piled high. An old, brown leather sofa sat against one wall, and several well-worn armchairs faced the desk in a rough semicircle. A thin, brown wool rug covered the floor like an Army blanket. Shabby, maybe, but familiar and comfortable. Farina took pride in the fact that he had never wasted money on frivolous upgrades in furniture or décor.

Between each pair of armchairs was one of those standing ashtrays so common on Army bases. Now that tobacco was becoming hard to obtain, Major Farina was looking forward to getting rid of the ashtrays, mainly because people were always knocking them over. He had given up trying to get the ashes out of the old rug anymore.

An American flag and an Army flag flanked his desk in floor stands. The room had only two real decorations. One was a framed color print showing American soldiers scaling a wall during the Boxer Rebellion in China with a written description of the action and the caption, "I'll try, sir!" The other, on the wall opposite the desk where Farina could see it while working, was his favorite, a framed photograph of the Washington Monument at night during a Fourth of July fireworks display.

Two other features of the room were not apparent under normal circumstances. Beneath the rug, under the work table, was a trap door leading to the main subterranean chamber where work on the most promising harmful substances was in progress. It was the commanding officer's private entrance, the soldiers' entrance being in one of the sunken ammunition storage rooms a mile away. Farina himself had never been to the underground work areas. His staff knew he had an inexplicable fear of caves, and they didn't force the issue. A personal visit to the work areas once in a while would have been good for morale, but fortunately morale was high enough anyway, and when Captain Leon or the other officers made inspection tours representing "the Old Man," they were able to carry some of his charisma with them. The trap door did get some use though. The Officer in Charge of Development, Second Lieutenant Edgar Duffle, frequently came up from below to announce some new discovery or to discuss an idea with Farina or his staff.

In Omaha, it was 10:00 a.m., or ten hundred hours at Camp Shafto. Punctual as usual, Farina's staff entered the office. After pleasantries were exchanged, they took seats in the armchairs. Major Farina began the meeting.

"Good morning, gentlemen. Iggy, where are those hourly news reports I asked for? Have there been any new developments?"

"Not much, I'm afraid," said Captain Leon. "About ten thousand Chinese-Americans in San Francisco staged a demonstration at City Hall to protest the ban on monosodium glutamate. That one's still going on.

"Some of the big labor leaders have made strong statements against the government, calling the retraining programs inadequate, and so forth. They're calling for a big meeting among themselves at some resort in the Pennsylvania mountains for next week, so that one could turn belligerent."

"What's the latest from the National Rifle Association?" asked Farina.

"They're for the military and against the government all right, but since private citizens can still have guns, they can't figure out whether the 2nd Amendment's been violated or not. Anyway, the NRA is telling its members to hoard ammunition, so now they're competing with the police on that, which doesn't make the police very happy. They're also telling everybody to buy pellet guns. Oh, and now the gun control people have had some kind of epiphany and are throwing the NRA's favorite slogan back at them, except now it's 'Guns don't kill people. Ammunition kills people.' Could be a big problem brewing there."

"That's confusing. What about the Sierra Club?"

"They're happy as clams, of course, which by the way will also be outlawed soon because in large servings they contain unhealthy amounts of selenium. The clams I mean."

"Okay, then how about the church leaders?"

"Not a factor, sir. Publicly they agree with the environmentalists who are fond of quoting the Bible about how mankind is supposed to take care of the earth."

"Yeah, I remember that from Sunday school," said Farina.

"On the other hand, common sense tells them the government's gone too far with the restrictions, but they don't say that to their congregations for fear of looking too political and losing their tax exemptions. So they're just riding it out from the sidelines."

"Gentlemen, planning our next moves is going to be more difficult than I anticipated," said Farina, but he spoke in confident tones as his gaze fell on each of the staff members in turn.

Captain Ignacio J. Leon, Executive Officer, a thin man almost as tall as Major Farina, was the son of illegal Mexican immigrants, and a naturalized citizen. The Army was now his whole life, and he was a good administrator.

Captain Horst Gruber, the Adjutant, blond, heavyset, with a ready smile. He had come to America as a German high school exchange student and liked America so well he returned when he was 21 and joined the Army. Farina considered him an even more efficient administrator than Captain Leon.

Captain Ernest Crockett, the S-2 or Intelligence and Security

Officer, with curly brown hair and a Harvard MBA, was good with figures and had an exceptionally analytical mind.

Captain Thomas Sims-Wellington, the S-3 or Training and Operations Officer, tall and gangly, but deliberate and methodical.

Captain Arnett Labouche, the S-4 or Supply Officer, a short man born in a French-speaking town in northern Maine. He couldn't read English when he was drafted, and he still made mistakes when filling out requisitions, but he got by with his quick wit, hot temper, and excellent command of the spoken language.

Sergeant Major Junior T. Williams, representing the enlisted men. A big man with thirty-odd years of service. Nobody tried to put anything over on Williams.

These men were hand-picked by Major Farina, with the influence and endorsement of his mentors in Washington. Most of them were older than he, and more experienced in the military. He had had an easy time convincing each of them of the importance of their official mission and turning them into an efficient and dedicated team. But Farina had gone beyond that. With his magnetic personality, he had made these officers blindly loyal to him, and six months ago he had taken the step of revealing to them, individually at first, his true intentions – his own self-appointed mission.

Not even the small group of zealous generals in Washington knew of it, yet.

Farina dreamed of the day he would sit in the Oval Office with a view of the Washington Monument while he and his "Cabinet" dispensed harmful substances as favors to the world population, accepting their grateful tributes of money, devotion, and, of course, women. The whole staff signed on with enthusiasm. After all, what better prospects did they have if they wanted to pursue true military careers?

All the training, hard work, and near celibacy of the past several years would pay off handsomely now, if only they could make the right moves in the next few days, weeks, months, or whatever it was going to take before they could safely pull off the coup.

Farina's fondest wish was for the coup to occur about seven months from now, on his thirtieth birthday. He was going to have the biggest celebration Washington, in fact the world, had ever seen. Bigger even than the Olympics opening ceremonies, which were pretty big.

His staff knew of this birthday wish and had already started planning something special with which to honor their leader on that day. In their loyalty to Farina, they had even gone so far as to falsify their reports of the progress of the stockpiling so he wouldn't suspect the wonderful surprise they were preparing. Blindly, sentimentally, they were stockpiling enormous quantities of one very special substance in particular, loading it into bombs for effective delivery. With this making up 80% of their arsenal, they believed their junta would be invincible after the coup, and Major Farina would be quite pleased with the militarily symbolic significance of the substance they had selected. When speaking of it in Farina's presence, the staff referred to it only as the "selective stockpiling" policy. Because of his fear of going underground, there was little danger of Farina discovering their secret and spoiling the surprise. Besides, they knew well that in the military, as in politics, a euphemistic and alliterative buzz word like "selective stockpiling" can aid greatly when obfuscation is required.

"The problem is this," Farina continued. "For our little coup to succeed, it must have the support of the people. The only way they'll support us is if they are truly angry at the restrictive laws. So let's review where we stand and see if we should change our course at all. Ernie, what do you think?"

Captain Crockett spoke up. "Well, sir, I agree the reports are spotty right now, but this is only the first day of the latest new laws. The meeting of the labor leaders looks good to me, and remember, even more laws are coming. It may take a few more before most people get truly fed up. After all, apathy has been an American hallmark for decades. I suggest we see how close we are to having the weapons stockpiled in the quantities required to pull off the coup. If we're pretty close now, we may want our undercover operatives around the country to stir up more trouble and get people really mad at the government right about when we move in."

Farina got the point. It's easy to excite people who have lost their jobs because of the laws. On the other hand, he thought, if we're not ready, and the people are spontaneously moving faster than we want, there isn't much we can do to slow them down. The only thing we can control is our own development and manufacturing operations, so we'd have to try to speed those up.

"Okay, Ernie, that's good thinking," he said. "Arnett, where do we stand, stockpile wise?"

Captain Labouche got up and moved toward Farina's desk. "Would you mind dropping the panel, sir?"

Farina flipped a switch under his desk, and the paneling behind the desk disappeared into the floor, revealing a large situation map. Pins in the map showed locations of all dumps in the Command, their colors denoting the state of readiness of each dump. Beneath the map was a bank of unfiltered television screens connected by closed circuit to hidden cameras located in strategic spots at this dump and others. Over the map were four clocks, each set to a different time zone.

"As we're all intensely aware, gentlemen, we're shooting for a 100% readiness level in six months, or a month before the major's birthday," said Labouche.

Everyone smiled indulgently.

"Let's look at the pins," Labouche continued. "Sergeant Major, would you hand me the pointer, please? Thanks.

"Now, looking in the Eastern sector, we have two greens and the rest yellows. And," he said ceremoniously, "today I hereby remove the yellow pin from the Philadelphia dump and replace it with a green."

The officers applauded briefly, and Labouche went on.

"Over in the Midwest and Western sectors, of course we're green here at Shafto, and at these three other dumps," he said, pointing as he talked. "The rest are yellow except for these two reds here in California."

"What are you doing about those two?" asked Major Farina.

"Well, I'm going to remove this one red one completely. That was the one small dump we set up on a trial basis outside the official Army Mundane Ammunition Dump Command. Its cover was the ROTC building at Stanford University, but we couldn't keep the FBI from nosing around all the time, so we hired some students to blow it up last Saturday."

"Too bad," said Farina, thinking at least that would have been fun to see, "but it was a worthwhile experiment."

"Yes, and nobody got hurt. Now this other one should turn yellow in about two weeks, even if I have to fly out there myself. Those guys were supposed to be stockpiling marijuana,. They started off pretty enthusiastically, but then their reports started getting kind of vague. Captain Sims sent a team out to move the marijuana to our dump in New Haven."

"Yes, you reported that operation at our last meeting," said Farina. "Tom, you and Ernie both deserve a lot of credit because that could have been a sticky one."

"It was simple, really," said Crockett. "We had them load the stuff in railroad tank cars marked 'Nerve Gas,' and nobody suspected a thing."

"Anyway," continued Labouche, "we've now assigned those guys to caffeine and nicotine. I think they'll straighten out soon enough."

"Okay, but the big question, Arnett, is how long will it take to make all those pins turn green?"

"I doubt if we can speed things up much, sir. Tom and Sergeant Major Williams feel we're pushing the men too hard now. It's not that morale is a problem—I think the men would work even harder if we'd let them—but there are physical limits to what they can do. At best, I'd say we could beat the schedule by two weeks, but I wouldn't want to count on it, sir."

Captain Labouche returned to his seat as Farina propped himself up on his elbows, resting his chin on his fists in a contemplative pose.

Captain Sims-Wellington stood and wandered over to the Boxer Rebellion print, speaking as he paced. "The problem is in the development work. That's the most time-consuming task initially for any harmful substance. We've got to refine the stuff and get it into some form suitable for delivery in one of our weapons systems. Take tobacco, for instance. Now, it wouldn't do just to load up a bunch of bombs with shredded tobacco and expect to have them do any harm beyond making a huge mess. What we have to do is extract the tars, nicotine, and other chemicals which, when properly activated, say, with heat or oxygen, can do some serious damage. Then, when we put that in a bomb or sneak it into a water supply, we've got a real threat."

"Yeah, but what are you leading up to, Tom?" asked Farina.

"I'm not sure. Just thinking out loud for a minute. We were lucky with tobacco because the industry had already done most of that kind of work, and it was a cinch to get our hands on it. Not so much work has been done yet, for example, on those nitrosamines in bacon and sausage, and they've got us stumped. We'd be ahead of the game if we could learn quicker how to make practical use of the substances ourselves. That would help us control our timetable."

"Well, what about the American Eco-Toxicology Association?" asked Farina. "They're the ones with the best track record. Aren't we still stealing their stuff as fast as they come up with it?"

"Yes, we are," said Captain Sims, "but we're getting it before the Association researchers have had time to do any of the good development work. What's worse, they're not even doing much development anymore. It's getting so all they do these days is identify something they think may have a harmful substance in it, and then they go running to some Congressional committee, waving their arms and crying 'The sky is falling' and first thing you know, 'zap!' and there's a law against it. Then the researchers run back to look for something else."

Captain Leon, who had sat quietly through all of this, finally could contain himself no longer. "It sounds like there's some kind of 'harmful substance race' going on. Maybe we ought to get into it."

"What do you think, Ernie?" asked Farina of his Intelligence Officer.

"Iggy has a point, sir. The head of the Association is a guy named Lavager – Dr. Gardiner Lavager, out of the Leland F. P. Mason Wesley, Jr., University, in Southern California. This guy is a real hot shot, a fanatic on harmful substances. He comes up with them faster than any of the other sources we're watching. Frankly, sir, and I've been thinking about this for a while, my recommendation is to kidnap this Dr. Lavager guy, bring him here, and get him to work on the development side of it for us."

Farina experienced a strange sensation, almost a *deja vu*, when Lavager's name was mentioned. But the feeling passed.

He pondered the kidnap idea for a few seconds before responding. "Lt. Duffle does a pretty good job in the development area, but it would sure help if he had a pro to give him some direction. I have to admit he's not always practical, and we'll need some help if we're going to speed up the timetable. Still, we've never pulled off anything like a kidnapping before. Do you think we can handle it?"

"I have some ideas on that, sir," said Crockett, "but I'm not ready to make a recommendation yet. The biggest problem will be to keep it a secret that he's missing so there won't be any panic."

"Yes, that would defeat our purpose," said Farina. "Who is our man assigned to this Dr. Lavager?"

Captain Gruber opened a notebook. "That's Staff Sergeant O'Grady, sir. We've had him there for two years masquerading as a gardener. He's a good man – very security conscious, too. He always makes his reports in person, leaving the campus on the pretext of some ethnic holiday or other, and flying up here. I think he'll be an asset to this operation, and his loyalty is above reproach."

"Are there any 'ethnic holidays' coming up soon?" asked Farina.

"I think we can arrange one, sir," said Gruber.

"Good. Send for O'Grady immediately, and work out some kind of kidnap plan with him. Let me know when you're ready to talk about it. Can you be ready in, say, 48 hours?" Farina was excited now.

"We'll try, sir," said Crockett.

Gruber had an inexplicable fondness for Wong Lee O'Grady, who had been a 38-year-old career soldier stagnating as a stockade guard at Fort Knox until Gruber singled him out for special espionage duty and assigned him to spy on Dr. Lavager. While working at the stockade, O'Grady often took prisoner details to the quarters of high ranking officers and had them do lawn and garden work. He had learned gardening by watching. That, plus his loyalty, work ethic and attention to detail, so important in the Army, and the admittedly sparse information about his background in his 201 File—mostly a record of his promotions and all his vaccinations—made him seem to Gruber an excellent choice for the Lavager assignment.

"Gentlemen, I believe the success of this operation will be critical to making our move with perfect timing," said Farina. "It's a heady feeling to know we've almost got the world in our hands."

Everyone nodded enthusiastic agreement.

Sensing the meeting should end here, as far as Farina was concerned, Captain Leon stood up and said, "Thank you, sir," saluting as he spoke. The others followed suit, snapping to attention and saluting their commander. Farina returned the salutes, and the men about-faced and strode out of the office, all except Captain Leon.

"Good meeting, Tony," said Leon. "What's on your agenda for the rest of the day?"

"Nothing much," said Farina. "Corporal Borgia got arrested for trespassing again, and I have to go talk to the Sheriff about it."

"What's got into that kid, anyway?"

"Beats me. Maybe we should get his sergeant to give him lighter duty for a while. Probably overworked."

"I'll take care of it," said Leon.

"Later this afternoon I've got to fake some more progress reports for my generals in Washington, and then I may go look for something to inspect. You know how it is … the loneliness of command and all that." Farina was feeling pleased with himself.

"But let's go over to the Officers' Club for a beer before we do anything else. We can use the back door so we don't disturb anybody out front."

Farina turned the map aside, revealing a secret rear entrance to the office. He and Leon strode outside into the daylight, adjusting their helmet liners as they went.

A boxcar was parked on the rail siding behind the building, and some soldiers from Supply were wrestling several large, heavy crates aboard. They were having a difficult time of it.

The sergeant supervising the loading was slouched against the side of the building, but he snapped to attention and saluted when he saw the two officers approaching. They returned the salute, and Farina gave the "As you were" command. Just then, one of the soldiers cried out a warning, and they heard the splintering sound of one of the crates crashing to the ground. Before the inevitable loosing of the "s" word all around, the sergeant intervened.

"Watch it, men!" shouted the sergeant. "You know the Major don't want to hear that kind of talk!"

"Thank you, Sergeant," said Farina.

"Sir!" responded the sergeant.

"What are those men loading, Sergeant?" asked Captain Leon.

"Oh, just some old machine guns, sir. They're our last ones, I think, and they ain't been fired since 1968, at least. Be surprised if they don't blow up on the first poor SOB who pulls the trigger."

"I wonder who requisitioned those," said Farina.

"All's I know is we got orders to ship them to the police force at some college out in California. They wanted some ammunition too, but we just ain't got any more of that."

The fallen crate had burst open on impact, and the soldiers were standing around grumbling. None wanted to be first to suggest getting a new crate and repacking the heavy gun.

Major Farina and Captain Leon strode off to look for Jenkins, the bike driver.

After the officers had disappeared around the corner, one of the soldiers stooped and picked up a piece of the shattered crate.

"Now ain't this some nuts, man?" he said, tossing the piece into the boxcar. The other soldiers began picking up pieces, too, throwing them into the boxcar with abandon. When the gun itself was the only item left on the ground, three of the men picked it up together and heaved it into the boxcar, grunting in unison. The gun landed with a clatter and broke into a dozen pieces. High fiving each other, the soldiers closed the boxcar door and sauntered back to the Supply room, followed by their sergeant. He walked slowly, shrugging and looking at the sky.

CHAPTER SIX

> They that go down to the sea in ships,
>   that do business in great waters;
> These see the works of the Lord,
>   and his wonders in the deep.
>
> Psalm 107:23-24 (KJV)

The octopus is among the strangest of God's creatures, odd-looking, like an alien cast ashore on earth without its UFO, lonely, formidable, and dangerous, but wonderful in its own way. It's usually a bottom feeder, hiding in the ocean sediment, at times indistinguishable from the rocks and mud in which it lurks. Sloth like, it slowly trolls for food or lies in wait for the passing of unsuspecting prey. Then with prey in range, it strikes with fearsome suddenness, quickly snatching the unwary victim in a rush of unbridled energy, suckered tentacles grasping tenaciously, drawing the doomed ever closer, closer, and finally into a venomous and seemingly cavernous maw, until then a harmless bird's beak at the confluence of languid arms.

A shape shifter, a color changing chameleon, able to insinuate its boneless body through impossibly small openings, its brain extending to its arms and surprisingly sophisticated for a lowly mollusk, the octopus sometimes likes to play with its food as much as eat it. Disturbed, it shoots a stream of ink like an overzealous newspaper columnist to hide itself from danger while it scurries to a new hiding place, a secret, moveable lair from which to sally forth when the coast is clear again.

The octopus can't help it; it was born that way.

Small ones, how cute. Average ones, how fascinating. Large ones, swim for your life!

Metaphorically, the octopus has its unseen tentacles in a multitude of places, its invisible fingers in a thousand pies, minding its own nefarious business by appropriating yours and mine. Hiding at the bottom of our lives.

At this moment, such a one was preparing for an early dinner in his castle nestled in a valley in the foothills of an obscure mountain range in the bowels of Eastern Europe. Lobster again. His favorite. Sitting at a long, wide table set with sterling and crystal, the front pages of a half dozen international newspapers spread before him, he tucked his linen napkin carefully into his collar and took a tentative sip of strong, hot coffee from a bone china cup.

"Let us see what the weasel governments of the West are up to today, eh?" he mused.

CHAPTER SEVEN

Wong Lee turned on the TV. The tube flickered to life. The talk show was just starting, and reception was good, but it took a few seconds for everyone's eyes to adjust to the darkening effect of the X-ray filter.

As he fiddled with the volume, a commercial came on.

"With all the controversy about laundry detergents and new pollution regulations these days," began an unctuous spokesman, "no one would blame you for being confused about how to get your family's clothes truly clean. But now the makers of Bolderdash are proud to announce revolutionary new Bolderdash II. Bolderdash II is completely safe for your family's clothes. It's pollution-free and it *really* gets clothes clean. By a patented process, scientists in the Bolderdash research labs take ordinary detergent and refine it to remove all traces of phosphates that may or may not pollute streams and rivers, whiteners and brighteners that cause your husband's shirts to disintegrate after several washings, enzymes that digest the water hoses and gaskets of your washing machine, and lemon fresheners that don't do anything. The result? A washday product that's safe as soap, because that's what it is.

"Naturally, Bolderdash II costs a little more, due to the special processing required. But you'll know it's well worth the few extra pennies a day for the safety of your family and the protection of our environment. With Bolderdash II, your clothes will be really, really clean, whether they look it or not, and there are no unexpected side effects. We predict within two years all laundry products will be like Bolderdash II. Try it today. You'll be glad you did!

"By FTC requirement, the makers of Bolderdash II certify that this product has been on the market for less than six months and therefore qualifies to be called 'new.' The claim that Bolderdash II gets clothes clean is substantiated by controlled laboratory experiments resulting in removal of a minimum of 96.4% of special synthetic laboratory dirt measured in test garments before washing in Bolderdash II. The claim 'pollution-free' is subject to pending rulings by the FDA on the ecological implications of plain soap. Base price information substantiating the Government-approved, cost-based differential between regular Bolderdash and new Bolderdash II is available by sending a stamped, self-addressed envelope to 'Bolderdash II Price Data' at the address on your screen. The Surgeon General warns that, if taken internally, Bolderdash II may be hazardous to your health. May not be available in all states."

The commercial ended, and the talk show host appeared.

"And welcome to 'What's Up Today'. As promised, during this half hour we are going to bring you a taped interview with the foremost authority on harmful substances, the man who has been called 'the father' of the new restrictive laws that are going into effect on this very day. He is Dr. Gardiner Lavager, a professor at Leland F. P. Mason Wesley, Jr., University, and unofficial head of the American Eco-Toxicology Association. And now, in the studio of our Los Angeles affiliate station, KIDU, here with Dr. Lavager and his assistant, Mr. George Smith, is our West Coast correspondent, Laslo Tjörds."

Wong Lee sat up straighter. He recalled vividly the day of the taping, when Dr. Lavager and George set out on the long trip to Los Angeles in Dr. Lavager's electric car. Lavager didn't like publicity to begin with and was upset even further by the fact that the network had been unwilling to send a camera crew out to the campus to do the interview. They had finally convinced him to go through with it by arguing the benefits of better popular understanding of his work and how helpful it truly was to humanity. It would be better for him to make more public appearances so people could see he was an ordinary human being and not merely some eccentric ivory tower professor.

Wong Lee happened to know it was Dr. Baldwin who had quietly discouraged the network from taping the interview on campus. In his view, the publicity could be harmful to the university, especially if the popular mood over the laws were to become violent. Suicides from the bell tower were one thing. Mobs slaughtered by machine gun fire from the roof of Dr. Lavager's laboratory were quite another. Identification of the university with Dr. Lavager's work was to be reserved for alumni publications and the like.

Another factor that had worried Dr. Lavager about the trip to Los Angeles was the danger of freeway driving in a vehicle whose top speed was only 30 miles an hour. In the end, they had made the trip with a Highway Patrol escort, staying in the shoulder "emergency" lane all the way. Wong Lee recalled that Letitia had moped around the lab all day until their safe return, biting her fingernails and consuming a week's worth of oatmeal cookies and diet milkshakes.

The little TV screen revealed a typical studio interview set. Around a low coffee table in a semi-circle facing the camera, Lavager, George and Laslo Tjörds sat in armchairs of tubular chrome and black vinyl. On the wall behind them was a stereotypical stylized cutout map of the United States, bisected from top to bottom and from left to right by slanted, two-headed arrows representing north, south, west and east. Lavager appeared to be drying his hands on a white paper towel, which he hurriedly stuffed into a pocket.

The scene moved to a close up of Laslo Tjörds.

TJÖRDS: Good morning. With me today is the man who has been called "the father" of the new restrictive harmful substance laws. Certainly the nation's foremost authority on harmful substances, he holds a half dozen awards for original work in toxicology and human ecology and has published fourteen papers and two books on the subject. He is, of course, Dr. Gardiner Mellors Lavager. With Dr. Lavager is his assistant, Mr. George Smith. We asked Dr. Lavager and Mr. Smith to give us a little background on their important research. Good morning, Dr. Lavager and Mr. Smith, and welcome to "What's Up Today."

LAVAGER: Thank you, Mr. Tjörds. It's good to be here.

TJÖRDS: "Laslo," please, Dr. Lavager.

LAVAGER: Of course. Thank you, Laslo.

GEORGE: Good morning.

TJÖRDS: Dr. Lavager, it must be a source of great personal satisfaction to see your work coming to fruition now. Have you planned any sort of celebration?

LAVAGER: It's very satisfying indeed, Laslo, but I don't think we'll have time for much partying. My niece, Letitia, is planning a little get-together of close friends for orange juice and oatmeal cookies, but that's about all. We feel there's no time to lose in this important work.

TJÖRDS: That must be the famous Lavager dedication we've all heard so much about, eh? Do you have experiments and research projects underway right now?

LAVAGER: Oh, several, in fact. For example, we are nurturing bacteria cultures taken from common lipstick and mascara to see if they produce toxins under certain conditions. Letitia helps out with those, of course. Right, George?

GEORGE: Right, Dr. Lavager.

TJÖRDS: Hmm, yes, and uh, Mr. Smith, how long have you been working with Dr. Lavager?

GEORGE: Oh, about six years now, Mr. Tjörds … uh… Laslo.

TJÖRDS: Very interesting, very interesting indeed.

LAVAGER: George was quite instrumental in the research which led to the paper dye legislation.

TJÖRDS: I'm sure our viewers would be very interested in hearing about the research techniques you used on that one. Could you tell us about it?

LAVAGER: Yes, I'm glad you asked that, Laslo, because I think this is the area of greatest confusion. When people see things they grew up with and learned to love— such as the automobile, tobacco, coffee, aerosol sprays, and tinted facial tissue, for example—singled out all of a sudden as "harmful" and then banned or restricted, why, it's naturally hard for them to understand, and I can appreciate their, uh, anxiety in these matters. But the fact is that we, by using our machines to do the work of nature, by synthesizing materials to substitute for those God put on the earth, by putting materialistic objectives in front of concern for our own bodies and the environment … by doing all this, we are rushing headlong toward our own destruction. Global warming may be only a small part of the problem. We are upsetting the fine ecological balance of the Earth at such a rate that we will have reached the point of no return very soon unless we are successful in bringing this trend under control.

TJÖRDS: Hmm, yes, I understand.

LAVAGER: Let me give you an example of what I mean, even though this example is not exactly about the kind of thing I myself and my colleagues in the American Eco-Toxicology Association, are working on. Ahem. Suppose in country A there seem to be too many of a certain kind of fruit fly which plagues the country's chief export crop. Traders bring back accounts of a certain small bird living in country B, which eats this particular fruit fly.

TJÖRDS: Yes . . .?

LAVAGER: So the government of country A imports some of these birds with the hope they will multiply and eradicate the fruit flies. Well, the birds do this, all right, and in fact life in country A is so good for these birds that they multiply incredibly fast. As they decimate the fruit fly population, they also begin to compete for the food supply of the other birds indigenous to country A, among which is a particular species whose bright feathers and tender meat are an important tourist attraction. So now if that species is to be preserved, it has to be raised in captivity and fed on insects imported from yet a third country, country C.

TJÖRDS: Intriguing . . .

LAVAGER: Meanwhile, the sparse population of other beneficial insects is not enough to pollinate the fruit trees, and the crop suffers anyway. Not only that, they soon discover the droppings of the fruit-fly-eating birds harbor a bacteria which attacks the nervous systems of rats, causing them to go into a frenzy and bite larger animals and children, thus spreading several other diseases. By now, you see, things have gotten so out of hand that country A should be quarantined. And there's no telling what that would lead to, including a potential brain drain as many of Country A's best and brightest business people emigrate to Country C to get into the insect export business.

TJÖRDS: Well, that certainly is a dramatic example! It reminds me of two imports from the Orient, Asian carp that are taking over our Great Lakes and kudzu vines in the South.

GEORGE: What's Asian carp?

LAVAGER: What is kudzu?

TJÖRDS: Uh, anyway, do you and your colleagues feel

America is headed in the wrong direction, ecology-wise?

LAVAGER: Yes, we most certainly do, and it's happening fast… which is why we have to conduct our research the way we do. Our rule has to be, "when in doubt, ban it." Then maybe later, when we're sure we've gotten everything under control again, we will have time to go back and reexamine certain things to see if perhaps we did act a bit more hastily than we needed to.

TJÖRDS: I see. Basically, then, Dr. Lavager, what is your technique for identifying harmful substances?

LAVAGER: Essentially what we do is take a fairly large quantity of a substance we suspect to be harmful, and we feed it or inject it into rats. If the rats get sick or die, then we conclude the substance is indeed harmful. It works quite well. This is exactly how it was discovered that cyclamates cause birth defects, hexachlorophene leads to brain damage, starch causes cancer, and saccharine causes bladder tumors.

TJÖRDS: Yes, Doctor, but that's in rats, not people. Also, some of your detractors have charged that the dosages of suspected carcinogens and other substances you give to laboratory animals are many times what a human being could use or ingest in a lifetime. What do you say to that?

LAVAGER: That's the point most people do not understand. You see, our philosophy has to be "better safe than sorry." Also, what most people don't realize is that a particular substance will be given to dozens of rats or guinea pigs, not just one or two, so we will know the harmful effects are not just chance occurrences. Now, it's true we're killing an awful lot of rats this way, and I suppose some criticism of that may be justified, although, come to think of it, I haven't heard any.

TJÖRDS: But still, Dr. Lavager, many would say sufficiently large doses of almost anything, even water for example, would kill rats. And humans too, of course.

GEORGE: Frankly, we hadn't thought about that. Have we, Dr. Lavager?

LAVAGER: Um, what is your next question, Laslo?

TJÖRDS: Ah, well, so uh, Mr. Smith, getting back to the paper dye research you participated in…could you tell us about that?

GEORGE: Yes, Laslo. For a long time, we had suspected the harmful dyes used in certain types of paper, particularly those disposed of through sewerage systems, such as facial tissue and bathroom tissue, and sometimes also crepe paper, for example – the dyes used are not broken down by conventional municipal treatment plants.

TJÖRDS: How did you verify that this was true and convince Congress to ban the use of these dyes?

GEORGE: One day, out of the blue, so to speak, I hit upon a surprisingly simple technique. I reasoned that since rats are well known for eating garbage, their systems must resemble municipal sewerage treatment plants in many important ways. The next step was easy. I took a handful of colored toilet paper, green, I think it was, and stuffed it down the throat of one of the laboratory rats. The rat died. Well, gosh, we knew we had it licked then!

LAVAGER: Of course, as I said before, we didn't stop with just the one rat. But after some two dozen rats died this way—George tried a lot of different colors of tissue paper, not just green—that was proof enough for us, and for Congress. I think the viewers should keep in mind, too, that these are simple tests anyone can perform in his own home. For example, we've just recently set aside one corner of our lab as the TV area. We have a dozen rats there watching television 24 hours a day, without the X-ray filter, just to confirm the findings of some of our colleagues in other parts of the country. Two rats have already died.

GEORGE: Of course, we're not suggesting everyone should go out and buy a supply of lab rats for their homes.

LAVAGER: Certainly not. That would drive up the price of rats astronomically, and they already make up a large percentage of our budget.

TJÖRDS: Sounds like it would be another good business for country C if that were to happen.

LAVAGER: Well, yes, I suppose so.

GEORGE: You do realize there is actually no country C, Laslo. That was just an example Dr. Lavager made up.

TJÖRDS: I think I got that. But, Doctor, can you tell us, in the few moments we have left, what other potentially harmful substances or habits you and Mr. Smith are currently working on? Some people are saying you are prepared to ban everything from loud music to loud ties.

LAVAGER: Ha ha. Well, I'm not sure we'd go quite that far, but to answer your question, we will have to choose our words carefully. The problem is whenever we do mention something we think might be harmful, lots of people immediately start hoarding it against the day it will be outlawed.

TJÖRDS: Ah, yes, in fact I remember the incident a few months ago when we journalists thought we were witnessing the outbreak of some horrible disease. Reports came in about people showing up for work with stomach aches and blue mouths and tongues. Then, right before airing a special bulletin which would have alarmed everybody, one of our correspondents recalled your niece, Letitia, had been quoted in a magazine that week as saying you were investigating blueberries for some reason or other. People had started buying up blueberries like crazy!

LAVAGER: Yes, that was Letitia's idea of a joke. She only said that to get rid of a reporter who had been harassing us.

GEORGE: Actually, it was cranberries we were worried about.

LAVAGER: And speaking of food, George, why don't you tell Laslo about the turkey project?

GEORGE: Of course. Everyone knows turkey meat contains tryptophan, which is why you get sleepy after Thanksgiving dinner. Obviously, this could be dangerous for people driving cars, flying airplanes, and so on, after they eat, so we wanted to confirm how serious it is.

TJÖRDS: Don't tell me: You fed turkey to some rats…

GEORGE: Exactly! Lots of it. And sure enough, the rats all fell asleep.

LAVAGER: I'm sure we don't have to tell you the implications of that.

TJÖRDS: No, I think I can imagine, especially when I put it together with the cranberries. Do we need to be worried about sweet potatoes and marshmallows, green bean casserole with mushroom soup and French fried onions, and pumpkin pie?

GEORGE: We're not sure.

LAVAGER: Yet.

TJÖRDS: Too soon to change my Thanksgiving plans, then?

LAVAGER: I would say so, yes.

TJÖRDS: Okay, well, what else are you working on now?

LAVAGER: To tell the truth, I could spend the rest of the day listing things. For example, we are studying anything that is not either biodegradable or recyclable. Lead and mercury have not escaped our attention. Why, do you realize that in the wrong hands, the common thermometer becomes a deadly weapon?

TJÖRDS: No, Doctor.

LAVAGER: Well, we should all think about that. Also, we are interested in habits which affect the heart and circulatory system. For example, we have ample evidence that common belts and shoelaces restrict circulation. We plan to recommend legislation against all such clothing, which would include panty hose, bras and girdles, wigs, tight collars, and so on.

TJÖRDS: You'll have to admit, that might be hard to get used to, Dr. Lavager. And of course it would mean more industries closing their doors.

LAVAGER: Well, yes, but between that and my pending legislation to require wide-brimmed hats to protect us from direct sunlight, I think we might have the makings of a new clothing style, which would once and for all end the wasteful practice of having new fashions every year. Just think of the benefits to society if every man, woman, and child wore an outfit that is nothing more than an open-necked bag, a wide-brimmed hat, and slip-on sneakers.

TJÖRDS: Or those loose galoshes you're so famous for. I see you're wearing them now.

LAVAGER: These protect me from certain insecticides and fertilizers which can be absorbed through the skin. You'd be surprised what you can pick up by walking on a lawn these days.

TJÖRDS: Very interesting.

GEORGE: I would say, too, that the outfits Dr. Lavager is describing might very well become an important factor in population control. Another good substitute for some of the substances currently prescribed by physicians.

TJÖRDS: An interesting thought, Mr. Smith. But, again, Doctor, what do you say to critics who point out how many people have lost their jobs because the products their companies make have been banned or severely restricted?

GEORGE: Let me take that one, Laslo. I can only say there are plenty of opportunities in government. The EPA, the FDA, the Consumer Product Safety Commission, the Surgeon General's Office, the Fish and Wildlife

Service, and the Centers for Disease Control are all hiring like crazy! Oh, and also the IRS.

TJÖRDS: That's certainly good to know.

GEORGE: I'm just glad I could remember them all!

TJÖRDS: Indeed. Well, gentlemen, it's been a pleasure having you with us this morning. Thank you for coming.

LAVAGER: Thank you, Laslo. It was good to be here and to have the opportunity to tell our story.

GEORGE: Yes, thank you. And by the way, Laslo, thanks for the idea about the loud ties. We'll have to give that one some attention.

TJÖRDS: Ladies and gentlemen, we've been speaking with Dr. Gardiner Lavager and his assistant, Mr. George Smith, of the American Eco-Toxicology Association. This is Laslo Tjörds in Los Angeles for "What's Up Today."

As Laslo Tjörds faded, a sign popped up on the screen:

How long has-your TV been on?

Remember the four-hour limit.

A service of the Advertising Council

Wong Lee turned off the TV and then joined Letitia and Dr. Baldwin in applause.

George beamed, and Dr. Lavager tried not to look too pleased with himself, stroking his goatee absently.

The rest of the morning was passed in pleasant conversation. George was ecstatic, having managed to kiss the *side* of Letitia's neck lightly three times.

Suddenly, Letitia shot out of her chair. "Quiet, everybody! I hear something!"

Everyone strained to hear whatever it was.

"There it is again!" she said. "What ... Wait a minute ... It's the telephone, Uncle Gardy, the telephone in your office."

"Could be trouble, Gardy," said Dr. Baldwin, already at the green door. "Maybe I'd better answer it."

All except Wong Lee rushed into the hall and ran to the door of Dr. Lavager's

office. Lavager's galoshes set up a rubbery echo in the corridor as he clomped along.

"Come on, Wong Lee," shouted Letitia. "We're all in this together, ha!"

"No, is okay, I stay here, Miss Retisha. That ritto office too smaw for five peopos anyway. I just stay and crean up some more. Besides, is not so far; I can risten flom here."

In the office, they all held their breath while Dr. Baldwin carefully picked up the receiver, composed himself, and said, "Dr. Lavager's office."

There was a pause, then, "Yes, thank you, I'll wait."

Excitedly to the group, "I think it may be the President!"

Everyone gasped. Dr. Lavager raised himself up to his full height and took a step toward the telephone.

"Yes, yes he is, sir, just a moment, please," said Baldwin. "Gardy, here, take the phone. It *is* the President."

"Gardiner Lavager here. Yes, Mr. President. Nice of you to call, sir. Do you mind if I put you on the speakerphone? There's an excited little group gathered here, sir. Thank you."

Dr. Lavager pushed a button on the small box beside the phone, and the President's voice filled the room and spilled out into the hallway. Even Wong Lee could hear it in the lab.

"Dr. Lavager, all of you are to be congratulated. Not since Pasteur has so much been done by so few in so short a time to make the world safe from harmful substances. I know today is only the beginning. If the restrictive legislation, which I signed into law to go into effect at noon, proves itself, as I am certain it will in a very short time, I expect Congress to be even more willing to act favorably upon all future legislation I will propose as a result of the efforts of you and your colleagues of the American Eco-Toxicology Association. As we all realize—and we pray our realization has not come too late—there is no time to lose in this critical area, where the quality of life, not only for those of us here in America today, but also for future generations of Americans, is so much at stake. We thank you, Dr. Lavager, we all thank you."

Dr. Lavager, nervous at first, now found his composure returning.

"We are indeed deeply touched by those sentiments, Mr. President, and we are proud to have been able to play a small part in the betterment of our nation. We are thankful for the opportunity to continue to contribute, until our work is finished."

Everyone felt a glow of satisfaction. In the drama of the moment, even the rats had again become still in their cages back in the lab. Wong Lee grabbed his cellophane tape dispenser and clutched it tightly.

"I know there are detractors," the President continued, "as there always are when there are issues which are difficult to understand or when special interests seem to be threatened. But the role of government is to lead and protect the people, especially in circumstances in which some of them haven't the incentive to do what is best for themselves. So keep up the good work. You have my support."

"Thank you for those encouraging words, Mr. President," said Dr. Lavager.

"You have my support (click) You have my support (click) You have my support (click)"

There was a brief scraping sound, some static, and then the dial tone. Dr. Lavager hung up the phone. The little group stood silent for a long moment, each absorbed in his or her own thoughts, deeply moved by the President's message. Especially Dr. Baldwin, who had written it at the President's request a few days before.

George was the first to awaken from his reverie. There was a strange sound in the distance which seemed to grow louder and more cacophonous. The others began to notice it too.

"Holy Toledo, what the heck is that noise?" asked George. "It's really awful."

They listened for a few more seconds, and finally Dr. Lavager said solemnly, "It's only the chimes in the Struthers Memorial Bell Tower. It is now noon."

"Well, it sounds more like somebody mugging the Good Humor Man."

The little group slowly filed out into the hall and walked back toward the laboratory. Dr. Lavager reached the door first, but didn't go inside. As the others peered over his shoulder or under his arms and through the door, they saw something very strange. Literally everything in the room, from the rat cages to the test tubes to the oatmeal cookies and the stereo, and including the armchair, the work tables, and the floor, was completely covered with a thick coating of yellow chalk dust. Even the crepe paper streamers had turned yellow. A dense yellow fog filled the air. Wong Lee could barely be seen, gesticulating wildly, at the other end of the greenboard near where he had plugged in the vacuum cleaner.

"Oh, Doc, Wong Ree so solly! (cough, cough) I tly crean off chawk tlay on gleenboard, but I forget put dustbag in vacuum creaner. Chawk dust brow ev'ywhere, is messee, messee. I so solly!"

CHAPTER EIGHT

Two days later, an excited Wong Lee O'Grady, no longer covered in yellow chalk dust, stepped off a steam bus at Los Angeles International Airport. Since traffic had been light, he found himself with time to spare before he had to board his flight to Omaha. Once inside the terminal, he found a men's room. He fished in his pants pocket for a dime, put it into the coin slot of a pay toilet, and entered the stall.

He placed his small carry-on suitcase on the toilet seat and began to remove his suit, which he hung on the hook on the stall door, once almost dropping his trousers in his eagerness to get on with his journey and find out what the mysterious summons from MADCOM was all about.

Although Wong Lee had made several trips to Omaha in the past two years, they had been on his own initiative, and only when he had something especially important to report. This was the first time they had sent for him. There was no denying the authenticity of the telegram. The telegraph company had called Dr. Baldwin's office trying to locate Wong Lee, and Dr. Baldwin scribbled the message on the back of an envelope and dispatched a student to deliver it at Dr. Lavager's laboratory. Wong Lee had unfolded the envelope to find the coded message: HAVE STOCK TO DUMP STOP CONSIDER THIS MAJOR EXPRESSION DESIRE FOR COUNSEL STOP, LOVE, MOM. Wong

Lee had thought quickly and immediately gone back to Dr. Baldwin's office himself.

Dr. Baldwin was full of questions, as Wong Lee had expected.

"Oh, Wong Lee," he had said as Wong Lee entered his office, "I couldn't help seeing

what was in that telegram, you know."

"Is okay, Doc. Wong Ree got no seclets."

"I didn't know your mother was in this country, Wong Lee. You must be very frugal, to have been able to save up enough money for your mother to be in the stock market," the old man had continued.

"Yes, is velly hard, Doc, but Mama an' me, we velly crose."

"Does this mean you'll be wanting to take a few days off?"

"Oh, yes; I hope is okay," Wong Lee had answered, bashfully. "Besides, tomollow is St. Seymour's Day, an' Wong Ree awrays tly to be with Mama on St. Seymour's Day."

"That's funny, I don't remember there being a 'St. Seymour's Day' last year," said Baldwin, scratching his head.

"Oh, well, I t'ink maybe my Mama come to visit me rast year, so I no take time off; I learry no lemember."

"All right, Wong Lee, I guess you deserve a few days, anyway. It's no picnic planting poison ivy."

"Oh, thank you velly much, Doc," Wong Lee had said with a low bow on his way out, pleased with his success at getting the time off and covering his tracks.

In the toilet stall, Wong Lee reached into the suitcase and

pulled out a carefully folded green U.S. Army uniform, complete with polished brass insignia, a black belt, a permanent-press beige shirt, a black wool tie, black socks, and gleaming black low-quarter shoes. He handled the garments respectfully, almost tenderly, in spite of his haste. And as he dressed, he tried to guess what was up. Could it be there was a general alert, with some stand about to be taken against the Enemy? He had been trained for that, but it still didn't prevent him from being nervous. Maybe he was going to get a promotion. That was possible, because being assigned to Dr. Lavager had given him a goldmine of good information to report back to Camp Shafto. Or maybe he was going to be transferred. That would be unfortunate ... for the same reason, unless, of course, the transfer was part of the promotion. The possibilities were endless, and they swam like slippery koi through his mind as he fumbled with his zipper and buttons. Whatever was going on, he was confident he could handle it.

Before the Army, life had been a confusing series of rejections. His origin was uncertain, even to himself, though he didn't like to admit it. He was a U.S. citizen by birth but knew nothing of his parents and spent his formative years being shuttled from one ethnically oriented or religiously sponsored orphanage to another because there was no place in which he fit properly. Along the way, he learned to play the harmonica, but little else useful. Finally, when he was 18 he ran away from a Jewish orphanage near Philadelphia and hitch-hiked to New

York City to try to become a professional musician. Unfortunately, at that time no one was looking for a Chinese-Irish Jew who played the harmonica, so Wong Lee joined the Army. It had been his home ever since.

Until he was tapped by Captain Gruber, he had found Army life dull, but these past two years had been more fulfilling. At last, he was proving he was useful, that his life had meaning. It was an opportunity he was going to make the most of. Wong Lee applied himself diligently to the espionage business. He liked spying. It was the only thing he had turned out to be good at, besides the harmonica and gardening. He went about his job efficiently and without emotion. To him, his "colleagues," such as Dr. Lavager, and his superiors, were merely objects. Their relationship to each other, while extremely important, was meaningless without himself as the catalyst to make the relationship operate. To Dr. Lavager, Wong Lee was a trusted subordinate. To Dr. Baldwin, he was a subservient and pitiable foreigner. To himself, he was what he had to be to get the job done. He made no judgments.

Wong Lee reached into the suitcase again and withdrew a soft Army garrison cap. He placed it on his head and began folding his suit for the suitcase. That done, he snapped the suitcase latches closed, opened the toilet stall door, and emerged as Staff Sergeant Wong Lee O'Grady, U.S. Army. He headed for the ticket counter.

Anticipating the inevitable challenge of making himself

understood, when it was his turn at the counter he pulled out a handwritten note he had prepared while on the bus. He handed it to the agent, who read:

I am Staff Sergeant W. L. O'Grady. Please pardon the note. I am recovering from a throat wound.

At this point, the agent furtively looked for, and found, the unauthorized Purple Heart Wong Lee wore on his chest.

I would like a round trip ticket to Omaha, leaving on the next flight this morning, and returning tomorrow morning. My orders are in my suitcase, if you would like to see them. I will be carrying the small suitcase on board, and I have no baggage to check. I would like to sit in the no-smoking section. Thank you.

As usual, the agent didn't ask to see Wong Lee's orders. If that ever did happen, Wong Lee had an official-looking document in the suitcase he would pull out with great ceremony. If the agent questioned it, Wong Lee would simply ask for a paper and pencil in awkward sign language and then begin to work on a laborious written explanation. Passengers in line behind him would begin to grumble, making the agent so nervous she would tell Wong Lee to forget about it, hand him back the worthless document, and issue a ticket. Even if there were no line behind Wong Lee, the agent would begin feeling like an ass for giving a wounded veteran a hard time and would cave in. This had never failed to work.

Having worked the trick again today, he put his boarding pass into his coat pocket and started for Gate 19, the boarding area for his flight.

Wong Lee walked between the uprights of the electronic metal detector under the watchful eyes of a security guard. For some reason he always breathed a sigh of relief after passing that hurdle unapprehended, even though he never carried anything more dangerous than loose change. Yet he knew from his training in the Dump Command there were deceptively simple means at his disposal if he should ever have to commandeer a commercial jet in the line of duty. One method involved picking up a new copy of *Ladies' Home Journal* or some other slick magazine, grabbing a flight attendant from behind, and threatening to give her deep paper cuts on the neck. Paper cuts could kill, if applied properly.

He heard his flight being called. In his haste, he had forgotten to do something else while in the men's room, and he now discovered he needed to make another visit. He checked his watch against the time on a large wall clock. If he hurried, he could still get to a men's room before boarding. He found one near the USO lounge and went in. He fished in his pants pocket for another dime, but came up empty handed. He was completely out of change. He looked around frantically, but there was no one in sight. Time was running out, and it was too late to find a newsstand. So, with great resolve, Wong Lee clutched his suitcase tightly and ran for the gate, muttering to himself. The gate agent smiled cheerfully at him when he arrived.

"You can board now, sir, right through the blue door to your left. Please show your boarding pass to the flight attendant."

Wong Lee became more and more uncomfortable as he shuffled to the tail of the airplane and took his assigned seat. He was going to have to sit between two overweight, matronly women. There were two things wrong with that. One was they would undoubtedly want to talk to him, since he knew he looked endearingly like Audie Murphy. The other was it would be a logistical headache for him to get up and go to the lavatory once the plane was in the air. There was only one way to handle the situation, and that was to become passively obnoxious.

As he sat down and bent forward to put his suitcase under the seat in front of him, he deftly reached into his breast pocket and withdrew a small piece of garlic, which he surreptitiously popped into his mouth. He chewed for a few seconds and then sat up and began to breathe deeply. The effect was instantaneous and satisfying. The seatmate on his left, next to the window, suddenly discovered the activity outside the plane was so fascinating she couldn't take her eyes off it. The other woman struck up a conversation with the passenger sitting across the aisle. Now all Wong Lee had to do was hold out until they were in the air and then put his hand on the aisle-seat woman's knee, gesturing with his body that he wished to get up. Chances are he wouldn't have to speak a word before the woman would be out of her seat like a shot to make way for him.

Wong Lee fastened his seat belt, relaxed as much as he could, and let his eyes close. The garlic actually didn't taste too bad. He dimly heard the engines rev up and a distant voice explaining about the window and door exits and the drop-down oxygen masks as he began to doze.

CHAPTER NINE

From *The Washington Post*
ENDANGERED SNAIL THREATENS TO CLOSE LANDFILLS

Washington, DC (UP) – The U.S. Fish and Wildlife Service has put yet another animal on the Endangered Species list. *Helix rapidus*, commonly called the darter snail, is found only in sanitary landfills in the Southeastern U.S. where it thrives on decomposing vegetable matter. Known chiefly for its unique ability to retract quickly into its shell and roll away in random directions at high speed, for a snail, it is apparently vulnerable to discarded coffee grounds which somehow render newly hatched snails unable to generate shells of sufficient thickness to roll well, leaving them unprotected from predators, including restauranteurs who harvest them as a delicacy. FWS estimates that at the current rate of population decline the darter snail will be extinct in five years.

"We're looking at several solutions," said FWS Director Duncan Feldspar at a news conference on the steps of the Capitol Building. "Regular coffee is already outlawed, and we could ban decaf too, but that wouldn't address the coffee grounds already in the landfills which will take many years to dissipate. Purging the landfills of existing coffee grounds would cost billions, although we've spent that kind of money on lesser problems in the past. Or, we could seize private farmland by eminent domain, open new, coffee-free landfills and relocate a sustainable population of darter snails to each one, which might cost less and be faster. Of course, we're immediately calling a halt to the harvesting of darter snails for restaurants."

"This is terrible news," said Chef Geoffrey Pierre, aka "Chef Jeff" of New York's famed *Le Cube de Bouillon* restaurant. "Although hard to catch, the darter snail is much tastier and to be preferred over French escargot, as long as you don't say it comes from landfills."

This reporter spoke to Mr. George Smith, chief assistant to Dr.

Gardiner Lavager of the American Eco-Toxicology Association, for his opinion. "We should definitely save the darter snails," he says. "Our tests show that laboratory rats don't die from eating them, even in large doses. So we should outlaw decaf coffee for sure."

An editorial in today's American Farm Bureau Federation's *Farm Bureau News* says, "Haven't we suffered enough? We know exactly what they can do with their darter snail."

Asked to comment, Senator J. Hooper Harper (R-SC), chairman of the Senate Committee on Environment and Public Works and vice-chairman of the Joint Congressional Oversight Committee to Oversee Oversight Committees, said, "Here we go again." He refused to elaborate.

CHAPTER TEN

Wong Lee awoke to find the airplane circling the Omaha airport and his bowels in an uproar. He had slept through the whole flight, and once again it was too late for relief.

Dumb thing to have to put up with in the line of duty, he thought, disgustedly. The garlic was tasting lousy by now, too, and there was no place to put it. The window-seat lady had had three Scotches while he slept. The flight attendant was removing the bottles and cup and putting up the woman's tray table. The woman was slumped in her seat, glassy-eyed, her head still turned toward the window. From the reflection, Wong Lee thought she might be about to get sick. The other lady had taken a bottle of perfume out of her purse and was holding it near her nose with the cap partly unscrewed. Though pretending not to, she was obviously inhaling the fumes and apparently had been doing so for most of the flight because to Wong Lee she looked almost as drunk as her counterpart to his left. Maybe I overdid it, he thought.

Wong Lee maintained his self-control as the airplane landed and taxied to the gate.

Once out of the plane, he ran to the nearest newsstand with his little suitcase bumping his thigh at every other step. Then, with a handful of dimes at last, he sprinted back down the concourse to a men's room and burst into a stall, just in time.

After a cup of decaf at a snack bar to try to wash away the

garlic taste, he stepped outside and got in line for the steam bus that would take him to the edge of the city. There he was to be met as usual by one of Captain Gruber's men.

He felt a lot better now, still confident he would be ready to respond appropriately to whatever challenge lay in wait for him at the Dump. Nevertheless, his eyes widened at the sight that greeted him when he alighted from the bus. There was Captain Gruber himself along with his driver and another officer whom Wong Lee had never met. And more surprising than being met by the adjutant himself was the fact that these men were not sitting in the usual jeep or staff car. They were on a buckboard, pulled by a mule.

Wong Lee walked over to the wagon and saluted the officers smartly.

"Staff Sergeant O'Glady leporting, sir."

"Good to see you, Sergeant," said Captain Gruber as he returned the salute. "Happy Saint Seymour's Day!"

Everyone laughed, and Captain Gruber introduced the other officer.

"This is Captain Crockett, the S-2. Captain Crockett, Sergeant O'Grady."

They shook hands.

"This is PFC Jefferson, our driver. Or what is it, 'wrangler' maybe?"

"'Driver' will do for now, sir," said Jefferson with a smile, nodding at Wong Lee.

"And this," continued Captain Gruber, indicating the long-eared creature in Jefferson's charge, "is Matilda."

Matilda looked at the men disdainfully and turned her head away, almost as if she knew the additional passenger would add to her burden.

"Climb aboard," said Captain Crockett. "We've got a lot to talk about, and not much time, so we might as well get started right now."

"Sorry about the transportation," said Captain Gruber, "but it was the best the Motor Pool guys could come up with until the steam jeeps arrive."

PFC Jefferson coaxed the reluctant mule into action, and the buckboard began to move down the road toward the military reservation. The men made ice-breaking small talk for a few minutes, including the inevitable comments comparing the types of pollution caused by automobiles and by mules. Then Captain Crockett became serious.

"How are the people out in California reacting to the new laws, Sergeant?"

"Not say for sure, sir, but seculity velly tight alound rablatoly now," said Wong Lee. "Doc Ravager spend rots of time washing hands and not go out much, and Doc Bawdwin nervous as cat awr de time, so maybe dey tink tings going be bad. Sometime when George Smith go liding bicyco, peopo makee obscene gesture, rike dis, at him. Wong Ree spend awr rast week pranting poison ivy alound rab building."

Captain Crockett laughed. "That's wonderful, really great security, isn't it?" he said sarcastically. "Boys, this job is going to be easier than we thought."

"I'll say," chimed in Captain Gruber. "Why, all they'll get with poison ivy in the bushes is a lot of coeds showing up at the infirmary with itchy backsides."

They all laughed uproariously at that idea, and then Wong Lee continued.

"But I not teow you about other stuff yet. Bloken grass on top of wall, bob wire, seclet TV camlas, and empracements for six machine guns."

That sobered them up a bit.

"Okay, Sergeant O'Grady, that's exactly the kind of information we need from you," said Captain Crockett. "I know you're wondering why we sent for you. Your two years of thankless, but excellently performed, duty at the university are about to come to an end. Wong Lee, we want you to help us kidnap Dr. Lavager himself and bring him here to the Dump."

"How you want me do this?" asked Wong Lee without emotion.

"That's what we have to figure out, with your help, Wong," said Captain Crockett. "Aren't you even a little curious why we want to do this?"

To Crockett, the concern wasn't over Wong Lee's lack of curiosity, but the need to make sure he didn't find out the real reason behind the mission. It wasn't yet time for Wong Lee to be let in on the secret-from-everybody plot to take over the world. For now, Crockett simply had to make up a story about how the kidnapping fit into the secret-from-the-government-only mission to stockpile harmful substances as a deterrent to Enemy aggression.

"Okay, how come, sir?" asked Wong Lee, dutifully.

Captain Crockett relaxed on the buckboard seat and told the story.

"So, you see, Sergeant," he concluded, "we need to move into a new phase of our operation. We're afraid if the public reacts quickly and violently to the new laws, it will create a political situation in which the American Eco-Toxicology Association will be muzzled and, worse, have its grants withdrawn until people cool off. We simply can't afford to suffer the consequences of that. Our agents assigned to various key researchers, like your Dr. Lavager, won't be able to send us any more information because their subjects will have to suspend their research and go back to teaching and writing letters to the editor. In the meantime, we've learned the Enemy's weapons stockpiles are at an all-time high, and there are signs he is massing troops along his western borders. Peru and Honduras are pretty nervous.

"So what we have to do is kidnap Dr. Lavager before the politicians silence him. We'll bring him here and convince him to work for us so our own development and stockpiling can continue. If what you've told us in your reports about him is true, he'll be glad to cooperate just to be able to continue with his work. He seems like an extremely dedicated man."

"He some kind of nut awr light," said Wong Lee, catching the spirit of the mission.

As he said this, another buckboard approached from the opposite direction, moving fast. It was smaller and lower slung than the Army rig and had wide rear wheels that were sprung higher than the front, giving it a racy tilt. Each wheel had mag spokes and oversize chrome lug nuts. There was a box full of storage batteries under the seat, with wires leading to a wooden dashboard on which a radio and an eight-track stereo tape player were mounted. There were two speakers in the front and one on the floor in the back. A Confederate flag flew from the antenna. Although small, the rig was drawn by two animals … sleek, black ponies, compact and muscular. They labored noisily in their chromed traces.

A sports buckboard.

Three teenage boys and a girl were on the vehicle, their long hair trailing in the breeze. They flashed by, jeering at the soldiers and openly displaying lit cigarettes. One of the boys shouted something about "wrinkled uniforms" and threw what looked like a small stone at the Army wagon before disappearing around a bend.

"Stupid kids!" said Captain Gruber, who had sat stolidly, eyes front, throughout the brief ordeal.

The stone turned out to be a firecracker, which exploded

nearby and frightened old Matilda into a frenzy. Braying loudly, she started to run, and it was all Jefferson could do to keep the wagon on the road. The men held on as best they could while the buckboard jounced along. The mule maintained the furious pace in spite of Jefferson's efforts to slow her down, and after about five minutes they arrived at the Camp Shafto gate. Matilda heaved a giant sigh, as of recognition, and dropped dead, causing the buckboard to stop with a bone-jarring lurch. Jefferson pitched forward, landing on top of the animal and then sliding off into the sand. Shaken but unhurt, the other men dismounted. After making sure Jefferson was okay, they all strode toward the headquarters building, Jefferson trailing behind, carrying Wong Lee's suitcase.

"What are you looking so sad for, Jefferson?" asked Captain Gruber.

"It's just that … well, Matilda and I were just getting to know each other, sir."

"But she died heroically for her country," offered Captain Crockett. "Don't worry, we'll call the Motor Pool and make sure she has a proper funeral."

"Maybe it's just as well the mule died," muttered Captain Gruber, "since we couldn't have spared a bullet to shoot her if she'd only been hurt."

"What you usuarry do?" asked Wong Lee.

"Well, remember we've only been using animals for a few days now, so we probably have a lot to learn. Never had one get badly hurt yet. Standard procedure would probably be to have somebody from the Chemical Development section come out with a bucket of glue and let the mule sniff it to death."

Gruber paused and looked at Crockett.

"Definitely some irony there, I guess," said Crockett.

Jefferson rolled his eyes, but the joke was lost on Wong Lee.

They entered the headquarters building, doffing their hats. To the soldier-clerks inside, Wong Lee must have looked like a visiting dignitary in his tailored and pressed Army greens next to everybody else in their droopy, wrinkled fatigues. Someone yelled, "Ten-Hut!" Everyone dropped work and stood up.

"As you were!" said Crockett, annoyed. "This is *Sergeant* O'Grady."

The soldiers grumbled and went back to their work. Wong Lee was embarrassed, but pleased by the impression he had made. He and the two officers entered Major Farina's office after Crockett sent Jefferson out to the PX Canteen for decaf and Danishes.

"The Old Man will be here in about an hour," said Crockett. "Meanwhile, O'Grady, let's work on the problem so we'll have a plan to recommend to him when he gets here. He's real anxious for us to move on this."

For the next sixty minutes, the three men sat locked in serious conversation, with Crockett taking copious notes. Jefferson came and went, delivering the decaf and Danishes which the three men devoured without interrupting their intense discussion. Wong

Lee filled the officers in on the layout of the laboratory, all the security devices and how they worked, and where the controls and monitors were. He detailed the daily habits of Dr. Lavager, George, Letitia, and the few other people who visited the lab, including Dr. Baldwin, not failing to describe his own duties and what Dr. Lavager and the others expected of him as their innocent gardener and sometime janitor.

"Okay, that's perfect, O'Grady," said Crockett when Wong Lee had finished. "Now, it seems to me it'll be easy to figure a plan for getting Lavager out of there. The only problem will be doing it in a way that won't cause a panic when people find out he's missing. We've got to think of a good cover story and plant it somewhere."

"Wong Ree velly good at pranting!"

It was perhaps the first joke Wong Lee had ever attempted in his life, but he was beside himself with pleasure at the prospect of the exciting adventure that lay ahead.

A little before noon, Major Farina strode into the office, returned the three salutes, and sat down behind his desk.

"Good of you to come on such short notice, Sergeant O'Grady," he said. "I hope it didn't jeopardize your cover, but this was important."

"No plobrem, sir. Is honor to meet you." Wong Lee bowed.

"Okay, Ernie, what have you got for me?"

"Sergeant O'Grady's been a great help, sir, and I think we've got something you'll like."

"Good. Let's hear it."

As Captain Crockett arranged his notes and rose to speak, a loud scraping and tapping sound filled the room. It seemed to be coming from under the work table. Everyone looked in that direction. The noise continued, and the rug under the table began to rise and fall fitfully, shaking the table and causing some shifting of the piles of papers on top.

Wong Lee was so startled he stood up and retreated behind his armchair, tripping on one of the stand-up ashtrays, which clattered to the floor.

That does it!" shouted Farina. "Gruber, send a detail in here after lunch and get rid of those nutty ashtrays! I don't care what you do with them. Make nicotine bombs out of them for all I care, but get them the nuts out of here!"

"Yes, sir!"

Wong Lee's confidence had momentarily vanished, and the noise and shaking were still going on under the work table. Wong Lee picked up the ashtray and placed it next to the sofa while Farina and Crockett moved the table. Then they pulled back the rug and lifted the trap door. To the surprise of nobody but Wong Lee, out popped a beaming Second Lieutenant Edgar Duffle. He greeted the three other officers effusively, then looked questioningly in Wong Lee's direction.

"This is Staff Sergeant O'Grady, one of our operatives on the West Coast," explained Major Farina. "Sergeant O'Grady, this is Lieutenant Duffle, our OIC Development."

"Pleased to meetcha, Sarge," said Duffle as he bounded over to shake Wong Lee's hand.

Farina had first run into Duffle one day while at the Pentagon. A private at the time, Duffle had gotten lost in the mammoth building while going from one medical station to another during a physical exam. He had been wandering in the corridors for three days wearing paper slippers and a bathrobe and carrying a urine specimen, subsisting on candy bars and coffee filched from empty offices at night, and afraid to embarrass himself by asking anyone for directions, not that there were many people to ask in the almost-deserted building. Farina took him in tow, haggard and unshaven, and returned him to the Dispensary.

Looking up his records later, Farina discovered Duffle had been a superior chemistry student in college and had an exceptionally high IQ. Farina sent for him, trained him, pulled strings to obtain a direct commission for him, and set him up as the Officer in Charge of Development.

Somewhat calmed, Wong Lee sat down again, but continued to eye the boyish lieutenant suspiciously.

"Sorry to interrupt, Major, sir," said Duffle, "but I've just got to tell you about this great idea we've come up with down below."

Farina looked at his watch, anxious to get on with the Lavager business, but he knew better than to do anything that might stifle the creativity of one of his best people. He let Duffle continue.

"One of our operatives in the San Francisco area, Sergeant Metcalf, sent us a detailed report on the work a Berkeley professor has been doing with artichokes. He says they've discovered artichokes contain a drug called cardinilis which, in sufficient concentration, causes the heart muscle to overwork itself like crazy and finally burn out after only a few minutes. In rats, anyway. Funny thing, too, the report also said in smaller doses the drug cures cancer in rats, but I guess we can't afford to take a chance on that, can we?

"So Sergeant Metcalf stole all the original files, reports, and data on the artichoke thing and sent them in. That puts the professor at least a year behind on redoing all his research, but meanwhile we have a leg up on everybody with this one. It's a real first for us."

"Sounds good, Ed," said Farina, "but what are we going to do with it?"

"That's the best part, sir. We've been fooling around down below, and we've come up with a way to refine cardinilis from artichoke hearts. What we can do is get a lot of this drug and spike ordinary artichokes with it. They'll be deadly!"

"How do you know it'll work on people?" asked Captain Gruber.

"Oh, it works, sir. We've already tried it."

Mouths fell open. Wong Lee clutched the arms of his chair so tightly his knuckles turned white.

"Oh, don't worry, there won't be any trouble," explained

Duffle. "We doctored up a boiled artichoke and took it down to skid row in Omaha the other night. We left it out on the sidewalk and then hid in an alley, waiting for a derelict to come along. You know, those guys are really desperate now. It's almost impossible to find cigarette butts in the gutters anymore, and the street price of wine has skyrocketed now that everybody's trying to make as much profit as they can before the government outlaws it. Anyway, one of them finally staggered by, and you could see when he spotted the artichoke on the sidewalk. His eyes got real big, and he stopped and just sort of stood there rocking back and forth, like he was trying to get it in focus and figure out what it was. Then he kind of tiptoed over and picked it up, almost losing his balance completely.

"I want to tell you, we were going crazy there in the alley. We thought everybody knew what an artichoke was, but this guy obviously didn't have a clue. He poked at it, put it up to his nose and sniffed it. He even pulled a piece of it off, lit it with a match, and tried to inhale the smoke. I thought that was going to kill him right there, the way he started coughing. We were about to die laughing ourselves while trying not to make any noise.

"All the commotion attracted the attention of another bum who came over from the other side of the street to see what was going on. The second bum said, 'Whuzzat there?' or something like that; it was pretty hard to make out what they were saying. And the first bum said, 'Don' know,' and held it up so the other one could see it. The second bum recognized it right away, and, boy, were we relieved! 'Azza artychoke,' he said. Quick as a wink, the second bum grabbed the artichoke and started stripping off the leaves, scraping off the soft parts with his teeth. The first bum just sat down on the sidewalk and started to cry, but by then we were only watching the second one. He ripped it open and popped the heart in his mouth, and then he tossed the rest of it on the first bum's lap and started to laugh. At least it sounded like it started as a laugh, but it went from that to a silly giggle, and pretty soon he started jumping up and down and waving his arms like a madman, yelling like a wild Indian, running back and forth across the street, bumping into the buildings and lamp posts, tripping on the curbs, then getting up and running around some more. A pretty good crowd had gathered by that time, so we slipped out of the alley and joined them. We were dressed like bums ourselves, of course. After about three minutes of the wildest gyrations I ever saw, this guy stopped right in his tracks, stood still for a few seconds, then grabbed his chest and collapsed in a heap."

"That's quite a story, Ed," said Major Farina.

"We were thrilled, sir, I can tell you. We came right back here and wrote up our report. Unfortunately, one of my men discovered his watch was stolen by one of those bums in the crowd. The dirty SOBs."

"Okay, so it works, Duffle," said Captain Crockett, "but how do you propose we use it against the Enemy? The artichoke is not an important part of his diet."

"Oh, that's easy, easy! We've dreamed up a beaut," said Duffle. "What we'll do, see, is we'll announce a 'culinary cultural exchange,' during which we'll introduce the Enemy to this delicacy. We'll make him jealous that we Americans have better artichokes than he does, and then we'll say 'Eat your hearts out!' Ha, ha, ha, ha, that's funny ..."

The others laughed too, not so much at the joke as at the scene Duffle presented with himself, rollicking, hardly able to stand up.

"You haven't been nipping any of the cardinilis yourself, have you, Ed?" asked Farina with amusement.

"Why, of course not, sir," said Duffle. "That's against regulations."

"Look, Duffle, your idea sounds fairly reasonable," said Captain Crockett, "but I don't think we can promise the artichoke ploy will provide the major thrust of our attack. You know how it is ..."

"Oh, of course not, sir," said Duffle. "'Selective stockpiling,' I know." With that, he gave Captain Crockett a wink, which was caught by Major Farina.

"One of these days," said Farina, "I swear I'm going to have to break my rule and go down below to see just what you guys are cooking up. It's a good thing I know I can trust all of you."

They all laughed self-consciously. Wong Lee sat there, taking it all in, trying to understand everything that was being said, and why. It was an unlikely tableau: a ruthless but charismatic major plotting to kidnap the nation's foremost humanitarian and put him to work manufacturing insidious weapons of suffering and death for an Enemy the government didn't think dangerous enough to defend against openly; two bright young captains, both trained for better things, acting as no more than cold, calculating henchmen, blindly loyal to the major; an idiot second lieutenant with no sense of professional decorum or propriety and absolutely no concept of the meaning of what he did each day in the underground labs; and, of course, Wong Lee himself, who knew in his heart he would do anything for the approval of his nearest fellow man.

Major Farina continued with Lieutenant Duffle. "Make sure you go ahead and stockpile some of that cardilinis. I'm sure it'll come in handy one of these days."

"Yes, sir," said Duffle. "There's only one little problem."

"What's that?"

"Well, you see, it takes about a hundred pounds of artichokes to get an ounce of cardilinis, and we used almost a whole ounce in the one we gave to the bum."

"Oh, brother," said Crockett, "here we go."

"So for the past few days I've had one of our men out quietly buying up artichoke farmland near Castroville, California, which as everyone knows is the artichoke center of the world. That's so we can ship artichokes here by the carload and nobody will get suspicious."

Duffle looked pleased with himself.

"Well, Ernie," said the major, "you'd better plan on getting those 'nerve gas' tank cars back from New Haven. Lieutenant Duffle, thank you for your report. As usual, a fine piece of work. We'll see you later, okay?"

"Yes, sir. Thank you, sir."

Duffle raised the trapdoor and took a few steps down inside. He started to lower the door after him, ducked his head, hesitated, raised the door, and stuck his head into the office again, at floor level. "There's just one more thing, sir."

"What's that, Ed?" sighed Farina.

"Eat your heart out, sir."

The door snapped shut a split second before both Crockett and Gruber jumped on it, their combat boots resounding from the hollow beneath the door. Laughing, they replaced the rug and the work table and returned to their armchairs.

Major Farina got right back to business. "All right, we've wasted enough time. What's your plan for grabbing Dr. Lavager?"

"Basically this, sir," answered Captain Crockett. "Sergeant O'Grady here knows the layout of the campus and the lab, and he knows everybody's habits. He can get a kidnap squad through the security defenses with no sweat. We'll send him back in charge of a squad of four other men, handpicked for their skill at working together in close quarters and their proficiency at hand-to-hand combat. O'Grady will go in first, the trusted gardener returning from his holiday. Then, when the coast is clear and Lavager is in the lab, O'Grady will signal the others. They'll show up dressed like landscape workers, driving a wagonload of trees to be transplanted on the laboratory grounds, inside the wall. O'Grady will supervise while they plant the trees, since that would be his job anyway if they were real landscapers, only they'll plant them strategically just inside the wall entrance so as to block the view of any passersby when the real action takes place. Then they'll get out a big plastic bag full of fertilizer, and they'll empty it on the trees, folding it up neatly afterwards."

Farina listened intently, nodding here and there and making notes as Crockett continued.

"By now, all that work will have made the men hot and thirsty, so O'Grady will invite them into the building for a drink of water. He'll proudly show them around the lab while Lavager is working away, not suspecting a thing. Then, at just the right moment, they'll spring the trap. They'll grab Lavager, give him a shot of sodium pentothal, and stuff him into the fertilizer bag. Then they'll haul him off in the wagon to the edge of the campus where they've parked a rented steam van for the drive to the airport. By that time, with the sodium pentothal, Lavager will be very cooperative, and the rest of the trip from there to here will be easy."

"Is that it?" he asked when Crockett paused to take a breath.

"Not yet. Now comes the clincher. Lavager reports to the university president, a guy named Dr. Baldwin who O'Grady thinks is very gullible. O'Grady will leave Baldwin a fake message from Lavager. In the message, Lavager will apologize for his hasty departure, explaining that he's been called away unexpectedly by the President to go on a special goodwill mission to offer information on harmful substances research to the peoples of Enemy countries. He'll say the mission is supposed to be secret until he actually arrives overseas. According to O'Grady, Baldwin will believe anything and probably won't bother to call the President to verify the story."

"And?"

"Almost done," said Crockett. "Now it's possible the kidnapping will be witnessed by a couple of Lavager's assistants. Our men can overpower them if they try to interfere, but naturally that'll blow the whistle on the 'secret mission' story. If that happens, at least the story will have confused Baldwin for a while, and it will suggest an explanation the President can use when he tells the nation about Lavager's disappearance.

"By that time, Lavager will be underground with us, and not even the CIA will know where to begin looking for him."

"That's beautiful, Ernie, really beautiful," said Major Farina. "I've got tears in my eyes, that's such a good plan. But let me ask you one thing."

"What's that, sir?"

"Back at the lab, when the kidnap squad shows up, why can't they just run in and grab Lavager without all that tree planting fanfare?"

"Oh, sir," protested Captain Crockett. "That's the kind of thing you'd expect to see in a B movie. But this…this has style. You know, planting trees for ecology and then kidnapping Mr. Ecology himself? That's class."

"It has your mark on it, all right. Okay, I approve it. It's great. Captain Gruber, pick the men you need and cut some orders that will get them back to California with Sergeant O'Grady. Ernie, take Sergeant O'Grady over to Supply to draw some linen, and get him a billet for the night. This thing gets going first thing in the morning."

Major Farina rose to signal the end of the meeting. Everyone else stood up too. Farina strode over to Wong Lee and shook his hand warmly.

"Thank you, Sergeant," he said. "Thank you very much, and good luck to you."

"A preasure, sir," said Wong Lee, beaming now himself, like Lieutenant Duffle earlier. He turned to leave with the two captains.

"And don't forget about these ashtrays, Gruber!" the major called after them.

CHAPTER ELEVEN

Wong Lee spent the rest of the day and most of the evening with the handpicked kidnap squad, going over the plan, getting acquainted, and getting the other men used to being in the presence of an Irishman with an Oriental accent. While they had to learn to get used to it, of course, it was just as necessary they learn to act as if it surprised them, so no one would suspect they were working together when they met again on the university campus. As a further precaution along those lines, Wong Lee wasn't told the names of any of these men. It would have been difficult for him to remember them anyway, since the men looked pretty much alike to him. All were dark, of average height (taller than Wong Lee, of course), and kept their faces buried in their collars, as if trying to get good suntans on the backs of their necks. They all had calloused hands with dirty fingernails, as would be expected of landscape workers. Muscles rippled appropriately beneath their droopy, wrinkled fatigues.

The next morning, a supply clerk issued faded overalls, scruffy shoes, and old khaki shirts to the four men. Captain Gruber came by with copies of their orders in case they should be stopped and questioned for any reason while in uniform. After goodbyes and good lucks all around, they were off to the airport, Wong Lee with his little suitcase and the others taking turns carrying the one duffle bag that served the four of them.

All five men wore the dressy Army green uniform. Only Wong Lee had a nametag on his. No one spoke.

At the airport they split up. Wong Lee would take the early flight to Los Angeles and the others would take the next one, two hours later. Wong Lee would return immediately to the campus, but the others wouldn't show up there until the afternoon of the next day. That would allow them time to rent a steam van and a wagon, buy a big bag of fertilizer, and dig up a bunch of trees out of a woods somewhere. It would also allow Wong Lee enough time to contact them and make alternate arrangements in case he found out Dr. Lavager was going to be away that day or that there was some other problem.

Wong Lee headed for his flight's boarding area, having this time remembered to arm himself with a pocketful of change, while the others went to the USO lounge. Playing their parts well, they sat in the lounge looking tired and bored, simultaneously sheepish and mad at the world, watching Captain Kangaroo.

Before boarding his flight, Wong Lee had a phone call to make. Making sure none of the others was following him, he ducked into a phone booth. He fished in his pants pocket for a dime. He slipped it into the coin slot, and dialed "0."

"Your call, please," said the operator as the relay clicked and released Wong Lee's dime to the coin return.

"Yes, opelator," said Wong Lee. "Thisee Misser Jorgensen. I gottee message to cawr Opelator Number Six in White Prains, New York, to leturn cawr of Misser Refkoritz, correct."

"I don't know, sir," said the operator.

"You don' know? What mean you don' know?"

"I don't know if that's correct, sir. I didn't take the message myself."

"No, no, opelator, that's *correct, correct*, not collect"

"You're not making any sense, sir. Would you like to speak to my supervisor?"

Wong Lee felt himself turning pale as his dilemma dawned on him. This was the agreed procedure for making contact; he had been over and over it in his head for almost a year, and he had it down cold ... only now, now when he had to do the real thing, he couldn't make this stupid operator understand him. Silently, he cursed his father, then his mother, since he didn't know which one of them had been Oriental.

"No, prease," he tried again. "I speo for you: see-oh-ow-ow-ee-see-tee, okay?"

"I'm sorry, sir, why don't you dial Information?"

Desperate now, with only a few minutes to flight time, Wong Lee's voice rose an octave as he fairly screamed into the mouthpiece. "You risten to me! Just get me Opelator Number Six in White Prains, an' I take care of it flom dere. You prease hully up. Not have awr day."

"Sir, as an employee of the Telephone Company in good standing, and a woman as well, I do not have to take any abuse from you or anyone else, is that clear?"

"Yes, opelator," said Wong Lee in a low voice, almost a growl, his fingers clawing slowly at the glass window of the booth, "just prace my cawr, …prease."

"Very well. I will connect you with Operator Number Six in White Plains, New York. That's Area Code 914, sir."

"Thank you," he whispered.

"I can't hear you, sir."

"I said, 'Thank you.'" He was perspiring profusely, and rubbing his free hand on his pants leg, trying to keep his palm dry.

There were lots of clicks and beeping noises on the phone as the operator attempted to contact her counterpart in New York. Finally, a female voice far away, said, "This is White Plains. May I help you?"

"Yes, operator," said Wong Lee's operator, "this is Omaha, Nebraska. I have some nut here named Jorgensen or something who says he wants to talk to you. I'll stay on the line in case he tries to pull anything funny."

There was silence from White Plains for a few seconds before that operator responded again. "Jorgensen, you say?"

"That's correct. I think he said he was returning a call from somebody back there … some Polish-sounding name, I can't remember."

"Ah, yes, that would be from Mr. Lefkowitz, I think. It's okay, operator, I remember the call. My party is paying the toll charges, so you don't have to stay on the line. Thank you, anyway."

"All right, operator," said Omaha. "I'm cutting out. So long, Bigmouth."

Wong Lee winced, but then heaved a sigh of relief.

"All right, let's have it, O'Grady," said White Plains.

"Twas blirrig, and the srithy toves," said Wong Lee. That was the sign.

"Did gyre and gimble in the wabe," said White Plains. The countersign. "Boy, you almost blew it, didn't you, O'Grady? I'll never be able to figure out why they picked you for that job when you can't even communicate. "'Twas blirrig.' That's just ridiculous!"

Wong Lee knew she was right, but he tried to appear un-intimidated. She was only a go-between anyway, not one of his superiors. She could complain about him, but as long as he did his job and asked no questions, he knew he had nothing to worry about. "Just a matter of being in light prace at light time," he said, gamely.

"Just give me the message," said White Plains. "I've got a busy board here today."

"Okay, Missee Refkoritz, risten carefurry as I can onry say once."

"Sheez, you'll be lucky if you can say it at all. All right, I'm listening."

Wong Lee tried to pronounce the words slowly and carefully. "Pigeon will be lobbed flom coop tomollow. Fright 94 from Ros Angeres. The prace is a dump. Inform The Octopus. Okay?"

129

"Gotcha. I'm sure it'll suffer a little in the translation, but we'll manage somehow. Don't take any wooden wanton." She clicked off.

Wong Lee hung up, retrieved his dime from the coin return, and got to the gate just in time to board his flight. He felt numb. It wasn't because he was a double agent – that suited him perfectly, and he'd had time to get used to that. No, it was the personal attacks on his ethnic background and his speech difficulty. New Yorkers are the worst, Wong Lee thought. He would never get used to it.

On the plane, Wong Lee ordered a "broody Maly," although he rarely drank. The flight attendant was nice about it. He gulped it down, buried himself in a day old copy of *The New York Times* he found in the seat pocket, and fell asleep.

CHAPTER TWELVE

In White Plains, Lefkowitz made another call. Her party picked up the phone in Scarsdale.

"Hello?" said the man in Scarsdale.

"Ahem. All mimsy were the borogoves."

"Oh, hi, Lefkowitz. And the mome raths outgrabe."

"Okay, Frank, listen carefully. I can only say this once. 'Pigeon will be lobbed flom

coop tomollow' … Oh, for Pete's sake, what am I saying? I mean, 'Pigeon will be robbed from coop tomorrow. Flight 94 from Los Angeles. The place is a dump. Inform The Octopus.' You got it, Frank?"

"Yeah, but I liked it the first way better."

"Oh, kiss off, jerk." She clicked off.

Two hours later it was lunchtime in Manhattan. The Chock Full o' Nuts Decaffeinated Coffee Shop on Madison Avenue was crowded. A tall man in a raincoat beat an old lady to a stool at the counter, next to a cab driver. He ordered a decaf. When the waitress brought it, he took a pencil out of his raincoat pocket and wrote something on his napkin, passing it unobtrusively to the cab driver.

"Beware the Jabberwock, my son," said the napkin.

The cab driver pulled a pencil out of his hat and wrote on his own napkin, passing it to the tall man without looking up from his strawberry diet frappé.

"The jaws that bite, the claws that catch. Hello, Frank," said the second napkin.

The tall man took his own napkin back and wrote on it, "Please don't call me by name."

The cab driver snatched his napkin back, scratched out "Frank," and wrote, "Sorry."

The tall man wrote on his napkin again. "Read carefully. I can only write this once. Pigeon will be robbed from coop tomorrow. Flight 94 from Los Angeles. The place is a dump. Inform The Octopus. By the way, I've always wondered, where do you guys park your cabs when you eat lunch?"

The cab driver studied the tall man's napkin for a moment, tossed some change on the counter, got up, and left. The tall man crumpled up the napkin and dropped it into his coffee. He stirred it with his spoon until it disintegrated, and then he drank it.

A woman got into an electric taxi in front of a fashionable Park Avenue apartment building. She was wearing a large fur coat and an expensive silk scarf.

"Cold enough for you, lady?" asked the driver.

"Such insolence," she responded.

"Ah, well in that case what if I were to say, 'Beware the Jubjub bird, and shun.'?"

"The frumious Bandersnatch. Ravi, I didn't recognize you," said the woman.

"Oh, that is perfectly okay. Now just listen carefully: Pigeon will be robbed from coop tomorrow. Flight 94 from Los Angeles. The place is a dump. Inform The Octopus."

"Very good, Ravi. Thank you very much."

That evening the Metropolitan Opera was performing Wagner. It was a full house, and as the performance came to a close, the audience was on its feet in a standing ovation. "Encore, encore!" they shouted. Siegfried and Brunhilde reappeared to sing a duet. It promised to be a powerful song, of warriors and dragons and fearsome breastplates.

In the second verse, Brunhilde assumed a particularly defiant stance and sang *a cappella*, "He took his vorpal sword in hand. Long time the manxome foe he sought – So rested he by the Tumtum tree, and stood awhile in thought."

Siegfried's eyes widened for an instant, but then without hesitation he took the identical stance opposite Brunhilde and sang the response.

"And, as in uffish thought he stood, the Jabberwock, with eyes of flame, came whiffling through the tulgey wood, and burbled as it came."

The crowd went wild, assuming this to be some newly discovered addition to the Wagnerian panoply.

Brunhilde continued her defiant song. "The pigeon will be robbed from its coop tomorrow. Flight 94 from LA. The place is a dump, so inform The Octopus."

Pandemonium broke out in the opera house. Siegfried and Brunhilde dashed out a side door together.

"You're a nut, you know that, Brunhilde?" said Siegfried as they ran two blocks and got on an uptown steam bus.

"That's what makes me so lovable, darling."

After ten blocks, Siegfried got off the bus. He entered a phone booth and dialed Western Union.

In Detroit it was one hour earlier. Jesse Jefferson had been sitting in his usual seat at the Tangiers Bar for almost four hours, ever since he had gotten the bad news from his foreman. He'd been laid off at the auto plant. Big Jesse Jefferson, the high living cool cat, had had it. He had had it every which way. Highly skilled worker? You bet. The best. Jesse Jefferson was the best damn cigarette lighter installer on the whole damn line. Shoot, he *ought* to be. That's all he'd done for five years. Five lousy years of working for the Man, but at least having enough money for a few beers and a trip downtown once in a while, and even a little left over to send home to Mama. All gone now. Poof! Just like that.

"Who needs a good auto worker now?" he mumbled as he downed his seventh beer. "Spesh'ly who needs a cigarette lighter auto worker? Sheeesh, man. Can't stay here, can't go back home and hold my head up, no way. Guess I better write to my little brother, Will. He's doin' all right there in the Army at least, bad as that is. Now he's just gonna have to make me one of his dependents, I guess. Sheeeeeesh, man."

A young man came into the bar wearing a jacket with a Western Union shoulder patch. He spoke softly to the bartender, who pointed in Jefferson's direction. The young man approached uncertainly.

"You Mr. Jesse Jefferson, sir?"

"Sir? Sir?" yelled Jefferson. "You hear that, man?" he called out to no one in particular. "He called me 'Sir.' Well, ain't that somethin' now? Hey, man, you sit down right here with ol' Mr. Jesse Jefferson Sir and have a beer."

He grabbed for the boy's jacket playfully. The boy jumped back like a cat.

"Hey, now you just take it easy there, okay, Jesse?" said the bartender cautiously.

"Awww, I am takin' it easy, man. You wouldn't believe how easy I'm takin' it. C'mon, boy. I won't hurt you. Whaddaya want from me anyway?"

"I ... I have a telegram for you, Mr. Jefferson," he stammered. He held out a yellow envelope, which Jefferson took and opened. His eyes widened as he read the message:

ONE, TWO STOP ONE, TWO STOP AND THROUGH AND THROUGH STOP THE VORPAL BLADE WENT SNICKER-SNACK STOP HE LEFT IT DEAD, AND WITH ITS HEAD STOP HE WENT GALUMPHING BACK STOP PIGEON WILL BE ROBBED FROM COOP TOMORROW STOP FLIGHT 94 FROM LOS ANGELES STOP THE PLACE IS A DUMP STOP INFORM THE OCTOPUS STOP RSVP STOP SIEGFRIED.

Jesse Jefferson was stone sober now. At least there would be one more paycheck coming after tonight's brief work was done. One the IRS need not know about.

"You wait right here, boy. Don't go away, 'cause I gotta message for you too."

He snatched a pencil from behind the boy's ear and wrote on the back of the yellow envelope:

SIEGFRIED, MESSAGE RECEIVED STOP AND HAST THOU SLAIN THE JABBERWOCK? STOP COME TO MY ARMS MY BEAMISH BOY STOP 0 FRABJOUS DAY STOP CALLOOH STOP CALLAY STOP HE CHORTLED IN HIS JOY STOP REGARDS JEFFERSON.

He gave the boy the envelope, his pencil back, and a ten dollar bill.

"Keep the change," he said, as he struck a match and burned the telegram he had received, crushing the charred remains in an ashtray.

The young man looked at Jefferson for a moment, as if they were both crazy, then turned and fled. Jefferson got up from the table without leaving a tip and dittie-bopped out of the Tangiers Bar, whistling to himself.

About 30 minutes later, outside the Athenaeum Hotel, a small, middle-aged woman walked up to a newspaper vending machine and paused as if reading the evening's headlines. She wore a black cloth coat and carried a large handbag. After a moment, a husky man wearing a brown leather jacket and blue jeans with a long comb handle sticking out the back pocket approached the newspaper stand. The woman didn't see him at first. He moved up close to her, until he was almost breathing down her neck.

He whispered, "Twas brillig, and the slithy toves."

The woman jumped about a foot off the ground. "Get away from me, you... you animal!" she yelled. "Help!"

She slugged him twice with her handbag and then took off running down the sidewalk, leaving the man standing there with his arms over his face and head. He lowered his arms and looked around to see if anyone had observed the incident. Apparently safe, he ambled to the newspaper vending machine at the other end of the block, where there was another woman dressed in a black coat and carrying a large handbag. This one was younger. He approached, cautiously.

"Uh..., excuse me, Ma'am," he began, with his hands out in a gesture of submission.

"Yeah?"

"Uh ...'Twas brillig, and the slithy toves?'"

"Okay, Jesse," she answered. "Did gyre and gimble in the wabe."

Jefferson sighed audibly. "That was close."

"Yes, Jesse, you're going to have to be more careful. For all we know, that other woman is a CIA agent, telling them the secret sign at this moment."

"All right, I'm sorry. Now listen carefully."

He gave her the message, and she hailed a passing electric cab and vanished into the night. Jesse Jefferson sat down at the curb with his head in his hands, trying not to close his eyes.

Four hours later and still in her black coat, the same woman window shopped a bookstore in the San Francisco International Airport. She was joined by a short man in a tan trench coat. They pretended not to notice each other.

"All mimsy were the borogoves," the woman whispered.

"So rested he by the Tumtum tree," he responded, still not seeming to be paying any attention to her.

"You're supposed to say 'And the mome raths outgrabe.'"

"Oh, no, that's Ralph," said the man. "He's got the flu and couldn't make it tonight, so they pulled me off another circuit and sent me over here. Of course, I said I was glad to do it. Anything for the cause, you know. Only they forgot to tell me what Ralph's countersign was, so I had to sort of fake it. See, that's what they call a field expedient, and I figured…"

"Oh, shut up," the woman whispered, somewhat shrilly. "As long as you're legit, I don't care. Now listen good."

As she gave him the message their eyes happened to meet in the reflection in the store window, superimposed on a display of Jackie Onassis' ghostwritten memoirs. There was a moment of uncertain recognition.

"Igor, is… is that you?" she said.

"Yes… and are you … Charlotte?"

"Oh, yes, Igor!"

"Charlotte!"

"Igor!"

They embraced passionately.

"Oh, Igor, I thought you were dead! No one's heard from you in six years," she cried joyously.

"I know," he soothed, "They've been keeping me sort of incommunicado, I think because I look so much like Richard Nixon. Look, I've got to take this message and run, you know, though God knows I'd much rather spend the evening catching up on old times with you."

"Don't you even have time for a drink?" she asked.

"No, I'm afraid not, Charlotte. But why don't you give me your number, and I'll look you up as soon as I get back."

The short man paused as soon as he said that, and he thought for a second. "No, that's too dangerous. It'd be a mess if we got caught. Listen, maybe I'll just ask my chief to get special permission for us to see each other, you know, through channels and everything."

"But that could take years again, darling."

Igor tugged nervously at his shirt collar, trying to think of a solution.

"Oh poop on them and their silly regulations," said Charlotte. "Here."

With that, she wrote her address and telephone number on a piece of scrap paper and handed it to Igor.

"Don't worry, it's written in invisible ink," she said, impishly. "It becomes legible only in the heat of passion."

Igor tucked the paper into his wallet. They embraced again, and kissed. Then Igor walked off toward the international departure area.

CHAPTER THIRTEEN

Dark, foreboding clouds scudded across the sky over the castle nestled in a valley in the foothills of an obscure mountain range in the bowels of Eastern Europe. A gleaming black Mercedes-Benz 300SD made its way up the treacherous, winding access road toward the manor. The grounds were enveloped in complete silence, save for the hum of the approaching engine. No birds sang. No squirrels dashed about on the lawn or dropped acorn shells from the trees. Not even a zephyr stirred to rustle the leaves or smack the dangling rope against its tall, empty flagpole. The ornate fountain in the center of the circular driveway was no more than a still reflection pool.

The Mercedes turned into the driveway, slowed as it came around the fountain, and stopped to discharge a passenger at the bottom of the marble steps leading to the massive castle door. A short man in a tan trench coat got out. He stood beside the car for a moment and looked around, as if seeing this place for the first time. He shut the car door, which caught the tail of his trench coat as it closed. The big Mercedes started to move. He pounded on the door. The car stopped. He reopened the door, cleared it of his coattail, and closed it again.

Then he turned and walked slowly up the steps as the car moved off. Just as he reached the great door, it opened slowly, revealing more gloom and darkness within. Taking a last look over his shoulder, the man stepped across the threshold. The door swung shut, catching the tail of his trench coat.

There was little to be seen inside even after his eyes had adjusted to the limited light. Its only source was a group of small, leaded glass windows far above the door through which tiny shafts of cloud-filtered sunlight passed. He waited, not moving from the spot because his trench coat held him in place. Presently, he heard footsteps approaching, and another man entered the room, alone.

This man was large, very large, with shiny, black hair combed straight back into a mass of curls at the nape of his neck. His eyes were unmistakably cold and calculating.

The short man in the trench coat spoke first.

"Uh, hi!" he said, nervously, but with great reverence. "I … I guess you must be Him. I mean … the, uh, head of our organization, known to us as 'LGM.'"

"Yes, that is correct," said the large man with a deep voice, rolling his "r"s. "I am in fact Le Grand Malfaiteur, sometimes called The Octopus, Chief of Espionage in the service of those powers who would see destroyed the weasels who govern your country. You have a message for me, yes?"

"Yes. Right. Uh, look, this is kind of embarrassing since it seems, you see, my trench coat is, uh, as you can tell, uh, heh, heh," said the short man.

"Nevair mind that. The sign, please. Give me the sign."

"Oh ... oh, yes. The sign. Uh ... 'So rested he by the Tumtum tree,'" said the short man, clearing his throat self-consciously.

Le Grand Malfaiteur, alias The Octopus, said nothing. He studied the short man carefully, passing cold eyes over him slowly, meticulously. Finally, he spoke.

"Where is Ralph?"

"Oh, Ralph ... Ralph ... right," laughed the short man in a tone of great relief. "Ralph had the flu and couldn't make it, so they told me to come in his place. I'm Igor." He spoke his name with childlike pride.

"Igor," repeated LGM, thoughtfully. "Very well, Igor. Give me the message."

"Sure thing. I've got it written down right here." Igor felt around inside his coat, awkwardly because its pockets weren't in their accustomed positions, and recovered the message, written on the back of a Pan Am boarding pass. "Okay, listen carefully. I can only say this once. No, wait a minute, ha, ha, I guess that doesn't apply to you, does it? Ha, ha, ha ... ahem. Well, anyway, here it is: Pigeon will be robbed from coop tomorrow. Flight 94 from Los Angeles. The place is a dump. Inform The Octopus. Hey, that's you, of course."

The Octopus pondered the message for a moment. "Hmmm, yes," he said, more to himself than to Igor. "Very interesting, and very appropriate. Naturally, I presume that by now tomorrow means today, and that would mean I will have to act quickly. I will put my plan into motion as soon as you and I have finished here."

"Wow, it sure sounds like I brought you an important message."

"My friend, Mr. Igor I-Do-Not-Wish-To-Know-Your-Last-Name, from The United States of America, all messages are important to me," said LGM. "Now let me give you a few, uh, how you would say, 'tips' on what spying is all about. First, you do not presume to take the place of another agent, even if authorized to do so, without learning the proper signs of recognition for his role. Second, you do not make arrangements to rendezvous romantically with agents of the opposite gender, thus jeopardizing yourself, and the lady, to compromise and discovery by authorities in the weasel government."

Igor was beginning to perspire.

"Third, you do not write a secret message on the back of a boarding pass. Fourth, you always ask for the countersign, even from such a one as myself. And fifth, Mr. Igor … fifth, and perhaps most important of all, you do not get your coat caught in a door in the presence of Le Grand Malfaiteur. *Mon Dieu, Monsieur* Igor, you are a fool. *Vous êtes un imbécile!* I will say goodbye to you now, *Monsieur* Igor."

LGM drew a Luger from his cummerbund and shot Igor twice.

"Give my regards to Charlotte," said Le Grand Malfaiteur. "*Je pense que vous verrez son très bientôt.* Yes, you will see her soon enough."

Hung up in the trench coat, Igor's body never hit the floor but instead crouched forlornly by the door.

LGM turned and vanished into the darkness, his footsteps echoing more and more distantly as he called to an unseen minion. "Clean up in the foyer, Andrei!"

CHAPTER FOURTEEN

In galoshes and sweat suit, Dr. Lavager rounded the ten foot brick wall on the last lap of his mid-afternoon jogging regimen. He detoured gingerly around a wagon loaded with trees from a local nursery which was parked just inside the gate, and jogged to the door of the laboratory building. Once inside, he walked briskly down the hall to his lab, opened the door and went in. He was breathing heavily and could only manage a muffled grunt by way of greeting to George and Letitia, working side by side by the rat cages. He went directly to his bedroom in the storage closet to change out of his sweat suit, shower, put on a different pair of galoshes, wash his hands, and brush his teeth.

Presently he emerged, just in time to catch George planting a kiss on the back of Letitia's neck. He smiled benevolently at the young couple. Along with his hi-top galoshes, Dr. Lavager was now wearing an olive drab one-piece muumuu with long sleeves that were cut extremely wide. Loose elastic drew the garment together at his neck and kept it from falling from his shoulders. Similarly, the hem at the bottom was drawn together by an elastic band just above galoshes-top level. It wasn't tight enough to restrict walking freedom, yet it didn't let the garment flare or flounce like a skirt. Several pockets were sewn on to the outfit around Dr. Lavager's middle, and he was using them for his wallet, pocket calculator, loose change, and keys. One of the pockets had a pocket protector with a pen and pencil set clipped in it. Midway down his back, dangling from a cord around his neck, was a simple straw hat with a wide brim like a rice paddy peasant's, only wider.

"How do you like it?" he asked, putting on a pair of cheap sunglasses and stroking his goatee.

George and Letitia looked up from their rat cages and stared at their beloved mentor in awe.

"It's … terrific, Uncle Gardy!" said Letitia.

"Thank you. I had it made up for me over in the Home Economics Department."

"You didn't tell them who it was for, did you?" said George.

"Why not? Besides, several of the girls saw our interview on television the other day, so it was no surprise to them," Lavager explained.

"Well, turn around and let's get a look at you, Uncle Gardy," enthused Letitia. "After all, it's dark in here. George installed ultraviolet filters on the fluorescent lights yesterday."

Lavager took a few steps, turned around, and struck a casual pose, modeling his prototype uniform of the protected future.

When standing still with his arms at his sides he resembled an immense hand grenade with feet.

"I'll wear it the rest of the week and see how it feels. Then maybe I'll have a few more made up and test them on some other people."

"Well, I know one thing," said George, "you're going to have a lot of fun with that when nature calls."

"Oh, George, really," cried Letitia.

"No kidding, Letitia, I really mean it!"

"Hmmm, you may have a point there, George, but I'm sure I can get things to work out," said Lavager.

"That's sort of a joke, right?" said George.

Lavager stroked his jet black goatee thoughtfully and changed the subject. "Speaking of work, how is yours going today?"

"It's a grind, but it's fun, eh, Letitia?" said George. Just then, he caught sight of the wall clock. "Hey, it's break time," he announced.

George went to one of the black composition-top tables and climbed on to a high stool. He opened a drawer and took out a newspaper and a Hostess Sno Ball. Letitia sat next to him at the table while Dr. Lavager settled into his armchair and, removing his sunglasses, began reading the draft of a report on iodized salt that was to be submitted to Congress in less than a week.

Softly, Letitia hummed the "Sunrise" movement.

In contrast to Dr. Lavager, Letitia was wearing a form fitting purple velvet jump suit – the kind with a zipper all the way up the front, with the inevitable large zipper handle hanging invitingly at the neck. George had trouble concentrating on his Sno Ball as he unwrapped it. Then, playfully, he lifted off the topping of the cake in one piece. It was a spongy mass of rubbery pink marshmallow sprinkled with shredded coconut.

He stretched it out and held it menacingly close to Letitia's face as he cried, "Bleah! Have some octopus liver!"

Letitia pretended to be revulsed, and then they both laughed, each taking a bite out of the confection.

George scanned the front page of the newspaper, looking for articles about possible harmful substances so he could circle them in red. As usual, there were several such stories, but today only one caught his eye.

"Hey, will you look at this?" he exclaimed.

"What's that, George?" asked Lavager and his niece, almost in unison.

"I'll read it to you. It's short, and I don't want you to strain your eyes in this light," said George.

MAN DRINKS NAPKIN, DIES

New York (UP) – A man identified as Frank Soggins, 38, of Scarsdale, collapsed and died on the sidewalk outside a decaffeinated coffee shop on Madison Avenue in Manhattan yesterday morning. Soggins, heir-apparent to the troubled Soggins International Machine Tool Company, one-time major supplier of arms to the U.S. government, had just come out of the shop, operated by the Chock Full o' Nuts chain. Cause of death was not immediately determined, but a preliminary investigation points to a paper napkin Soggins reportedly ingested along with a cup of coffee.

According to waitress Flora Higbee, Soggins was a regular customer. In a statement to police, Mrs. Higbee described Soggins as a quiet man who came in about once every two weeks. "He always wore a raincoat and never spoke to nobody except to order a coffee," she said. "I never paid much mind, right? But today I seen him wad up his napkin and stir it in with his coffee. I remembered that because it's out of the ordinary, you know. Never seen nobody do that before."

Police are continuing their investigation today.

Soggins is survived by his uncle, General Ulysses S. Soggins (Ret.), and his grandmother, Mrs. Constant Krupp, both of New York. Funeral arrangements are pending.

"What do you make of it, George?" asked Dr. Lavager. "New York does have more than its share of strange people, you know."

"I know that, but it's the napkin itself that interests me. It was probably white, right?"

"Yes, I believe that's correct," said Dr. Lavager, laying his report aside. "At least the last time I was in a Chock Full o' Nuts the napkins were white. A dull white, and very flimsy."

"Okay, now listen to this," continued George. "The other morning, after we had the little celebration in here and cleaned up all the chalk dust, some of the crepe paper decorations had fallen down. A couple of strips were lying across the rat cages, and when Letitia and I came in we found two rats dead, apparently from eating the crepe paper. The crepe paper was white, too, of course, as you'll recall."

"Say, that's right. Just like the napkin," said Letitia.

"Exactly," said George. "Today, Letitia and I have been experimenting with stuffing white crepe paper down rats' throats. I've done it a half dozen times, and the rats die every time. So when some nut in New York also dies after swallowing a white napkin, I have to wonder if there's a correlation."

"Well, it certainly suggests an interesting hypothesis," said Lavager.

"Yes," said George, "it sure looks like there is some other harmful substance in paper in addition to colored dyes. I wonder how we missed that before."

"Now, don't blame yourself, George," said Letitia.

"Well, darn it, I was so sure we had the paper thing licked. It's frustrating."

"George is right," said Lavager. "And if we can't identify the offending substance in a hurry, we may have to seek a ban on paper altogether. At the very least, we would have to set up a program of instruction in the safe use and handling of paper – maybe even require people to have a license."

"Oh, wow," exclaimed Letitia. "We'd better think of something to print the licenses on, then. Maybe cotton cloth."

"Hmmm, quite possibly. But first things first. George, get started right away analyzing and testing the ingredients in the paper. You know the routine."

"Right," said George.

"Letitia, you write to the Chock Full o' Nuts people and ask for some sample napkins. Don't tell them who you are; there's no point in scaring anybody yet. Just say you want them for Show and Tell as souvenirs of New York, or something. Make up anything."

"Oh, this is so exciting," gushed Letitia, absently fingering her zipper handle.

Dr. Lavager sat back and contemplated his immaculate fingernails for a moment. "You know, this may fit in well with some other thoughts I've had lately. It could result in a complete package of paper legislation. I have become very concerned about the problem of paper cuts. Do you realize we don't have any statistics on paper cuts, and yet that's one of the most common injuries suffered in modern life?"

"Golly," said Letitia.

"One thing we might do," continued Dr. Lavager, "is require that all paper be cut to a deckled or soft and uneven edge, the way they used to do books to make them look high class."

"I think some of the book clubs still do it," observed George.

Just then, the door in the greenboard opened, and Wong Lee came in, followed by four workmen in overalls and old khaki shirts.

"Hi, Wong Lee," said Letitia.

"Herro, Missee Retitia. Solly to intellupt, Doc, but these men flom nursely been pranting tlees awr afternoon ou'side, an' Wong Lee t'ink maybe it nice they take ritto blake now. I show them rab, maybe we have some juice, okay?"

Wong Lee looked around the lab and up at the ceiling.

"Hey, how come is so dark in rab today?" he asked.

"Just a new precaution," said Lavager, "ultraviolet filters on the lights. You'll get used to it."

The workmen looked hot and tired. Their hands and overalls were dirty, and all four had sunburns on the backs of their necks. Dr. Lavager saw the sunburns immediately and felt a wave of compassion. He stood up to invite the men in formally.

"Yes, please, Wong Lee, feel free to show them around," he said. "Letitia, we still have some orange juice in the refrigerator, don't we?"

"Yes, I'll get some." Letitia went to the storage closet and returned with a pitcher of juice and some plastic cups as Dr. Lavager continued to greet the men.

"So you're the ones who were planting all those trees, eh? Well, that's honorable work, you know. More trees, more oxygen."

Even in the artificial twilight and with their chins buried in their shirt collars, the men could see very well, although they weren't sure they believed what they saw. Could this muumuued apparition with galoshes and a Gook hat speaking to them in fatherly tones be the famous Dr. Gardiner Lavager, head of the American Eco-Toxicology Association, protector of Man from his environment, and soon to be key to the success of the Army's defense of the United States of America? Well, great men are often eccentric. One man stifled a laugh by disguising it as a cough. The others nudged Wong Lee inquisitively, but he assured them with his eyes that this was indeed *the* Dr. Lavager, their target.

"You men really ought to watch those sunburns, you know," Lavager went on. "Could lead to cancer. Soon, I'm going to recommend everyone wear a hat like this."

Lavager put on the wide-brimmed hat and sunglasses, but by this time the men had noticed Letitia and the way she filled out her purple jump suit, the contents shifting provocatively with each step as she went to the front table and began pouring the orange juice.

Wong Lee began to sense a certain potential for trouble with the mission, so he spoke up in an attempt to get everyone back in the proper frame of mind. "Thank you velly much, Doc. Prease, you go back to work. Not mind us. We be velly quiet; just rook alound rab a ritto and go back ou'side."

"Well, make yourselves comfortable, and take your time," said Dr. Lavager heartily.

With hat and sunglasses still on, Lavager settled back down in his chair, took a small sip of orange juice, and picked up the report he had been reading. George went back to his newspaper, and Letitia, when she finished pouring the juice, went back to the storage closet to put the pitcher away. Eight eyes followed her hungrily.

When she had gone, the four men moved silently around the room, as if taking in all the sights Wong Lee seemed to be pointing out to them: the testing equipment, the rats watching television, the armchair. One of the men had stationed himself by the greenboard door, another by the storage closet. The other two, and Wong Lee, crept up behind Lavager's chair. George and Dr. Lavager were too absorbed to notice what was happening.

Suddenly, the two men grabbed Lavager and pinned his arms to the chair. There was a struggle as Wong Lee, advancing on him through a shower of orange juice, took a hypodermic syrette out of his pocket and plunged its needle into Lavager's thigh. Lavager's body jerked, and the two men lost their grip on him momentarily as he tried to stand up.

George sat still and open-mouthed, too stunned to move.

Regaining their hold on Dr. Lavager, the two men braced him in the standing position. Wong Lee pulled an empty folded plastic fertilizer bag from the overalls of one of the men and opened it. It had small air holes punched in it, near the bottom. Standing on tiptoes, he drew the bag over Dr. Lavager's hat and pulled it down over his body so the air holes were now at the top. The man at the greenboard door, the same one who had smirked earlier, laughed openly this time. With the fertilizer bag completely covering him, Dr. Lavager's appearance hadn't changed a great deal.

The figure in the bag began to slump as the drug took effect. The two men laid the bag down carefully, and Wong Lee tied it closed with a length of heavy twine. The bag lay motionless.

George was standing now, and the man at the storage closet door tensed, ready to spring if George tried anything. Just then, Letitia returned.

"What's happening?" she cried, instantly aware that all was not right. "Where's Uncle Gardy?!"

She rushed toward the fertilizer bag at the same time George started for her, but both were roughly elbowed out of the way by two of the men and crashed to the floor. Letitia recovered first, got up, screamed, and rained furious little blows to their heads with her fists, to no avail.

George was mobilized now too. An uncontrollable fury rose in him as he watched Letitia struggling among the dirty ruffians as they tried to fend off Letitia. He gathered himself to his full height and approached the two men slowly, relentlessly, breathing heavily, and with a fearsome expression on his face. Wong Lee stood rooted to the spot next to the fertilizer bag. He had never seen George like this before. By this time, even the other men sensed something powerful in George's menacing demeanor. They braced themselves for the worst and looked up at his hulking figure. Then George let them have it.

"You guys stop that right now!" he yelled. "I'm warning you! No telling what I might do!"

The men were so surprised at this that they abandoned their struggle with Letitia, who fell to the floor again, and simply stared at George, bewildered and unbelieving, as his fury rose even higher.

"You get away from her!" he continued, his voice so firm and loud it could be heard throughout the building. "Why don't you pick on somebody your own size? I'm going to call the police, and you'd better watch it or I may be forced to take matters into my own hands!"

The men stepped away from Letitia. George grabbed his raincoat and wrapped it around her, embracing her protectively He closed his eyes and began kissing her profusely on the back of her neck.

He hardly noticed the scuffling noises receding down the corridor outside the door to the lab, and when he opened his eyes moments later he was still holding Letitia. She looked up at him with adoration.

"You were wonderful, George, just wonderful," she said. She kissed him then, *on the lips*.

George felt elated, but at the same time rotten, and somehow drained. He wanted to sit down. As he did so his normal senses started to return. He looked around the lab. Orange juice was everywhere. The four workmen, along with Dr. Lavager and Wong Lee, had vanished.

CHAPTER FIFTEEN

At that very moment, in his office in the university Administration Building, Dr. Theodore Lighthorse Baldwin was reading for the fourth time a typewritten note with Dr. Lavager's signature on it. Someone had left it in his IN box while he was out attending a protest meeting. The students were accusing the Food Services concessionaires of putting saltpeter in the mashed potatoes again, and this time they had a petition asking that saltpeter be declared a harmful substance. Anticipating such a request, Baldwin long ago had asked Dr. Lavager to feed large doses of saltpeter to some rats. The rats did not die. That was a blow to the students, when Baldwin told them about it that afternoon, and it sent them scurrying back to their dorms for more strategy sessions. Of course, Food Services weren't using saltpeter, and never had been, but there was no way to prove that to the students. The whole thing bored Dr. Baldwin immensely. On the other hand, it gave him an idea about how the university might save some money by breeding its own rats.

But now this note from Dr. Lavager. There was something funny going on. Dr. Lavager never wrote notes like this. If he had something to tell Dr. Baldwin, he always called him on the phone or told him in person. Still, it looked like Lavager's typewriter all right, and it looked like his signature. He read the note once more.

Dear Ted,

Sorry to be so secretive about this and not give you more notice, but the President wanted it this way. He has called me to Washington to brief me on a top secret goodwill mission. By the time you read this, I will be on my way. I can tell you this much on a "need to know" basis. I will be making a tour of Enemy countries, offering their governments all our information on harmful substances as a humanitarian gesture. The President believes this will reduce world tension. But, he wants it kept a total secret until my first appearance overseas is publicized by the Enemy press. I do not know how long I will be away—perhaps a month—but George and Letitia will carry on my work.

Again, sorry to have to tell you about it this way.

Sincerely,

(Signed) Gardy

Baldwin put down the note and picked up the phone. He dialed "9" for an outside line, and then "0" for the long distance operator. He didn't want to go through his secretary and alarm her needlessly.

"Operator, please connect me with the White House in Washington, D.C. I'd like to speak to the President. Yes, I'll wait." He gave the operator his university credit card number.

The story sounded plausible enough. It was just that, well, why hadn't Dr. Lavager told him in person? Why this secrecy and already being on his way to Washington before Baldwin could ask any questions? And, perhaps most annoying of all, why hadn't the President himself told Baldwin? What kind of an omen might that be?

"Thank you, Operator. Hello… White House? Yes, well, with whom am I speaking? Oh. Oh, this is Dr. Theodore Baldwin, president of Leland F. P. Mason Wesley, Jr., University in California. May I speak to the President, please? All right, I'll hold."

This was the same routine he always had to go through when he called the President, not that he did it frequently. Come to think of it, if he did it more frequently, they would be used to it, and he wouldn't have to go through all this waiting. He made a mental note to call the President more often.

Right now they were probably feeding a tape recording of this conversation into a computer and comparing his "voice print" to the one on file.

"No, I am not at liberty to tell you exactly what it is about which I wish to speak to the President."

More waiting.

"Yes, I'm sure you are duly authorized to take any message. However, there is no way I can be certain it's really you to whom am speaking, is there? For all I know, this is not the White House at all. Maybe the line has been tampered with. Now, there's no need to get angry. I just feel it necessary to demonstrate that I am as security conscious as you people are. Yes.

Well, if you'll just tell him who I am – you have verified that, haven't you? Good. Just tell the President who it is and that I have uncovered some secret information which I believe he considers of grave importance. I'd like him to be aware of how I found out, in case it's an unauthorized leak. No, I cannot just tell you. Please put the President on the line."

Another wait. Finally, the President's voice.

"Hello, Ted? Is that you? What's all this they're telling me about top secret information?"

"Ah, Mr. President," said Baldwin, "it's a good thing I wasn't calling to tell you the White House was on fire."

"Now, Ted, you know how careful we have to be these days," soothed the President.

"Yes, I know. In fact, I have the same problem here. Anyway, Mr. President, I received this mysterious note from Gardy Lavager … you know, Dr. Gardiner Lavager, of the American Eco-Toxicology… Right. Well, it said something about you sending him on a top secret goodwill mission to Enemy countries, and I thought I should just verify it with you."

The President expressed ignorance. Dr. Baldwin read him the note from Dr. Lavager, twice. The President thought for a moment.

"What do you think we ought to do, Ted? I certainly don't know anything about this mission he's talking about. Are you sure he's gone?"

"To tell you the truth, sir, I haven't checked," said Baldwin, feeling vaguely foolish. What if this were just some student prank? Now that he had gone so far as to disturb the President, he certainly hoped Dr. Lavager was missing. All these conflicting thoughts were beginning to confuse the old man. He began to feel guilty, about everything, yet he had done nothing.

"Mr. President, let me put you on 'hold' for a moment. Thank you, sir. I'm sorry."

Dr. Baldwin pushed the 'hold' button, then another button to get an inside line. He dialed the laboratory extension while the President's hold button light flashed on and off. The phone rang at the other end. And rang, and rang. After what seemed like forever, an out-of-breath Letitia answered it.

"Hello?" she said.

"Letitia? This is Dr. Baldwin. Is everything all right down there?"

"Oh, Dr. Baldwin!" cried Letitia. "Some awful men came and took Uncle Gardy away in a fertilizer bag! Wong Lee was one of them!"

"Okay, Letitia," said Baldwin. "You stay there. I'll be right over."

That was a relief. At least he hadn't embarrassed himself before the President. He pressed the President's button.

"Mr. President, Dr. Lavager is indeed missing. I've just learned he's been kidnapped. What are we going to do? It's probably some extremist pro-harmful substance group. I'm afraid the public might react violently."

"Well, now, let's not get too excited, Ted," said the President. "I think I see a way of handling this that will keep everybody calm for a while and also further our political aims. I'm going to request immediate television and radio broadcast time to make a nationwide announcement. Meanwhile, I'll get the FBI into this. You'd best just see what you can do to keep things quiet out there. Go along with the story in the note; it's believable."

"Yes, Mr. President."

"And, Ted…"

"Yes, sir?"

"Thanks, Ted."

Dr. Baldwin hung up and went straight to Dr. Lavager's laboratory. In spite of the confusion and the possibly tragic disappearance of Dr. Lavager, or perhaps because of it, Dr. Baldwin realized he felt good. He, too, was on a sort of mission for the President, and he was on the inside of something that could turn out to be very big. He felt young and excited, pleased to be part of an important mystery. He hadn't lost touch, then, as he had feared. Still, he thought as he hurried to the lab, he couldn't make much sense out of what was happening, but as long as it didn't turn out to reflect poorly on the reputation of the university, it would probably be all right.

But who would kidnap Dr. Lavager? Ransom was out of the question, since public opinion would be strongly against Congress appropriating the money to pay it, and the university certainly couldn't afford to do so. Could it be the Enemy? But many columnists daily pointed out how Dr. Lavager's work gave the Enemy nothing but aid and comfort because of its effects on the economy. No, it had to be radicals. They would hold Lavager hostage, perhaps in Canada, and demand repeal of the harmful substance laws. Congress would never give in to that either, since it wasn't an election year. But what did the President have in mind? Why did he instruct Baldwin to go along with the secret mission story? It was too much to figure out while hurrying across the campus, so he tried to put it out of his mind. For him, it was enough that he was on the team. That was what was important now.

Dr. Baldwin entered the lab through the greenboard door and found Letitia mopping the floor, trying to get up the stubborn orange juice stains.

"Letitia!"

"Oh, Dr. Baldwin, this is awful!" said Letitia.

"Yes, it looks like orange juice. Very sticky."

"No, no, I mean about Uncle Gardy and those dirty men! And to think, Wong Lee was helping them. Oh, it's terrible."

"Why don't you turn some more lights on in here?"

"They're all on now."

Baldwin looked up and, seeing it was true, continued his questioning.

"What about George Smith? Was he here?"

"Oh, yes. He saved me from a fate worse than death. He's in

Uncle Gardy's office, addressing an envelope for my letter to Chock Full o' Nuts."

"Oh… excellent, Letitia," said Baldwin. "Come to the office with me, then. I want both of you to tell me everything that happened."

In Dr. Lavager's cramped office, George and Letitia spilled out their whole story to Dr. Baldwin. Then he told them of the phony note he had received, his call to the President, and the President's instructions. After that, they just sat and looked at each other. None of it made any sense. Should they call the police? But no, the President had said to keep things quiet for now. Should they call the President back? No. Maybe it was best at this point to watch and see what the President had to say on television.

"Well, I guess there's nothing left to do but see what the President has to say on television," said George, as if reading Baldwin's thoughts. He switched on the TV.

There was a knock at the office door. Baldwin opened it. A campus policeman stood in the hallway.

"Well, come in, Commander Cartwright, do come in," said Baldwin heartily.

"Hello, Dr. Baldwin," said Commander Cartwright as he stepped inside. Everyone shifted position to make room for him. "I was told I might find you here. Have you folks had any trouble today?"

"Trouble? What kind of trouble?" said Baldwin with a laugh.

"Why, no. Where did you get that idea? We haven't had any trouble ... have we, everybody?"

"No, sir," said George. "No trouble here."

"It's just that it looked like there was orange juice on the floor back in the lab, and I wondered if ..."

"Oh gracious, yes," said Letitia. "George had a little accident and we haven't had time to get Wong Lee to clean it up yet."

"Glad to hear it, folks. Just doing my job, you know."

"And we do appreciate it, Commander Cartwright," said Baldwin.

"Sure thing, Dr. Baldwin," said Cartwright with a shrug. "Anyway, I came to tell you the machine guns have arrived. Well, five of them showed up, I guess I should say. We don't know where the sixth one is. One of my men is trying to trace it with the railroad. We're going to start installing the others now, if it's okay with you."

"Yes, that's fine, Commander Cartwright," said Baldwin.

"It's just that there may be some noise, with the men on the roof and everything," said Cartwright.

"That's perfectly all right," said Baldwin.

"You're sure it won't bother Dr. Lavager, now? We could come ba..."

"Take my word for it, Commander. Anything else?"

"No, I guess not. Well, thanks." Cartwright turned to leave.

"Thank you, Commander," said Baldwin, closing the door and breathing a sigh of relief.

On the TV screen the Presidential Seal appeared through the X-ray filter. Off camera an announcer said, "Ladies and Gentlemen, the President of the United States." The President's face replaced the Seal. He spoke.

"My fellow Americans. First, let me offer my sincerest thanks to our friends in the broadcast media who so cheerfully cooperated with our request to go on the air at this time. It was very short notice, and for that we apologize. However, as I am sure you will see, it was necessary.

"Today, I wish to speak to you about one of our most respected friends, Dr. Gardiner Mellors Lavager, known to most of you as head of the American Eco-Toxicology Association. My office has received erroneous ... let me repeat that... *erroneous* reports that Dr. Lavager has disappeared or has been abducted. Perhaps some of you listening and watching this telecast today have also heard such reports. If these reports were true, or if they were to be believed, whether true or not, I feel sure the American people would wish to rise up indignantly against the perpetrators of such an evil deed, even setting aside individual personal differences of opinion about the value of Dr. Lavager's fine work ... and I know these differences do exist. The result of this righteous concern might well be civil disturbances. This, of course, would be deplorable, for we are a peace loving nation.

"And so, my fellow Americans, it is my duty to set the record straight regarding Dr. Lavager's whereabouts and to assure you that he has not been abducted.

"Dr. Lavager is missing; that much is true. Because of the delicate nature of this matter, with its national security implications, I had not originally planned to make public the information I am now about to share with you until we were more certain that our plans were being implemented successfully. A premature announcement of our intentions, followed by failure of the plans for any reason, might have precipitated a grave diplomatic crisis. Now, however, since news of Dr. Lavager's departure is apparently known, I must tell you what this matter is all about.

"Today, I have dispatched Dr. Lavager on a very important—and what was to have been a secret—mission of goodwill. At this moment he, along with a specially selected group of my closest advisors, is in the air over the Atlantic Ocean, winging his way toward a rendezvous with our neighbors in the Eastern Bloc. On my personal instructions, Dr. Lavager will offer to the peoples of those nations all information such as they might find useful concerning this country's research into harmful substances and human ecology.

"It is our fervent hope that, by this gesture of humanitarianism and sincere goodwill, we can further mutual understanding between nations, help to improve the quality of life for all peoples, ease tensions between our two hemispheres, and further reduce this nation's wasteful defense budget.

"I know that all of you, regardless of what your feelings might be toward some of the restrictive harmful substance laws, join with me in wishing Godspeed to Dr. Lavager on this critical mission.

"Dr. Lavager has promised not to report to me until concrete progress has been made. This is the measure of the man's dedication, ladies and gentlemen. Thus, I cannot tell you at this moment when we might hear some word, encouraging or otherwise. But, let me assure you that, when we do, we will release it just as soon as we receive it. Thank you."

Dr. Baldwin, George, and Letitia sat in silence for a few moments. The announcer appeared on the screen to say a special panel of Senators and Congressmen was about to be interviewed by key network TV correspondents in a Washington studio to discuss the implications of what the President had said.

"Well, I do hope it works," said Dr. Baldwin, "I hope it buys some time for us."

"Gosh, me too," said George.

Letitia nodded her agreement.

"So now we just wait for the FBI," said Baldwin. "George, can you and Letitia keep Dr. Lavager's work moving ahead until this is cleared up? George?"

"Huh? Oh, sorry Dr. Baldwin. I guess I wasn't paying attention," said George.

"What's the matter, George?" asked Letitia.

"I'm not sure … Dr. Baldwin, come take a look at this piece of paper I found next to the typewriter. I wonder what the heck this is."

"Hmmm," said Baldwin, as he and Letitia leaned forward for a closer look. "It appears to be some sort of official document."

"Yeah," said George. "Like Army traveling orders or something. I'm going to have to work on this thing for a little while and see if I can figure it out. Pretty doggone strange, if you ask me!"

CHAPTER SIXTEEN

At this moment, Dr. Lavager was not in the air over the Atlantic Ocean, winging his way on a goodwill mission for the President. Dr. Lavager was being carried into Los Angeles International Airport in a fertilizer bag.

The kidnappers were still wearing their overalls, old khaki shirts and scruffy shoes. Stranger groups have been seen in Los Angeles International Airport, so they didn't attract much attention. Most people were either hurrying to catch a flight, hurrying to wait for their luggage or catch ground transportation, or watching the President's speech being analyzed to death by talking heads on television. The rest were too busy trying to avoid the ubiquitous saffron-robed Hare Krishnas handing out poppies for donations in every terminal to notice five men in work clothes carrying a gigantic fertilizer bag.

The kidnappers found a men's room and went inside with their load. They fished in their overalls pockets for dimes, put the dimes into the coin slots of five pay toilets, and entered the stalls, leaving the fertilizer bag propped up against a wall.

Once inside the stalls, they stripped off their dirty disguises and changed into their green Army uniforms, passing their duffle bag from man to man under the stall walls. After a few minutes, they opened the stall doors and emerged as U.S. Army soldiers, nameless except for Sergeant O'Grady.

The fertilizer bag was beginning to show signs of life, rocking to and fro, jerking occasionally. The soldiers quickly formed a semi-circle around it to shield it from the view of anyone else who might come into the men's room. Wong Lee cut the twine at the bottom and removed the bag briskly from Dr. Lavager's body.

"There's our pigeon," said one of the men.

Wong Lee was startled by that, and he opened his mouth to say something. Then he thought better of it and returned to work.

"Rook rike dlug working velly weo," he said. "C'mon, Doc. We you fliends. You do what we say, and come with us, an' evyting gonna be okay, okay?"

The sodium pentothal was making Dr. Lavager cooperative. He had no idea where he was or who these soldiers were, but he vaguely recognized Wong Lee's soothing voice, and his face, under the garrison cap. What was Wong Lee doing in a uniform? It didn't matter, though. Wong Lee was his friend, and Dr. Lavager would do anything Wong Lee said. Anything.

"Come on, let's get out of here," said another of the soldiers.

They got Dr. Lavager to his feet and determined he could walk under his own power as long as at least one of them guided him. His will power was almost completely depressed by the drug. Almost, but not quite. On their way out of the men's room it was all the soldiers could do to keep him from stopping to wash his hands. Finally, though, they managed to get him out.

He was still wearing his protective galoshes, muumuu, sunglasses, and now-rumpled wide-brimmed hat-on-a-string, and there was nothing the soldiers could do about it. Fortunately, he had a goatee, so most people would think he was only an aging hippie freak, certainly not a Hare Krishna in spite of his muumuu, although either way it might seem incongruous for him to be traveling with a group of soldiers.

By the time they all got their boarding passes and herded Lavager to the gate, their Omaha flight was boarding. Once on the plane they made their way to the tail section. Seats were three abreast on both sides of the aisle. They put Lavager in a window seat, and Wong Lee sat next to him, with one of the other soldiers in the aisle seat. The other three took scattered seats nearby so as to arouse as little suspicion as necessary.

So far so good. Wong Lee was pleased with how smoothly the whole operation was going, in spite of the unpleasantness back at the lab. Fortunately, these men were well trained, and their discipline and focus had returned as soon as Wong Lee had asserted his authority. Otherwise, he knew, they would have torn George limb from limb. He made a mental note to report the incident to Captain Gruber.

The airplane taxied out to the runway and began its takeoff maneuver. As the plane gathered speed and lifted off, Wong Lee and the soldiers relaxed in their seats, looking forward to their arrival in Omaha and their delivery of Dr. Lavager, finally, through the back door to Major Farina's office.

Dr. Lavager sat motionless, looking out the window, hat and sunglasses askew, his seat belt mashing the contents of his muumuu pockets. The dazed expression on his face was like that of a child on a carnival ride. He stroked his goatee absently.

CHAPTER SEVENTEEN

Back in the lab, George sat in Dr. Lavager's armchair, puzzling over the document he had found after Wong Lee and the kidnappers had left with Dr. Lavager.

"Well, George, what do you think?" asked Dr. Baldwin.

"It's Army orders, all right," answered George, with deliberation. "See, it says 'Headquarters, Mundane Ammunition Dump Command, United States Army, Camp R.H. Shafto, Omaha, Nebraska.' Then there's a date and a lot of mumbo-jumbo letters, commas and hyphens. See?" He held it out so Dr. Baldwin could look at it.

"Yes, George, but it's full of abbreviations, initials, incomplete sentences, and backwards dates, like that one at the top," lamented Letitia.

"Well," said George, officiously, "I think my experience in the Marine Corps Reserve should help us out here. Those letters and hyphens are simply a file code."

"How helpful is that, George?" asked Dr. Baldwin eagerly.

"Not much, really," George admitted.

"Oh, my. What are we going to do?" wailed Letitia.

"Now, just keep your shirt on," said George. "These orders are addressed to somebody named Staff Sergeant Wong Lee O'Grady."

Letitia's mouth dropped open. "You mean ... Wong Lee is in the Army? But, but that's impossible! Isn't it?"

"How many other Wong Lee O'Grady's do you think there could be in the world? No, it has to be our Wong Lee. And it looks like he's been in the Army for a long time, judging from his rank."

"And I used to think he was cute," said Letitia.

"So, our own little Wong Lee O'Grady is in the Army," said Baldwin, more to himself than to anyone else. "What else do the orders say, George?"

"Yes, why did he help those men kidnap Uncle Gardy and act so nasty?" asked Letitia.

"I must admit Army gibberish isn't exactly like Marine Corps gibberish, but as best I can make out here, this seems to be authorizing Sergeant O'Grady to travel from Omaha to Los Angeles, to perform some kind of duty for a couple of days— it's either unspecified, or disguised somewhere in all these initials—and ..."

"Right," Letitia interrupted, "and kidnap Uncle Gardy, is that what it says?"

"Could be. You know, I doubt they'd come right out in the orders and say something like, 'Proceed to duty station and abduct Dr. Gardiner Lavager.' After all, they sometimes have to show these orders to people, so they couldn't just write it out in plain language for everybody to read."

"But why would the Army want to kidnap Dr. Lavager? It's crazy."

A terrible thought struck Dr. Baldwin. Could it be the President knew all about it and wasn't letting him in on it? What on earth was going on?

"Oh, George, I'm scared," said Letitia. "We've got to do something."

"Lucky for us Wong Lee dropped these orders," said George. "We can make some deductions about where they might be taking your uncle."

"You found them by the typewriter in Uncle Gardy's office," said Letitia. "Why, then it must have been Wong Lee who typed that note to Dr. Baldwin and forged Uncle Gardy's signature on it. George, where do you think they might be taking him?"

"I think it says here they're to take him back to Omaha, to this Mundane Ammunition Dump Command, whatever that is."

"We've got to rescue him, then," cried Letitia, grabbing the orders away from George. She scanned the document, comprehending nothing but Wong Lee's name. Then her gaze rested briefly on the name of the commanding officer typed in the signature block: Henry A. Farina, Major. It seemed to ring a bell, but she couldn't quite place it.

"What do you think, Dr. Baldwin? It'd be a whole lot better than sitting on our duffs here, waiting for the FBI," said George.

Yes, Dr. Baldwin couldn't help thinking, especially if the President has no intention of "finding" him. But he couldn't be sure of that. "Yes," he said, "I suppose there might be some value in having you go to Omaha and have a look around. Then you'd have more to tell the authorities when they get there."

"I'll pack a few things and leave right away," said George.

"I'm coming with you," said Letitia.

"No, Letitia," protested George. "It could be very dangerous out there."

"I'm coming, darling," she murmured.

They packed quickly and took Dr. Lavager's electric car to the airport. This time, there was no danger on the freeway for the little car as it plodded along at thirty miles an hour. It was almost the only vehicle on the road, except for a couple of electric Highway Patrol cars.

How things had changed. George and Letitia had been working in the lab practically around the clock ever since the day the new laws went into effect. Meanwhile, some transformations had taken place in the outside world. The smog was almost gone, for one thing. Along the roads were dozens of plain white billboards where cigarette ads had been painted over. Service stations were running half price sales on gasoline (newspaper reports had been suggesting most of the buyers were people planning to make Molotov cocktails). Water for batteries and steam engines was 50¢ a gallon, air had risen to 75¢ per tire since George's bicycle incident near the campus, and even getting a windshield washed cost a quarter. About half of the stations had closed completely.

In every industrial area through which they passed, there were two or three picket lines. Not strikers, these were workers who had been laid off in industries affected in one way or another by the new laws. They were demanding their jobs back. George recalled the words of a worker quoted in a newspaper article: "Ain't nothin' left but pickin' fruit, and the Chicanos got that locked up tighter'n a drum."

Occasionally in one of the picket lines they would see a man lying on the ground, his body twitching erratically, other men standing close by as if trying to help. Later they would read of the hospitals filling up with "nicotine fit" cases, and about how, in areas of heavy population concentration, whole trees were stripped of their leaves as people experimented with everything they could think of to substitute for tobacco.

Alcohol was still legal, and as they passed one empty liquor store after another, George and Letitia realized the extent to which people were hoarding it. For some, it was a satisfactory substitute for tobacco. Others were simply saving it up against the day when it, too, would be outlawed. Consumption was definitely up. There had been several reports of disgruntled merrymakers ambushing electric cars late at night and persecuting the occupants for "selling out" to the government. Battery acid sometimes got thrown around, and things became messy.

Undaunted, George and Letitia realized this was all to be expected at first. It was just a transition the people had to go through until they readjusted to a new, and better, way of life without harmful, polluting substances. Dr. Lavager's work, and that of others like him, had to continue. They had to rescue him, and quickly. Even the time they were taking from their own work now could hardly be afforded if it weren't for the importance of getting him back safely.

They left the car in an almost empty parking lot close to the terminal building and went inside, detouring only as far as a mail box, where George posted the letter to Chock Full o' Nuts. After a few minutes in the restrooms to freshen up after their drive, they purchased coach tickets on the next flight to Omaha.

"Golly, I hope this is a dinner flight," said Letitia, interrupting her humming as they walked to the gate area.

George looked at his watch. "Should be," he said.

"This is so exciting. I feel just like a spy," said Letitia. "Only, whenever I remember that it's Uncle Gardy we're trying to save, it's no fun anymore. Poor Uncle Gardy."

"Well, at least now I'm pretty sure we're on the right track," said George.

"How come?"

"In the men's room back there..."

"Yes ... what?"

"There was an empty fertilizer bag—a big one—behind a trash can."

When it was time to go, they boarded the plane and took seats near the front of the coach section. Letitia took the window, George the aisle, leaving the middle seat empty.

"If we don't look up, maybe no one will sit between us," said George, studying his shoes.

The airplane was about half full when the doors closed, and they taxied to the runway.

CHAPTER EIGHTEEN

Somewhere over Colorado, Wong Lee realized he had been dozing. Something about being on an airplane always seemed to make him sleepy. It was impossible to say what had awakened him. The plane was flying smoothly. Dr. Lavager still sat staring, glassy-eyed, out the window. Everything seemed to be normal. And yet, somehow, Wong Lee felt uneasy.

He rose from his seat, got past the knees of the aisle-seat kidnapper, and headed for the lavatory in the rear of the plane. One of the other soldiers in the kidnap squad rose and followed him. As Wong Lee opened the lavatory door, he felt a shove from behind which sent him headlong into the padded wall behind the toilet. He turned around and reoriented himself just in time to see the other soldier, inside with him, locking the door.

"Son a bitch! Whatza matta, you clazy, sojer?" cried Wong Lee, trembling with rage. "What you doing?"

"Take it easy, Sarge. Keep your voice down," said the other soldier. "Listen: 'Twas brillig, and the slithy toves.'"

Wong Lee's eyes narrowed. Sure enough, this was the same kidnapper who had said "There's our pigeon" about Dr. Lavager back in the airport men's room.

A mixture of relief and anxiety went through Wong Lee's mind.

"Oh, so my message get thlough," he said. "You awso work for Octopus."

"Yes, and I got the word just in time. I got a tipoff in the USO lounge," said the soldier.

"Okay, so what we do now?"

"First, just to keep everything on the up and up, you have to give me the countersign."

"Oh, uh, 'Did gyre and gimbo in the wabe,'" sighed Wong Lee.

"Good enough. Now, there are two women dressed as nuns up in First Class. They're working for The Octopus, too. One of them's the one who clued me in on the operation." The double-agent kidnapper-soldier checked his watch. "In about 90 seconds from … now, the same nun—the big one—is going to grab a stewardess from behind and demand to be let into the cockpit. She'll use the standard gambit, probably … you know, where she picks up a copy of *Mademoiselle* and threatens the stewardess with paper cuts. There will no doubt be a little commotion at first, and some of the passengers will see this happening and get nervous. That's where you and I come in."

"But what we do?"

"We give the nun about another 30 seconds to get into the cockpit. Then we appear in the aisle. Our uniforms will command authority. We'll say things like, 'Don't panic, everybody. We'll try to straighten this out.' That will calm the passengers down. Then we'll head for the cockpit ourselves. The two nuns will take it from there while we sort of act as lookouts."

"Sound rike velly good pran."

"Yeah, uh, on second thought, Sarge, better let me be the one to talk to the passengers. You just stay close behind me, keep your mouth shut, and follow my lead."

They looked at the watch and waited. Then, when it was time, they opened the lavatory door and peered into the cabin. The door to the cockpit was closing, presumably with the nun and her stewardess hostage inside, and several passengers were on their feet, gesticulating and looking about frantically. Wong Lee and the other soldier moved out smartly into the aisle and began to march up toward the cockpit.

"Don't panic, everybody! We'll try to straighten this out!" announced Wong Lee's companion.

The effect of this on the passengers was anything but calming. They began clamoring for the two soldiers to sit down and mind their own business.

"You want us all to get blown up or something?" pleaded a balding gentleman, who had already spilled his drink, or something, on his pants.

Just then the airplane lurched, as if it had hit an air pocket. Wong Lee knew that was the moment the pilot discovered the cockpit had been invaded. The two soldiers struggled to retain their balance. The P.A. system crackled into life, and the pilot's voice came on.

"Ahem, uh, sorry about that, folks. Wow, that was something, all right. What we call clear air turbulence. Uh, you'll notice that we've, uh, turned on the 'fasten seat belt' sign, and this is just a precaution in case we do encounter any more unexpected bumps. Thank you."

Wong Lee and the other soldier had reached the cockpit door. The soldier tried once more with the passengers.

"Please, don't worry, folks. We've got everything under complete control."

With that, the other nun—the smaller one—rose from her seat, drew a Browning automatic rifle from under her habit, and pointed it at the standing passengers. They sat back down and shut up. The cockpit door flew open, and the stewardess was ejected into the aisle. Seeing the nun's gun, she immediately found an empty seat. Wong Lee had a good view of everything now. Vaguely, he wondered how the nun had gotten the gun past the metal detector. Maybe she had made several trips back and forth to the plane, carrying only a few pieces at a time, not enough to be detected. Maybe the gun was a plastic fake.

Inside the cockpit, the big nun had a pistol pointed at the pilot and seemed to be giving him instructions. The navigator was desperately leafing through the Unabridged Edition of the "Conversational Commercial Piloting" handbook, which is issued to all airline pilots upon graduation from flight school. At last, he found what he was looking for. Laboriously, he handed the cumbersome book to the pilot. It was opened to Section 199 (Air Piracy), Paragraph 5 (Not Arguing with Hijacker).

More static on the P.A., and the pilot spoke again.

"Uh, this is your captain speaking to you from the flight deck. As some of you may have gathered, we do seem to be faced with the necessity to change our plans a little bit today, but I don't think it's anything to worry very much about. Fact of the matter is, there are some people up here with weapons, and they say they want us to take them to Cuba. Well, we're not going to argue with them. So, just sit back, relax, and enjoy your flight, and, uh, we'll try to point out various landmarks as we fly over on our new route. Now, if you'll excuse me, we do have an awful lot of work to do up here right now. Uh, oh, and our, uh, guests have suggested that I declare the bar open, and naturally everything is on the house today, ha, ha, ha. So, bottoms up. Thank you."

In the tail section, three surprised kidnappers looked at each other in amazement as they realized what was happening. They were supposed to be the official kidnappers. Yet, here they were, being kidnapped. And Dr. Lavager was being kidnapped from the kidnappers.

Dr. Lavager's expression didn't change.

CHAPTER NINETEEN

Before the new laws went into effect, the strip of main highway near the access road to Camp Shafto was on its way to becoming just that—a strip. This stretch of road had been authentic Americana in the making. Here, along three solid miles of three-lane concrete (center lane for turning left or, if you had the guts and the traffic was light, for passing illegally), was the typical line-up of fast food drive-thrus, dairy bars, junk yards, gas stations, gift shops, reptile gardens, tire recappers, bowling alleys, Army-Navy stores, tattoo parlors, bail bondsmen, palm readers, storefront churches, gun shops, package stores, dime store "shopping centers," auto parts stores, motorcycle shops, drug stores, convenience stores, banks, pawn shops, adult book stores disguised as newsstands, movie theaters, music stores, motels, and a Walmart. Only a year before, the Governor's Traffic Safety Commission had declared these three miles the most treacherous stretch of highway in the whole state of Nebraska.

Now, of course, owing to the demise of the internal combustion engine for surface transportation, the highway was almost as safe as one's back yard, if not quite as safe as a playground. Drugs were still easier to get on playgrounds.

Half the places were closed and boarded up. Many of the others were on the verge of ruin. Nobody was going to take a steam bus to a fried chicken drive-in, and there wasn't much money in recapping bicycle tires. Some of the motel owners, those with a little capital, were feverishly trying to convert their units into efficiency apartments by having small, modular kitchenettes installed. A few of the others were just hanging on, hoping to cover expenses until the inevitable and glorious time when some other, non-polluting, mode of fast personal transportation would return the strip to its glory days as the most dangerous, and profitable, highway in the state. Or until torched for the insurance.

Lester's Motel, located about a quarter mile west of the intersection of the highway and the Camp Shafto access road, was one of the still-optimistic businesses. It was a squat, one-story, ranch style building with twenty units, half of which the owner now kept permanently locked. The fifteen-foot neon sign flashed its hopeful message to the world: "Lester's Motel. Triple AAA. Deluxe units. Singles from $8. Free TV. Air conditioned. Vacancy."

Neon strip lighting trimmed the roof at one end of the building, and outside the door was a pole on which were displayed an old plastic placard stating "Your BankAmericard Welcome Here" and a hand lettered sign saying "Office."

Inside, behind a pine-paneled Formica topped counter strewn with free matchbooks and postcards depicting Lester's Motel in happier days, sat Lester Grunion, the owner, bravely manning a silent switchboard and gazing wistfully at the open guest register. There was only one entry, and that was for a Mr. and Mrs. George Smith.

Ordinarily, Lester would have been suspicious of a name like that, especially when the couple themselves had seemed somewhat nervous when they checked in. But these days you took what business you could get, and you didn't bother to ask too many questions. After all, they had been here now for a full week. Still, it was odd for them to have insisted on separate rooms. And, come to think of it, no one had ever stayed more than one or two nights at Lester's before. Well, it was none of Lester's business. "An idle mind is the Devil's plaything," he reminded himself, closing the register. He got up and went to the big plate glass window at the front of the office. Through it he looked longingly down the highway, hoping to catch a glimpse of some traffic of any kind. After all, the Smiths, if that was their real name, hadn't caused any trouble. They paid their bill every day, even though Lester didn't require it. Every morning, nevertheless, Mr. Smith would come to the office with his BankAmericard. After that, he and Mrs. Smith pedaled up the highway to the Western Buckaroo Flapjacks place on rented bicycles, and Lester never saw them again until the next morning.

George and Letitia sat on separate beds in George's room, waiting for the six o'clock news to appear on George's free TV. It was equipped with the Government's combination X-ray filter and monitoring device with optional automatic shutoff to insure only four hours of viewing in a twenty-four hour period. They usually didn't watch much television, but it had been an especially tiring and fruitless day of reconnoitering over at the Dump, and they wanted to relax a little before going to dinner at the Polynesian Surf 'n Turf.

"Golly, George, this isn't working out at all," lamented Letitia. As she sat on the bed, her shapely hips strained the material of her tapered yellow slacks. George was having a great deal of trouble relaxing. After all, they had been in this motel for a whole week. Every night, it was the same excuse: "It just wouldn't be right, George. Not until we know Uncle Gardy is safe." It was driving him crazy, but at least it deepened the commitment he had to finding and rescuing Dr. Lavager.

Alas, they weren't making much headway there either.

"Yeah, I know what you mean," said George.

"You're sweet, George."

"Well, it is kind of frustrating. It's been a whole week, and there's been no word from your uncle. Wong Lee just disappeared off the face of the Earth, seems like, and we haven't seen anything interesting at all over at that old Army ammunition dump. In fact, the place always looks practically deserted. We've called Dr. Baldwin twice, and he says the FBI is still trying to turn up clues at the lab, but they won't tell him when they're going to come out here to work with us. I'm getting sick and tired of eating those same stupid flapjacks every morning, with imitation maple flavor syrup. That reminds me, we've got to take some of that syrup back with us, because there's bound to be something harmful in it if we look hard enough."

"If you feel that way, George, we could always try the Lost Dutchman Golden Omelet Mine across the street," said Letitia, trying to be helpful.

"Sometimes I just wish I had something to drink," said George.

"If it would get you to relax a little, I'd almost welcome it."

"Holy moly!" said George, jumping up. "You know what I think?"

"What, George?"

"I think the FBI is already here, working in secret. Yes, come to think of it, why do they need *us*? They made a copy of the orders I found in your uncle's office, and they can snoop around as well as we can ... probably better. I'd bet my bottom dollar they're here, and they're just ignoring us."

"But, we've never seen anybody else looking around over at the Dump."

"Right, but don't forget, we've never been there at night."

"Oh, George, you're so smart."

Letitia yawned, stretched, and then settled down on the bed, her head propped up on two pillows so she could still see the TV on the desk across the room.

"I feel useless here, Letitia. It's no good sneaking around, finding nothing. We have to take some action. Tomorrow night, when nobody's looking, let's get into that bloody Dump and see what's really going on!"

George had other hopes for tonight.

"If you say so, George. Golly, that means we'll have to get to bed early 'cause tomorrow will be a long day."

"Nuts," said George, under his breath.

"Look, George, it's the President!"

George hadn't been paying any attention to the TV. Sure enough, there was a still photo of the President, looking somewhat haggard and drawn. The network anchorman was talking about something the President had said. George turned up the volume.

"…to report no new encouraging developments in the mysterious disappearance of Dr. Gardiner Lavager," the news-caster was saying. "The nation was shocked to learn today that his whereabouts are unknown, scarcely a week after the President announced that Dr. Lavager was going to the Eastern Hemisphere on a goodwill mission. Now, according to the Ad-ministration, there never was such a mission, but rather the President was trying to cover up for Dr. Lavager's disappearance. This has, naturally, put a strain on the Administration's credibility. Here's a portion of the President's statement to the press earlier today at the White House."

Letitia moaned and sat up straight on the bed.

The President mouthed several words in silence before the network engineers got the sound working.

"… with a heavy heart. As you can imagine, it is very difficult for me to come before you today and admit a mistake has been made. But let me assure all of you this mistake was made with only the best of intentions. Last week this Administration received a report from Leland F. P. Mason Wesley, Jr., University in Southern California that Dr. Gardiner Lavager had disappeared. Dr. Lavager, as you know, is the nation's foremost authority on human ecology and the inspiration for much of the recent harmful substance legislation, some of it controversial. The report we received indicated Dr. Lavager had been, well, abducted, by a group of strangers disguised as workers planting trees on the grounds of Dr. Lavager's laboratory building. At about the same time, Dr. Theodore Baldwin, president of the University and a long-time trusted advisor to this Administration, received a note apparently from Dr. Lavager indicating Dr. Lavager was leaving on a top-secret goodwill mission for the government. This note, of course, turned out to be a forgery."

George and Letitia, eyes glued to the TV, listened with rapt attention as the President continued.

"Naturally, we were very sensitive to the possibility the kidnapping of a public figure of Dr. Lavager's stature could create confusion. Public safety was uppermost in our minds when we made the decision to go along with the forged note and announce the goodwill mission while attempting to locate Dr. Lavager. Frankly, we were overly optimistic. As you know, nothing has been heard from Dr. Lavager, or his abductors, since he disappeared last week.

"In the interest of Dr. Lavager's safety, we now feel we should no longer keep this terrible crime a secret. We urge all Americans to stand behind us now as we work together to expose the perpetrators of this evil deed. I have assigned all appropriate agencies, including the FBI, to devote their full attention to this case. At this time, we have very few meaningful clues that can be revealed without jeopardizing Dr. Lavager's safety. There has been no word from the kidnappers. No ransom demand. Our allies abroad report nothing, and intelligence reports give no indication that either the Eastern Bloc of nations or China is in any way involved."

"Oh, George, I'm so scared."

"We do have Dr. Lavager's photograph, of course, and his co-workers have given us a description of what he was wearing on the day he was abducted," the President continued.

The President turned to a large easel behind him and removed a cloth drape, revealing a composite photo-drawing of Dr. Lavager. He was wearing his galoshes, muumuu, sunglasses, and wide-brimmed hat. The microphone at the President's lectern picked up gasps from the press audience, including a few derisive snickers.

"Apparently, Dr. Lavager was testing some new protective clothing that day," the President explained. "We do not believe this costume was forced upon him by the kidnappers."

"I still think it's kind of cute," said Letitia.

"What? Shhh!"

"But . . ."

"We appeal urgently to all Americans to aid us in the search for Dr. Gardiner Lavager and in bringing the perpetrators of this heinous crime to justice," finished the President.

"Mr. President, Mr. President!" Reporters were clamoring to ask questions.

"Mr. Vandever."

"Mr. President, does this mean Dr. Lavager was actually kidnapped, and the goodwill mission was just a hoax?"

"Not exactly a hoax, I would say, Mr. Vandever," said the President. "Remember, I promised during my election campaign that I would never lie to you. We were just trying to buy some time in hopes of finding Dr. Lavager right away and thus avoid divisive confusion. Mr. Wallis."

"Mr. President, are you saying then that Dr. Lavager has been abducted and that his whereabouts at this time are unknown?"

"Yes, I believe that is essentially what I have tried to say, yes."

"Thank you, sir."

"Mrs. Fillmore."

"Sir, is it true, then, that nothing has been heard from Dr. Lavager or his abductors? No ransom note? No indication that foreign powers are in any way involved?"

"That is correct, Mrs. Fillmore. Mr. Beaton."

"Mr. President, can we take it, then, that you have assigned the FBI and other appropriate agencies to this case?"

"Uh… yes, that is correct. Mr. Talps."

"Sir, is it safe to say your Administration is appealing to the American people to help solve this case?"

"Is that what I said, Mr. Talps?"

"More or less, yes, sir."

"Very well, then." The President appeared to be turning toward his Press Secretary, who had been hovering nervously near the easel. The President put his hand over the microphone and said what sounded to George and Letitia and millions of other viewers very much like, "How much did you say we're paying these morons?"

The network anchorman reappeared.

"Law enforcement agencies involved in this strange case have been very tightlipped regarding what evidence, if any, has been found linking the kidnapping with any of a dozen dissident groups who might be suspected of being involved," he said. "Since the Administration's admission that the truth was withheld from the public, there have been minor disturbances in several cities, and the Federal Building in Des Moines, Iowa, was bombed this evening a few minutes before we went on the air. No one was hurt, and we'll have more on that later in the program.

"At this hour, protesters are so thick in front of the White House that Capitol Police have re-routed traffic on Pennsylvania Avenue. There seem to be at least 30 different organizations represented, as well as a large number of individuals who have shown up to demonstrate their displeasure with the President. Many carry signs calling the President a liar and expressing distrust of the Administration. Only a few of the demonstrators seem to be supporting the President, if backhandedly. These people are carrying rather lackluster signs saying things like 'Bring Back Dr. Lavager' and 'Ban Harmful Substances.' The majority of the signs, however, bear such slogans as 'Hurray for the Kidnappers' and 'Kidnappers Si – Lavager No!' and there are scores of 'Dr. Lavager is a Harmful Substance' T-shirts. Fights have broken out between groups of protesters with opposing views, and police have moved in on parts of the crowd with tear gas and Mace, both of which, incidentally, will be outlawed as harmful substances in pending legislation. At least 25 arrests have been made. About a dozen empty police cars, parked a few blocks from the White House, were reportedly festooned with multi-colored crepe paper streamers by a roving gang of apparently anti-Administration demonstrators. One police officer required hospital treatment after he was hit in the face by a paper bag filled with wet monosodium glutamate."

"This is terrible, George!" said Letitia.

"Shhhh!"

"How could they do such a thing?" wailed Letitia. George tried to comfort her by kissing her neck, but it only seemed to make things worse. "Please, George. Stop, and help think of something to do about Uncle Gardy."

The program moved on to other news, including a report that the passengers and crew of an airliner hijacked to Havana last week were released after questioning by Cuban authorities. The plane had landed safely in Miami early this morning. The hijackers and four of the passengers remained behind in Cuba, apparently of their own volition. George turned off the TV.

"All right, Letitia," he sighed. "Let's put our heads together, and..."

"That's not one bit funny, George Smith! Oh, you men are all a..."

"Dang it, I didn't mean anything. For Pete's sake, Letitia, settle down." He plopped down disgustedly on his bed, his Hush Puppied feet grinding streaks of dirt into the white chenille bedspread. He didn't care.

"All right, now look," he said. "We know your uncle has to be on that Army base somewhere. The problem is we don't know exactly where, and we don't know why. For all we know, the whole thing is legitimate, and the President just has him working on some secret project. I have to admit sometimes I don't know when to believe the President and when not to anymore. Of course, if it were legitimate, the 'kidnappers' should have had a bit more self-control."

"Well, I should think so, too!"

"Unless they *really* wanted us to be thrown off the track. Anyway, so if it is on the up and up, we'd look pretty stupid busting into the place and raising Cain. We'll have to sneak in and prowl around. The place is surrounded by a double fence that's patrolled by guys with M-1s. From what I've heard, the Army doesn't have any bullets anymore, but, after all, this *is* an ammunition dump, so I don't feel like taking too many chances."

"Why can't we just go up to the gate, pretending like we're doing market research or something, and casually ask if a Dr. Lavager is on the premises?" asked Letitia.

"Please, Letitia, I'm doing the best I can."

"I'm sorry."

"Now, I do think once we got inside we'd be pretty safe, since there's hardly anybody in there, from all appearances."

"You could dress up like a soldier," suggested Letitia. "There's one of those Army-Navy surplus stores down the road. We could both get uniforms."

"Now, that's not a half-bad idea, Letitia. Okay, tomorrow we'll buy some fatigue uniforms and combat boots and stuff, and some wire cutters. Then, when it gets real dark we'll sneak in. We'll head right for that headquarters building—after duty hours there probably won't be anyone there—and see if we can find any clues, like papers or more orders or something, that'll tell us where your uncle is being hidden."

Letitia stood up and did a sort of pirouette, with her arms in the air. "Oh, George, that's wonderful. I'm so excited ... and still a little scared." She shuddered girlishly.

George joined her in the middle of the little motel room.

Approaching from behind, he put his arms around her waist and began kissing her on the back of the neck. She moved her head back and said "Mmmm," seeming to enjoy this stimulation. Slowly, he hoped unobtrusively, George let his hands creep upward.

"Not now, George."

"All right then, let's go eat supper."

CHAPTER TWENTY

Twenty-two hundred hours the next night. Major Farina's office in the Camp Shafto Command Post building. Present: Major Farina, Commander; Captain Leon, Executive Officer; Captain Gruber, Adjutant; Captain Crockett, Intelligence Officer; Captain Sims-Wellington, Operations Officer; Captain Labouche, Supply Officer; Sergeant Major Williams, Sergeant Major; Staff Sergeant Wong Lee O'Grady, apparent failure. Lights (and spirits): Low. Expressions: Grim. It was not going to be a pleasant staff meeting.

"Sergeant O'Grady," began Major Farina, "I know you've already explained everything to each of my staff officers repeatedly, and they have repeated it to me I don't know how many times since you straggled back in here this morning from Cuba, but if you don't mind, I'd like very much to hear it one more time, from you yourself." His voice was a study of controlled impatience, mixed with disbelief.

"I no mind, sir," said Wong Lee tiredly.

It wasn't that Wong Lee was concerned about slipping up somewhere and being inconsistent in the stories he had told the other officers. No, that would be too fundamental an error for a spy like Wong Lee O'Grady. He had his story down pat. The problem was the simple one of making himself understood. He had discovered during the course of this day of interrogations, or "de-briefings," that about halfway through his story the person listening usually lost interest. A blank expression would come over the listener's face, and his responses became like those of a person hypnotized. Then, before Wong Lee had finished, the listener would start acting as if it had been an exceptionally successful and thorough interview and would end it, thanking Wong Lee very much. There had to be a way of avoiding this same phenomenon with Major Farina, while at the same time somehow managing to tell the whole story.

"Ret me tly make rong stoly sholt, sir," he began, bringing as much earnestness to his voice as he could command. "That way I not bole you with detaos."

Major Farina nodded, gravely. All eyes were on Wong Lee.

"First, I t'ink you know on way to Ros Angeres the airrine rost duffo bag of kidnap squad, awrmost forcing us to deray kidnapping unteo it found."

"Yes," sighed Major Farina while the others nodded, gravely.

With that inauspicious beginning, Wong Lee capsulized a description of what had happened, padding slightly here, omitting a little there, and generally telling the story in such a way that no one would suspect him of being a double agent.

The plane carrying Dr. Lavager and the MADCOM kidnap squad had been hijacked to Havana. Wong Lee had tried to keep the passengers calm, but was forced by the hijackers—the two "nuns" and one of the soldiers—to work with them since somehow they knew of his relationship of trust and friendship with Dr. Lavager. Wong Lee was horrified to discover one of the men on his kidnap squad was working with the hijackers, but he was unable to find out who the hijackers were working for. Since they had been taken to Cuba, it was doubtful the American authorities were behind it. (This was comforting to Farina because at least it meant the secret mission of DEATHCOM and his own secret mission were both still safe.)

When the plane landed in Havana, the hijackers got off, taking Dr. Lavager, Wong Lee, and the traitorous MADCOM kidnapper with them. Cuban authorities got on the plane to question the passengers and crew. Strangely, most of the questions had to do with the passengers' opinions about the chances of various American major league baseball teams. Although in uniform, the three remaining members of the MADCOM kidnap squad sat quietly during the inspection and drew little attention.

Having whisked Lavager away from the airport in a Russian made automobile with the hijackers, the Cubans wanted to let Wong Lee return to Miami with the plane. However, the passengers and crew refused to let Wong Lee re-board because of the role they thought he had played in the hijacking. The plane took off, leaving Wong Lee behind.

"Well, that jibes with what was said at the press conference at the Miami Airport when the plane returned, and what our three guys said when they got back here," observed Major Farina. "It's a good thing Lavager was listed under a false name on the passenger manifest. So far, no one has linked the hijacking with his disappearance, in spite of what he was wearing."

"We just forrowed orders, sir," said Wong Lee, taking no credit for that fortuitous circumstance.

"Right," said Farina, "now tell me how you got back into the country." No one else had sat still long enough for Wong Lee to get to this part before, but he continued without betraying any nervousness.

"Cubans question me a ritto bit, but they no understand much I say, so they decide again they no want me stay. Then is velly simpo. They put me in ord motor boat with some money and a Cuban sandwich flom airport coffee shop, and I head nolth unteo I rand somewhere in Frolida. Then I get steam bus ticket to Omaha."

Major Farina sat in silence for several seconds after Wong Lee had finished. This was always the most difficult time for Wong Lee, somewhat like waiting for a jury to return. He had told his story and told it well. There were no holes in it. Still, there was always the possibility Major Farina knew more than he was supposed to know. Somehow, he might have found out about Wong Lee's double allegiance and was toying with him for a while before bringing in the MPs. Or there was always a chance Major Farina and his staff—all very intelligent men—had figured out the truth in some way and were now about to try to trip Wong Lee up and make him expose himself. While Major Farina sat deep in thought, Wong Lee went over the story one more time in his mind, noting where the story stretched or departed from the truth and where it didn't, searching for any false note that could have made the whole thing sound suspicious.

Actually, the truth on the surface at least was pretty much as Wong Lee had claimed, and these men had no real reason to doubt him other than the sheer unexpectedness of the hijacking. Although Wong Lee had been helping the hijackers, he and they had successfully made it seem he was a victim of circumstances. True, the passengers had refused to let him re-board, but then if he were guilty of anything why would he have gone to so much trouble to return to Omaha and make his report to Major Farina? Well, that one was debatable, he had to admit. But no one had asked that question. In Farina's command, complete loyalty was assumed, the one traitorous kidnapper notwithstanding.

How did the hijackers know when and where to strike, and on such short notice? That was easily explained by the traitor, a convenient scapegoat for Wong Lee.

But who were the hijackers? Who were they working for? What did they want with Dr. Lavager? Wong Lee knew the answers to those questions, or some of them, and these were the most crucial of all. But it wouldn't be appropriate for him to try to explain them, given his role as a simple operative in the kidnap mission. No, that was Farina's job, to figure out the whys and wherefores.

Nevertheless, all this silence from Farina was making Wong Lee nervous. The major had gotten up from behind his desk and was pacing the floor, striding from one side to the other and back again, the neutral expression on his face changing to one of anguish and concern. Wong Lee knew the hijackers worked for The Octopus, just like he did. The Octopus was the Enemy. The Enemy, thanks to Wong Lee and others like him, professionally speaking, knew of the secret mission of DEATHCOM—the development and stockpiling of harmful substance weaponry to be used against them in a war of nerves and brinkmanship. If DEATHCOM felt it had to have Dr. Lavager in order to accomplish its mission, then the Enemy must see to it that Dr. Lavager wasn't available. Precisely what the Enemy was going to do with Dr. Lavager even Wong Lee didn't know.

At last, Major Farina spoke. Wong Lee felt as if his pounding heart was going to pulverize his ribs as he waited for the verdict.

"All right, Sergeant O'Grady, you did the best you could."

An acquittal. An adrenalin warmth originated under Wong Lee's belt in the small of his back and spread throughout his body, seriously hampering his motor and sensory responses. He suddenly felt like a limp dishrag, and he was scarcely able to hear what Major Farina said next.

"But it's obvious the Enemy is on to us, at least as far as the official secret mission of the Dump Command is concerned."

Something deep inside Wong Lee's burning brain told him he should have listened more closely to that last statement.

The other officers murmured among themselves. Captain Crockett addressed Major Farina.

"It does look bad, sir, but there's nothing here to suggest we shouldn't continue with our plans."

"Oh, nutnuts, Crockett, it seems to me we're right back where we started from a week ago, only now we know the Enemy knows our official plans, and they know we know they know. How can you say we should just go on with business as usual?"

It was unlike Farina to talk this way to his subordinates, especially those on his staff. This went beyond sternness, firmness, and decisiveness, the three nesses so necessary to a command position. He was plainly shaken up, and it would take great self-control for his staff not to follow suit.

"How many more Dr. Lavagers are there in this country?" he continued.

"He's the only one, all right," conceded Captain Crockett.

"That's what I thought. Then we're screwed if we still expect to be able to speed up our weapons development."

"Maybe not, sir," ventured Crockett. "The Enemy could have known about this for only two years at the most. Frankly, I think we still have a two year head start on them, even if they do have Lavager. Our intelligence suggests they haven't been doing any work at all in this area."

That was true, thought Wong Lee. He happened to know the Enemy thought the whole idea of a harmful substance arsenal was stupid, although they'd been keeping a close watch on its progress and obviously now felt threatened enough to want to remove Dr. Lavager from the equation, or to use him somehow.

"So you think if we keep working at our current pace, we'll still be able to make our move before the Enemy is in a position to retaliate?" asked Farina.

"I'm certain of it, sir," said Crockett.

Crockett looked knowingly at the others who, like himself, knew better than Farina what the true state of affairs was in the underground labs and storage areas. "Selective stockpiling" indeed. Just a few more days and the special surprise weapon, their birthday tribute to their commanding officer, would be ready. With it, there was no chance of failure. The other officers voiced agreement with Crockett.

"Okay," sighed Major Farina, "so much for the Enemy. But we still don't know where we stand as far as the American civilians go."

There it was again. What did that have to do with anything? Wong Lee looked up in hopes of gaining some information from Major Farina's expression. He found Farina staring him directly in the eyes.

"Sergeant O'Grady," he said, "I'm either going to have to throw you out for a while or let you in on something so big you won't know what hit you when I finish telling you. I hate to keep you on edge like this, but I'm going to have to ask you to leave for a few minutes while we talk this over."

Surprised, disappointed, and slightly embarrassed, Wong Lee stood up, still striving for a cool dejectedness.

"Velly weo, sir. I go ou'side, maybe watch TV in Message Center. You cawr me when you leady." He left the office, closing the door behind him. For a moment he considered hanging around by the door in hopes of eavesdropping, but he thought better of it and walked away. Sure enough, when he had gotten about halfway to the Message Center, he heard the office door open and, after a few seconds, close again. He didn't look back. In the Message Center, SP4 Jenkins, the major's driver, was watching the last scenes of a movie on television. Wong Lee joined him and immediately laid down a smokescreen just in case Jenkins might think they had thrown him out of the meeting.

"Is the news on next?" asked Wong Lee. "Ol' Man ask me to check on ratest news on any tloubo flom civirians."

Jenkins nodded silently in acknowledgment of this gratuitous explanation. The movie was reaching a climax.

"How you rike new steam jeep?" asked Wong Lee, trying to ingratiate himself.

"Beats nuts out of a bike," said Jenkins, curtly.

"I sooprise they not make erectlic jeep instead. How come they not do that, huh?"

"Because in the field or in combat you're more likely to find water to boil and something to burn for fuel than you are to find a place to plug in a battery recharger," said Jenkins, paraphrasing the technical manual.

"Ah, velly smart," said Wong Lee.

"C'mon, Sarge, let's just watch the flick, okay?"

Ordinarily, Wong Lee would have pulled rank and straightened out a Jenkins for talk like that, but he was feeling meek at the moment and decided to let it pass. He sat down.

Meanwhile, in Major Farina's office, the conversation centered on the domestic situation.

"All right, Ernie," Farina said to Captain Crockett, "assuming we still have the jump on the Enemy after we're set up in the White House, what about the public? How long before they'll be ready to support us? Is there any way we can make our move earlier than we'd planned?"

Captain Labouche, the Supply Officer, stood up. "I think I can answer that last question, sir," he said, "if you'll drop the panel covering the situation map."

Major Farina did so. The assorted colored pins looked exactly as they had looked a week ago.

"As you know, we're still several months from a complete 'Go' position," said Labouche, surveying the map with an outstretched right hand. "However, we do have enough greens to start a few good ruckuses if we want to."

"Right," said Captain Crockett, "We think we're close enough now we could bluff with a small move. Call it a 'show of force' or something."

"How about it, Tom?" asked Farina.

Captain Thomas Sims-Wellington, the Operations Officer, spoke up in agreement with Crockett. "I think we could do it, sir. We have one advantage, and that is the Government doesn't know our state of readiness, nor do the people for that matter."

"Not entirely true, Tom," said Farina. "Don't forget, I've been filing periodic reports with my little generals in Washington, telling them how things are behind schedule and assorted other malarkey so they won't figure out our plans. So at least they think they know our condition, and if they see us trying to pull a coup they'll blow the whistle on us."

"Hmmm, let me think about that one for a few minutes, Major," said Captain Crockett. "Meanwhile, Tom, go ahead and tell him what the plan would be, if we can pull it off."

"Amazingly simple, really," continued Sims. "We pick one or two of our green pin areas and get ready to pollute them. Then you commandeer the Emergency Civil Communications System and go on the air with your speech about taking over the country for its own good and so forth. Then announce that, to prove you're serious, you're going to do a warning demonstration in a certain city. Then do it, right away. If they don't cave in immediately, you can do it a few more places until they get the idea there's no stopping you. Then, after we're in power, we'll have plenty of time to finish the development and stockpiling we need before anybody can mount a counter coup. And we doubt anybody will want to anyway."

"You really should go underground on an inspection tour one of these days, sir," said Captain Labouche. "I think you'd find we're a little further along than we've been letting on."

The others chuckled their agreement to this.

"You guys are something else. Ernie, what about my generals?"

"I think I've got it, and if I do, it's beautiful." Crockett was glowing with pride as they all looked at him expectantly. "All you have to do is cut them in. I mean, how hard would it be to convince those guys that what you're doing really *is* good for America? I can think of a half dozen appeals that are sure to work. Plus, if you promise them all powerful posts in your new government, say, where they can run a real he-man Army again, you can't miss. Naturally, you'll 'promise' to step down as soon as it's safe enough to hold free elections."

It was almost overwhelming, the way these problems were being faced and solved right before his eyes, and it made Farina giddy. He fought the urge to be swept along on the wave of optimism that was building. Still, it was hard to cope objectively with the thought that much sooner than he had planned, he was to see his dream become a reality. Major Henry A. Farina, President of the World. No, no: The Honorable H. Anthony Farina, his Excellency and Majestic Benevolence, Ruler of the Earth. Oh, but that was nonsense. Even as dictator, Major Farina would insist on being just "Tony" to his friends. Opulent uniforms and fancy titles wouldn't be required. Well, maybe he'd make himself a Colonel at least. That had a nice ring to it. But other than that, definitely there would be no pomp and circumstance. He would be a man of the people. He would allow smoking, and no one would mind if he regulated tobacco production and consumption, and therefore prices and taxes. Coffee breaks would again mean something to millions of workers. And television … yes, television. He would remove all "Off" switches, and televisions would be on at all times, and his staff would select the entertainments. Books, magazines, newspapers … those would have to be regulated, of course. Small print causes eyestrain anyway.

He would take a mistress. No, several mistresses. But there would be a number one mistress who would be First Mistress. She would order tinted toilet paper for all the White House bathrooms, and soon housewives all over the world would follow suit. And he would get himself only one major personal luxury: the most expensive sports car he could find, with an internal combustion engine, of course. And he would drive it as fast as he wanted to.

But that wasn't a reality, yet. Reality was still right here in this dinky little office with a young staff facing a blown kidnapping, an Enemy who knew too much, an unpredictable civilian population, and not enough green pins in the situation map. Farina brought himself back down to earth.

"Even if all these ideas work," he said, "what about the public? Without them, we're dead. You know that. How do we read them?"

Captain Crockett opened his mouth to speak, but before he could utter a sound, the door burst open. It was Wong Lee, out of breath and in such a state of excitement he had momentarily forgotten some basic military courtesy.

"Terevision!" he shouted. "You guys teo Ol' Man turn on terevision. Go channawr thlee! Doc Ravager on the News!"

Captain Leon, the Executive Officer, who had sat quietly through the meeting, got up and switched on the TV built into the secret panel behind Farina's desk. Sure enough, there was Dr. Lavager, or at least someone who resembled him. The figure on the screen was wearing what appeared to be galoshes, a muumuu, sunglasses, and a floppy, wide-brimmed hat. But the face looked like Dr. Lavager.

"That's the famous Dr. Lavager?" asked Captain Gruber incredulously, turning to Wong Lee.

"Shhhh!" whispered Major Farina as loud as he could. "Turn it up!"

Captain Leon turned up the volume, and everyone looked at the screen in wonder. One thing no one had asked Wong Lee was how Dr. Lavager had been dressed during the kidnapping, other than in the fertilizer bag. And Wong Lee hadn't considered it relevant to his story, so he hadn't mentioned it. Now it was obvious the officers were beginning to wonder just what kind of a fruitcake they had almost brought into their midst to act out a key role in the most important undertaking of their lives.

Dr. Lavager was standing before a microphone, accompanied by three other men wearing baggy 1950s-style business suits.

They appeared to be at a news conference. It was shot in black and white film, not videotape, so the quality was poor, and the voice coming from the TV wasn't Dr. Lavager's, but that of a network news commentator. Lavager was smiling, but he looked tired, and maybe a bit disoriented. Occasionally he stroked his goatee. Absently. Wong Lee thought he could see traces of the same vacant expression Lavager was wearing when they parted company in Havana. Evidently, he was still, or again, drugged. The commentator was excited.

"… seen in this news film released today by the Eastern news agency, Borscht. According to Borscht, Dr. Lavager is shown here talking to newsmen in the Polish coastal town of Stupsk, where he had gone to confer with local authorities about the effects of recent oil spills in the Baltic Sea. Borscht also published tonight what is claimed to be Dr. Lavager's itinerary for the next two weeks, during which he is to visit a dozen other cities in Eastern Europe as well as inside the Soviet Union. Dr. Lavager's unusual attire in these film clips is not explained.

"Earlier this evening, the Soviet Embassy in Washington made public an official communiqué from the Eastern Bloc to the President of the United States, thanking him for sending Dr. Lavager on the 'goodwill mission.'

"Just yesterday, of course, the President announced the goodwill mission story was a hoax perpetrated by the Administration in hopes of buying time while trying to solve the alleged kidnapping of Dr. Lavager. Official Washington is in a complete uproar over these latest developments, and so far there has been no word from the White House acknowledging the communiqué."

The news film ended with Dr. Lavager shaking hands with a group of men and women in peasant dress, not much different from his own, in fact, and climbing into a shiny Mercedes. The commentator appeared, seated behind a news desk. A map of the United States was projected on a screen over his left shoulder. Here and there on the map were little rebus symbols for fire and explosion.

"And in other news tonight," he continued grimly, "reports have come in from several major cities in the United States of fires and explosions at government buildings, as well as demonstrations organized against the Administration. At least one such demonstration has already resulted in bloodshed. We switch now to Laslo Tjörds in Los Angeles."

On the screen, Laslo Tjörds stood before the Struthers Memorial Bell Tower.

"Good evening. I'm not actually in Los Angeles, but instead on the campus of the Leland F. P. Mason Wesley, Jr., University, which for the past two years has been the home and headquarters of Dr. Gardiner Lavager, now the central figure in what may turn out to be the most bizarre diplomatic and political story of the decade. There has been trouble here this evening.

"Shortly after the dinner hour here in California, when news came of the goodwill mission communiqué from the Eastern Bloc, demonstrators representing several anti-Administration organizations began gathering where I am now standing in front of the Struthers Memorial Bell Tower, the main campus landmark. They carried signs and placards denouncing the harmful substance acts and calling for the dismissal of Dr. Lavager from the university, as well as direct attacks against the Administration in Washington for the way it has handled the Lavager kidnapping / goodwill mission situation. Approximately one thousand people gathered here, and after a few brief speeches by their leaders they moved off in that direction toward the building which houses Dr. Lavager's laboratory."

Tjörds pointed in the direction of the lab, but the camera didn't move.

"Campus authorities and local police are not permitting the media in the area of the lab after what happened tonight, and in the turmoil it was hard to determine what did take place. I can only say the mood of the demonstrators when they left this spot was a mix of anger and confusion. Apparently, the crowd tried to storm the lab building, and the order was given to campus police to fire over the heads of the demonstrators. Warning shots were fired, and the crowd dispersed, but only after many had been injured by rocks and bottles, and several people were trampled. One campus policeman was lowered from the roof of the lab building and taken to a hospital in serious condition after his machine gun exploded. This is Laslo Tjörds reporting."

The commentator in the studio reappeared.

"Thank you, Laslo. And I've just now been handed this bulletin from Pittsburgh. Unknown persons in a helicopter have dropped a large plastic bag filled with raw sewage through a skylight into the offices of the Internal Revenue Service there, causing extensive damage to the water filter records and the files on household television viewing.

"Ladies and gentlemen, it promises to be a long night of news. Stay tuned, as we will interrupt regular programming as necessary to bring you breaking developments. More news, plus weather and sports, in a moment, after this word …"

Captain Leon turned down the volume. The officers sat in stunned silence. Wong Lee searched their faces for some clue as to how he should act. He said nothing.

"Looks like all hell is breaking loose, Tony," said Captain Leon, finally.

Captain Crockett spoke next. "Sergeant O'Grady, was Lavager wearing that outfit on the plane?"

"Yes, sir," answered Wong Lee. "He wole it first time, day we kidnap him. I t'ink it some kind of expeliment."

"How about the passengers on the hijacked airliner?" continued Crockett. "If any of them watched that broadcast, they most likely would have recognized Lavager as the man the hijackers took off the plane, right?"

"Light, sir. Passengers not know it Doc Ravager, but rots of them weo lemember garoshes. They raugh a rot when he get off prane," said Wong Lee, earnestly.

Nobody in the room had to voice what they all were thinking. Some of the passengers would talk to the media. More confusion would result. Nobody would trust anybody, and nobody would know what story to believe. First a goodwill mission. Then no goodwill mission, but a kidnapping. Then proof of a goodwill mission and an Administration hoax, or hoaxes. Then a kidnapping / hijack to Cuba prior to the goodwill appearance. Next, people would start making up their own stories. Rumors would abound. There would be a national nervous breakdown.

Worst of all, from the standpoint of the officers of the Dump Command, since it would now be revealed a uniformed American soldier was involved in the hijacking, the Army would be implicated. The mission would be in jeopardy. Both missions, actually, although Wong Lee still knew of only one.

Of everyone in the room, Wong Lee noted curiously, only Major Farina didn't look very grave. Farina had a sly smile on his face and a twinkle in his eyes.

"Gentlemen, don't you see," he said slowly, trying to contain his obvious excitement, "our time has come at last. This is the moment we've been waiting for."

"Why, of course!" shouted Captain Crockett as the meaning of the major's words dawned on him. "With the people in such an uproar and the Government in disarray, now is the perfect time to make our move."

The others caught on immediately, and for a moment they were overcome with relief, joy, and enthusiasm. They whooped and slapped each other on the back. Sergeant Major Williams took a flask from inside his shirt and offered it to Major Farina. They passed it from man to man, and everyone took a long swig. Except for Wong Lee. The jubilant scene made no sense to him at all.

Then they told him they were planning to take over the world.

He didn't believe it.

"You're in this thing up to your eyeballs now, O'Grady," said Farina, "so you'd better believe it."

Farina told Wong Lee the whole story as the other officers looked on approvingly, adding appropriate details here and there as Farina spoke. He told him of their plan to threaten to overwhelm the country with harmful substances unless their demands for power were met. Maybe it wouldn't frighten the public, who continually demonstrated their affinity for harmful substances, but it would sure scare the government. Having no effective conventional or nuclear weapons at its disposal, the government would capitulate. Then, having gained the White House, Farina and his men could threaten the whole world and win it. They showed him the situation map and explained what it meant. They described for Wong

Lee the weapons and delivery systems they had been developing. They showed their resolve, determination, dedication, and expertise.

He believed it.

What they didn't tell him was the exact state of readiness of the special harmful substance weapon they had been preparing in honor of their commanding officer. That would have spoiled the birthday surprise.

They made it clear Wong Lee was expected to help them.

"The 'show of force' idea is the way we should go, gentlemen," said Farina. "And I have just the place in mind to stage our little show. Knob Lick, Kentucky, has a certain personal attraction for me, although it wouldn't interest anyone here, I'm sure. Can we be ready to move tomorrow night?"

"What'll it be, sir?" asked Captain Labouche. "Hexachlorophene in the water supply? Or Lieutenant Duffle's latest development, a bacterial spray derived from carrots and radishes that can digest six million times its own weight in concrete? Give the word and in twelve hours we'll have the whole town looking like leftover oatmeal!"

"Perfect, Arnett. You guys set it up for tomorrow evening, on my signal. Right now, I'm going to head for Washington and have a little talk with my generous generals to get them in the boat with us. Tom, prepare the dumps in the Washington area for a major troop movement sometime tomorrow afternoon. And start cashing in those IOU's you've been piling up by giving little harmful substance favors to the Air Force boys. We're going to need planes tomorrow.

Iggy, you and O'Grady are coming with me. O'Grady here, trusted friend of the departed Dr. Lavager, is going to add a touch of drama to the scene tomorrow afternoon when we pay our little call on the President. I won't even have to commandeer the airwaves to make the coup announcement. I think old Mr. Pres himself will do that just by saying he wants to have a press conference. This is going to be something to see!"

Wong Lee's mind was racing. All he could think of was he had to find some way to tip off the other side. There was so little time. Should he go through channels, starting with that shrew, Lefkowitz? Who knew how long the message would take to get to The Octopus by that route? Besides, this was an unexpected event, and there was no pre-arranged code phraseology to cover it. What an opportunity to take a lot of crap from Lefkowitz, all right! No, somehow he had to get a message straight to the top and in the clear. And he had to do it between here and Washington in fewer than ten hours.

Just then, the door to Major Farina's office flew open, and two disheveled and bewildered soldiers were hustled into the room at billy club point by a very large MP.

CHAPTER TWENTY-ONE

Another fateful event was beginning at 10:00 p.m. that night. Even as the staff meeting was getting underway in Major Farina's office, George and Letitia were putting the finishing touches on their disguises in George's motel room.

"Golly, George, you look pretty snazzy as a soldier," said Letitia.

"You've seen me in my Marine uniform before, haven't you?" said George, pseudo-indignantly. "I think that one looks better."

"You're just not used to this one. It's cute. Besides, green becomes you."

"I'm not sure the Defense Department had that sort of thing in mind when they designed all the service uniforms. Anyway, you don't look too bad yourself there."

"Do you think so, George?" asked Letitia, preening before the wall mirror. "I must say, these heavy combat boots pinch a little."

"That's because they're new."

George regarded his own image. Everything was on straight, and the placement of the insignia looked correct to him, although he couldn't be certain since the Marines and the Army might do things differently. Tonight he would wear sergeant's stripes. A little rank would come in handy if they were forced to bluff their way out of a tight spot once they got inside the

Dump. And it was the same rank he held in the Marine Corps Reserve, so he felt comfortable with it.

Satisfied with his own readiness, George turned to look at Letitia's costume again.

"Not bad at all," he repeated. She, too, was wearing the rank of sergeant. Her hair was tucked up under her fatigue cap, out of sight. She wore no lipstick or makeup, and she had trimmed her fingernails short and square like those of a man.

"Of course, there is one problem with the whole thing," said George.

"What's that, dear?"

"Well, two problems, really, come to think of it. In the first place, you're, uh, not shaped like most soldiers."

Letitia giggled at that. George could feel his hands getting sweaty.

"Okay, George, I'll wear a sweatshirt underneath, and maybe then it won't be so obvious."

"Good idea," said George, somewhat ruefully.

"The other thing," he continued, "is your voice. You'd better let me do most of the talking if we meet anybody."

"Right," she said, trying to sound guttural.

Letitia was pinning another piece of insignia on the collar of her fatigue shirt, above the sergeant's stripes. She turned toward George so he could admire the effect.

"Do you like it?"

It was the gold oak leaf insignia of the rank of major.

"What is that for, Letitia?"

Letitia pouted at that reception.

"Golly, I thought you'd like it. I thought of it all by myself. With the stripes and the oak leaf, I can be a sergeant major. Don't you think it's a nice touch?"

"I think it'll get us thrown in the brig. I mean the stockade. A sergeant major just has stripes, lots of them, with a star in the middle. We can't impersonate anybody with that much rank anyway. There's probably only one sergeant major in the whole place, and everybody's bound to know what he looks like."

Letitia removed the insignia.

"Are we ready to go now? I've got the wire cutters right here."

"George, I'm scared again."

George seized the opportunity and embraced Letitia tenderly, lowering his lips to the

back of her neck out of long habit.

"You still want to go through with it, don't you?" he asked.

"Oh yes ... we have to get Uncle Gardy back. It's just ... oh, I don't know."

"Listen, I'm nervous, too, Letitia. But it's just stage fright. After all, what's the worst that could happen if they catch us?"

"Oh, I don't like to think about it!"

"What I mean is, the worst that could happen is they put us on trial for impersonating soldiers and trespassing on government property. But if they do have your uncle, that would cause too much publicity, so they'd have to let us go instead. Dr. Baldwin would help us anyway."

"But, George, what if they've done something horrible to Uncle Gardy? Then we'd know too much, and they'd have to 'rub us out,' wouldn't they?"

"You've been watching too many mobster movies. Don't worry; everything's going to be all right."

George had to admit to himself that last thought was unsettling to say the least. But they were committed now. Besides, all this bulky fatigue uniform material didn't make for a satisfactory embrace. The best way to make Letitia more receptive was to get her uncle back safely, so George was anxious to get started. Letitia went back to her room to put on a sweatshirt underneath her fatigue shirt.

A few minutes later they met outside, unlocked their bicycles, and started off toward Camp Shafto.

It was a clear night. The stars shone brightly, but the moon was new, so it was dark as George and Letitia pedaled up the access road, Letitia humming the "On the Trail" movement. About two hundred yards from the entrance gate, they pulled their bicycles off the road into the tall grass of one of the vast, treeless fields surrounding the camp.

"Watch where you step," cautioned George. "Don't forget, we've seen cows wandering around out here in the daytime."

"Oh, George, it looks so different at night!"

Indeed it did. Although they had spent almost every daylight hour of this week prowling around in these same fields, to the point where they felt they could find their way even if blindfolded, it did seem somewhat different from what they expected now that they were faced with it in the dark. In the distance they could see the light in the guard house at the entrance gate. As usual, there was no traffic through the gate. Streetlights were on in the camp, and light could be seen in the windows of the Officers' Club as well as in the area of the PX and other troop services buildings. Except for a porch light here and there, the barracks were dark. From this distance, there was no way of detecting any activity near the headquarters building.

They walked a few yards in from the road, chain-locked their bikes together, and stood looking toward the camp. George hefted the wire cutters in his right hand, holding Letitia's right hand in his left.

"What we'll do," he said, "is creep up to the fence over there." He indicated a spot behind the BOQ's. "Then we'll wait until the sentry goes by on his patrol. We'll have about twenty minutes before he comes by again. That will give us time to cut through both sides of the double fence, replace the cut part so it looks normal, and slip into the camp. Then we'll head straight for the headquarters building, acting as if we belong there."

They crouched low in the tall grass and looked at each other.

"Ready?" asked George.

"I guess so."

"All right, let's go."

They started walking toward their objective, hunched over

229

as if to avoid low-flying birds. George led the way, about two steps ahead of Letitia.

"Spread out," he ordered.

Letitia complied by widening the distance between them to about fifteen feet. Then, without warning, Letitia let out a short yelp of surprise and fell to the ground with a thump.

"Letitia, what is it?" asked George, backtracking.

"I tripped over something!"

"Darn right you did!" said something. "Watch where you're going!"

George stopped dead in his tracks and dropped to all-fours, a cold sweat breaking out on his forehead. He crawled the rest of the way to Letitia and helped her sit up. She wasn't hurt. They both looked in the direction of the strange voice, straining their eyes in the darkness. Something sat up. Silhouetted against the faint light from the dump, it resembled a man in a business suit and fedora.

"Who are you?" demanded George as best he could, considering his voice was shaking.

"FBI," said the man firmly, "and I'll ask the questions from here on…"

"Oh, George, you were right," gushed Letitia. "They've been here all along!"

"You've got a funny voice for a soldier," said the FBI man. "And did I hear you call this guy George? Who are you people?"

"I'm George Smith, and this is Letitia Lavager, Dr. Gardiner

Lavager's niece. Where have you guys been? Do you realize we've been here a week waiting for you to show up?"

"Now take it easy, Mr. Smith. I've got my orders, and we were told not to make contact with you yet. There's been some mighty strange things going on, you know."

"All we know is my poor Uncle Gardy is missing, and some awful men have him hidden somewhere," cried Letitia. "We thought you were going to help us!"

"Please, Miss Lavager, you'll just have to trust us," explained the FBI man. "Now I'm afraid you're going to have to tell me what you're doing out here dressed up like soldiers."

George was still suspicious. "May I see your identification, please?"

"Oh, for Pete's sake!" the FBI man muttered. But he fished out his badge and ID card and displayed them for George. It was too dark for George to read a word of the credentials, so he had no choice but to be satisfied with them.

"All right, I guess," he said finally. "Look, we're going to sneak into the camp and try to find out where they're keeping Dr. Lavager."

"That's pretty risky, isn't it?" asked the FBI man.

"We've got to do it," said Letitia.

"It's not advisable," said the FBI man curtly. "We don't think the sentries have any ammunition, but we can't be sure. Besides, I could arrest you both right now for unauthorized wearing of U.S. military uniforms."

"But you won't, because that's not what you came out here for, right?" asked George, triumphantly.

"No. I won't because I've been ordered not to make contact with you yet."

"I don't believe this," said Letitia. "Can't you help us?"

"Like I said, no contact," said the FBI man. "But then I can't stop you, either."

"Oh, well that's very encouraging," said George.

"No need to be sarcastic, Mr. Smith. I have my job to do."

The FBI man produced a walkie-talkie, extended the antenna, and began to speak softly into it.

"All units, all units. This is Fibby One." He paused. "Two soldiers in fatigue uniforms will be approaching the perimeter fences. They are Mr. George Smith and Miss Letitia Lavager in disguise. Let them pass, with no contact. Repeat: no contact. Over."

"How many more of you are there out there?" asked George.

"Stand up and see for yourself. Only twelve from the FBI, actually, but we've got company."

Their eyes had adjusted to the darkness by now, and when George and Letitia stood up they recoiled in surprise. Dark lumps were scattered everywhere in the tall grass. Scores of them, as far as their eyes could see. There must have been two hundred people hiding in the fields, on this side of the camp alone.

"My gosh!" exclaimed George.

"Yeah, I know," said the FBI man quietly. "The President is directing this operation personally, I understand. Naturally, he doesn't want it to fail. And I guess he doesn't want to slight anybody either."

"But who …?" Letitia started to ask.

"The CIA is here in force," said the FBI man. "About forty of them, I'd say. All disguised as college boys. Two squads of Secret Service people are over there." He pointed off to the right. "Army Intelligence has a couple of platoons out here too. The Army spying on the Army … weird, if you ask me. Oh, and there's a bunch from the Coast Guard down that way."

"Really, the Coast Guard?" said George.

"Yup. And other than the homeless people scattered here and there the rest are from the Teamsters Union, the AFL-CIO, UAW, IBEW, and so forth. They're here as observers. There sure are a lot of people interested in your uncle, Miss Lavager. All this fuss over one man who's not even a politician. I've never seen anything like it in my whole fifteen years with the Bureau."

"Homeless people in Nebraska too?" said Letitia.

"Tons. They can't find jobs, and they come out here and sleep. They beg from us too, which is kind of a new twist on government handouts, I have to say. Anyway, we've put a stop to that."

"Doesn't that mean your cover is blown?" asked George.

"I guess it might be, but they don't seem to talk to anybody but each other."

"But what does everybody do? I mean other than the homeless people. What's your plan?"

"Mainly, we come out here every night and lie on the ground awaiting further orders. The only action we see is slapping mosquitos. Even the FBI can't get any insect repellent these days."

"Maybe your orders will come through tonight," suggested George, hopefully. "We could sure use some help if things get sticky."

"Well, like I said, Mr. Smith, no contact. Now you'd better be on your way."

The FBI man went back into the prone position, facing the dump, and began ignoring George and Letitia.

George sighed disgustedly. "Stupid bureaucrats," he muttered.

"Now, George, they're doing the best they can," said Letitia. Silence passed between them for a moment. "Why are you looking at me that way, George?"

"Never mind. Let's just go."

They moved off through the dense grass, picking a route as they went which avoided the large, lump-like figures scattered about, and trying to avoid contact with any smaller lumps of bovine origin which might also be lurking in their path. It was impossible to proceed in a straight line, and more than once they had to climb over a lump, with a perfunctory "excuse me" going unacknowledged. With all the required zigging and zagging, careful stepping, and eyes-to-the-ground crouching, it took about fifteen minutes to reach their first objective, the outer fence.

Creeping up to the fence at last, they, too, took prone positions and waited for the armed sentry to pass. They hardly breathed, for fear of attracting attention.

Presently, the sentry approached. He was carrying an M-1 rifle at right shoulder arms and whistling to himself. Incredibly, it was the "On the Trail" movement, from "The Grand Canyon Suite." Letitia felt herself tense up. She longed for a Philip Morris filter. George tried to relax, knowing there would be less likelihood of an involuntary twitch giving him away. The sentry slowed as he approached their position, but he didn't act as if he suspected anything. He looked out through the fabric of the outer chain-link fence, surveying the fields. He halted only a few feet from George, whose heart was beating so loudly the sentry must surely hear it. The sentry stopped whistling and began muttering to himself.

"I swear, I thought cows were supposed to go back to the barn at night," he mused. "Look at 'em all out there. Must be two hundred of 'em, every night for a week now. Yet there's hardly ever any in the daytime. Stupid cows got their days and nights mixed up."

The sentry shifted his weight and looked around, first to his left, toward the entrance gate on the horizon, and then behind him, toward the troop area. No other soldiers could be seen. He leaned his rifle against the fence, unbuttoned his fly, and relieved himself in the general direction of George's position.

Letitia closed her eyes, as did George but not for the same reason. Then the sentry recovered his rifle and walked off toward the entrance gate, whistling a country music tune.

After a full minute, George lifted his head and rolled over to Letitia.

"Oh, George, I'm so sorry I got you into this," she whispered.

"It's all right. I'm okay," George insisted gamely. "Now let's get through that fence."

They belly-crawled forward, George with the wire cutters out and ready. At the fence, George began snipping away at the strands of wire, pausing after each snip to make sure the sound of his work hadn't reached the sentry's ears.

"It's a good thing he's whistling," said George. "I should have brought a piece of a blanket or something to muffle the sound."

Soon he had cut a flap large enough to crawl through. He did so and assisted Letitia in following him. She carefully re-bent the flap into place so the cut wouldn't be noticeable on the sentry's next round while George worked on the inner fence. It was covered with grape vines, which made his job more difficult. Nevertheless, more experienced now, he made quick work of the second flap, and then they were both inside the dump. George heaped a few weeds over the bottom couple of links of the flap to heighten the "undisturbed" effect. Crouching low, he and Letitia sprinted the distance to the rear of the Officers' Club and hid under a propane tank until the sentry passed again from the opposite direction.

The sentry noticed nothing amiss and kept walking, still whistling. Then he was gone. George and Letitia were home free.

They eased themselves out from under the propane tank and stood up, brushing dirt and grass off their uniforms. Adopting we-belong-here postures, they walked around from behind the Officers' Club and then into the street in front of it. Staying on the left side of the street, in order to be safely facing traffic if there were any, they walked toward the headquarters area. There was no one else around, but even if there had been, thought George, they would fit in perfectly. He felt relaxed, and he found himself walking too jauntily. He corrected that. Letitia, likewise, was feeling the relief of having gotten through the first trial of the evening successfully. She was giddy with all the excitement, and she took George's arm and squeezed it warmly.

"Watch it, Letitia. Sergeants don't do that sort of thing to each other, you know."

"Oh, right. I'm sorry." She released his arm and increased the space between them.

"Not that I don't like it, you understand."

"You look a little odd yourself," she said, "swinging those wire cutters around like that."

"Oops, I forgot."

He stuffed the tool into his pocket, where it rode on his thigh uncomfortably, chafing him as he walked.

They rounded the corner on to the street with the headquarters building. This area was well lit by streetlamps, but even here it was almost deserted. A few soldiers were hanging around the door to the PX Canteen, and three or four others could be seen walking across the parade ground, but it was definitely not as many as one would expect to see in a camp this size. It was very mysterious.

Suddenly, out of nowhere, a steam jeep chugged up from behind, barely missing them as it passed. Before they could react, the jeep turned in front of them, blocking their path. Two burley MP's jumped out and cornered George and Letitia between themselves and the jeep.

"Get your hands on top of your heads, you two! You're under arrest," said the bigger one. He brandished a nightstick.

Surprised and overwhelmed, George and Letitia did as they were told. Before they knew what was happening, they were being marched off toward the headquarters building.

"We better take these two right to the Old Man," one of the MP's declared. "We've never had any infiltrators before. He'll prob'ly want to see 'em right away."

"Yeah," said the other one. "Maybe we'll get a medal for this. Ain't been anything like this happen since the cannon got blowed up a couple years ago."

"Boy, I never seen such a glory hound as you. We better just hope the major don't get mad at us for interrupting his special staff meeting."

With a fanfare of unnecessary pushing and shoving, the MP's

got George and Letitia into the headquarters building. They marched them through the outer office, past a sleepy-eyed SP4 who was watching TV in the Message Center and toward a closed door in the rear.

The larger of the two MP's threw open the door to Major Farina's office and hustled George and Letitia in, disheveled and bewildered, at the point of his nightstick.

CHAPTER TWENTY-TWO

Captain Leon started to protest the intrusion on behalf of the commander, but the MP managed to speak first.

"Awfully sorry for the interruption, sir, but we found these two infiltrators snooping around outside, and we thought you'd want to see them right away. They were carrying these."

He held up George's wire cutters.

"Infiltrators, my ass!" shouted Major Farina, clearly upset over this apparent breach of security. "What's the meaning of this?"

Farina was on his feet. The other officers, and Wong Lee, followed suit. The infiltrators stared at the floor, their hands still on top of their heads. Wong Lee had a feeling the smaller one looked familiar, somehow. In fact, they both did.

"They look like a couple of ordinary sergeants to me," declared Captain Labouche, trying to side with Major Farina. "What makes you think they're outsiders?"

"Yes, have you checked their identification?" asked Captain Gruber, in his turn.

"Didn't have to, sir," said the MP adamantly. "One look and it's obvious they don't belong here. We spotted them a mile away."

"Now that you mention it, I think I see what you mean," said Captain Crockett, his eyes narrowing.

"What are you talking about, Ernie?" Farina asked.

"Look at their fatigues, sir. They're starched. That's against regulation."

"Well, I'll be … You're right!" exclaimed Farina. "Good work, you men!" he said to the MP's, who beamed.

"Now the question is, who are they?" shouted Captain Labouche, attempting to redeem himself. "Stand at attention, you!"

George snapped to the position of attention. Letitia's reaction was slower, not having had any military training, but she attempted to follow George's lead. In the process of removing her hands from the top of her head, she accidentally knocked off her hat. Her hair spilled forth.

Wong Lee felt himself falling apart. They were familiar, all right. He had to think fast. At least they hadn't yet recognized him.

Letitia stood erect again, looking at Major Farina for the first time. He and the other officers were still not over the shock of discovering one of the intruders was a woman, and not a bad looking one at that, from what they could see.

Letitia and Farina looked hard at each other for several seconds, as recognition dawned. Memories reawakened. The past caught up to the present. For Letitia a spring day with blue sky and green leaves, a budding relationship, then trauma and shame behind a bush outside a cave, and finally the stultifying shock of explosions, falling stalactites, and a family put asunder.

An experience to be repressed, shut up in the mind, and denied. And yet, when recalled by the overwhelming stimulus of Tony Farina's presence, the memory seemed much more of pleasure than of pain.

For Farina a day of grass-stained knees, hopes disappointed, a handful of cherry bombs tossed into a cave, and a ghastly accident. Self-preservation, hasty flight, and phobia. Was there a statute of limitations for such a crime? He struggled to sort it all out, and he braced himself to cope with this new situation and old responsibility. Somehow, though, he felt good about it. It was going to turn out all right.

Finally, Farina spoke. "Letitia? Letitia *Lavager*?"

"Tony?"

"Do you know her, sir?" asked Captain Leon.

"We …," stammered Major Farina, "we're, uh, old … friends."

"Tony."

"Letitia."

They rushed toward each other. They met in the center of the office and embraced warmly, kissing repeatedly and deeply, moaning and sighing as if they were alone in the room.

The other officers were bewildered now, and embarrassed at witnessing such a scene. The MP's were dumbfounded. George was devastated. Wong Lee tried to shrink.

After what seemed to the others like an eternity of unabashed necking, the loving couple parted, and Major Farina spoke, his voice quivering with emotion.

"Gentlemen, I'd like to present Miss Letitia Lavager. Letitia, this is my staff."

He introduced each man in turn, leaving out Wong Lee who had slipped into the latrine unnoticed during the embrace.

"You know, I thought the name Lavager sounded familiar when the boys and I first started talking about it a couple of weeks ago, but it's been so many years, I never connected it with you. That means you must be … Dr. Lavager's niece … right?"

"Oh, yes, Tony," said Letitia dreamily.

"And who might this other 'infiltrator' be, then?" he asked, referring to George.

"Oh, that's just George Smith," she cooed. "He's my uncle's assistant. We came here to rescue Uncle Gardy."

Letitia was transformed. Tony Farina was the only thing that mattered. Without knowing he was the missing link in her life for all these years, she had found him, her first and only lover, or almost-lover, and now she was fulfilled. Never mind the circumstances of her parents' death at the hands of this man. Never mind, for a moment at least, the whereabouts of her beloved uncle. She was complete now. She had Tony Farina, and she was going to keep him.

Farina felt the same way toward Letitia, although she wasn't the only woman he had known, and certainly not the first. But the shared trauma of that fateful day outside the cave in Knob Lick drew them together as if by some divine force. He had no control over it.

"This can't be happening," thought George. But there was no mistaking it. Letitia was not going to be his.

He couldn't accept it. He couldn't bear the thought of being away from his beloved, even if his love were unrequited. He had to stay with Letitia, to seek her favor, to serve her, to have her approve of him, even if she would never give herself to him. George's mind snapped. It didn't show on the outside, but he turned into a puppy then and there. He created an invisible leash running from his neck to Letitia's lovely hand. Right now it was time to heel.

"By the way, what did you all do with my uncle?" murmured Letitia. It sounded like no more than idle curiosity.

"He never got here, Miss Lavager," said Captain Crockett. "We had some men bringing him here, but the plane got hijacked to Cuba, and the hijackers took your uncle with them. Then, just a few minutes before you came in, we saw Dr. Lavager on television in some news film taken in Poland. They said he was on a goodwill mission, which is the story we planted when we kidnapped him in the first place."

"The whole thing is very confusing," admitted Captain Labouche.

"However, my dear," said Major Farina, "you stumbled upon us at a most opportune time. Have I got some news for you. Babe, we've got the world in our hands, and tomorrow we move!"

He was talking too fast for her; she wasn't ready to hear that story yet. Letitia was still turning Captain Crockett's last speech over in her mind.

"Those men, Tony … the ones who took my uncle away from the lab. They were your men? They were nasty men."

"Yes, I suppose it would seem that way, but we had to do it. You see…"

"No, I don't mean nasty for being kidnappers. That's just nasty. I mean *nasty* nasty. They did something nasty to me, sweetheart, and I want you to punish them."

"But what did they do to you, Letitia?" asked Farina. "As a matter of fact, they're all asleep in their barracks right now… that is, all except Sergeant O'Grady, and he never mentioned any…"

"Sergeant *O'Grady*?" she said. "Oh, you must mean Wong Lee. He was with them! He helped them!" She was becoming shrill.

"That was his assignment, Letitia. Tell me what happened. Where is O'Grady, anyway? He was here a second ago. O'Grady, where are you?"

"In ratline, sir." Wong Lee stuck his head through the door.

"There he is! There's Wong Lee, that awful man! Get him!"

Letitia charged toward the latrine, pausing long enough to pick up the heavy stand-up ashtray Wong Lee had placed in the shadow of the sofa and Captain Gruber's men had missed.

"Prease! Prease, Miss Retitia! Wong Ree can exprain! Not hit Wong Ree, prease!!!"

Letitia advanced on him, swinging the ashtray so fiercely no one dared try to disarm her. The officers scattered to the four corners of the room. The MP's both leaped up on to Farina's desk, as if to protect their commander, who more or less cowered behind it, having abandoned his place with Letitia in the center of the office. Only George, out of sheer bewilderment, held his ground.

Letitia's first swing went wide, but Wong Lee stumbled over an armchair and fell to the floor. As he struggled to regain his footing she hit him a glancing blow to the head which sent him headlong into the Boxer Rebellion print, shattering the glass in the frame. He caromed off the wall and, aided by a second blow to the small of his back, pirouetted into the doorway of the latrine.

As Letitia hefted the ashtray for another sally, Wong Lee's flailing arms dislodged the fire extinguisher. It dropped to the floor with a thud and began to discharge, its black rubber hose writhing like a snake as it sprayed foam all over him. He lurched backward into the latrine and went down, his head striking the lip of the urinal. He didn't get up.

Sergeant Major Williams felt for Wong Lee's pulse as Letitia calmly replaced the ashtray where she had found it and rejoined Farina at the desk. The MP's got down from the desk and looked into the latrine.

"It's bad," pronounced Williams.

"Are you sure?" asked the smaller MP.

"I've been in the Army longer'n you can count, son," said Williams with fatherly reproach, "and I know bad when I see it."

"Oh gosh," said George, without emotion.

A pool of blood was forming under Wong Lee's head.

"Letitia, tell me what happened back there," beseeched Farina. "It must have been truly awful."

"Now no one need ever know, Tony," she said. "I simply don't want to talk about it."

"George, you tell me what happened," tried Farina.

"It was awful," said George. That was all he would say. Farina saw he would have to give up on the subject.

"All right, everybody," he commanded, "let's all calm down now. Back to your seats. You MP's, uh, take O'Grady to the infirmary and, uh, I'll make my report on it for the record tomorrow, or I'll send Captain Leon over to take care of it."

"Right, sir," said the larger MP. They took Wong Lee out and wiped up the blood with paper towels.

"Thanks again, men," Farina said. "That was a nice piece of work, all around."

The MPs saluted and left. Everyone else sat down, including Letitia, who sat with Farina behind his desk, in his lap, fondling his ear lobes.

"All right, gentlemen," Farina said, "the plans remain essentially the same as before, except of course now I'll take Letitia … and George … with me when I call on the President.

Letitia, I'll explain all this to you and George right after the meeting. Any questions, anybody?"

There were none.

"Fine," he said.

The officers rose and saluted their commander. Then they left to begin carrying out their assignments for the next day … the day that would, they hoped, see them become the new government of the United States of America.

When they were alone—Farina, Letitia, and George—Farina relaxed in his swivel chair and regarded Letitia warmly. She was still in his lap.

"Well, well," he mused. "Letitia Lavager. Of all the happy coincidences. I can hardly believe it. You haven't changed much, except for this funny uniform, of course."

"How do you know, handsome?" she teased.

His left hand, which had been around her waist, slid down along her hip, tracing its graceful curve to her thigh, where it rested, stroking her leg gently. His right hand, which had been no place in particular, began unbuttoning her fatigue shirt. Somehow, it didn't matter to the two of them that George was still in the room.

George got up and began studying the tattered Boxer Rebellion picture on the wall.

"What's this, baby?" asked Farina, discovering Letitia's sweatshirt. "Are you cold?"

"Not anymore," she murmured. She and Farina kissed long and ecstatically.

George moved over to the Washington Monument picture and marveled at the fireworks.

"There's just one thing," mumbled Farina, between kisses.

"Mmm, and what's that, darling?" asked Letitia, nuzzling his ear.

"Don't you wear any deodorant?"

Letitia climbed out of Farina's lap, rearranged her sweatshirt, and buttoned up her uniform. Then she sat down on the top of the desk, facing Farina, the heels of her combat boots putting small dents in the bottom drawer.

"I'm sorry," she said. "I didn't mean to offend. I just didn't think."

"That's okay, really," said Farina gently, hoping to recapture the mood. "But I'm curious. Why not?"

"Uncle Gardy always frowned on it, so I got out of the habit. He said the anti-perspirants were especially bad for you."

"That's absolutely right," said George, rejoining them. "They have aluminum chlorhydrate in them. I remember one day we fed it to some rats. Whew!"

"Well, what happened?" asked Farina.

"Oh, they dried right up. It was fantastic. One of my best experiments."

"I see," said Farina. "So that's the kind of thing you've been working on, eh? We could have used you around here, believe me. Now if you want to hear about something really fantastic, you'd better listen to what I have to tell you. Honey, I don't exactly know how this is going to get your uncle back from wherever he is, but it's going to change the history of the world."

For the next half hour, as Letitia listened adoringly, Farina told her and George the whole story of the Mundane Ammunition Dump Command and the secret mission of DEATHCOM, revealing his personal plan to take over the world, starting tomorrow. It was a long story, and he relished the telling of it. As he made each point, he became more and more excited and confident the plans would work out successfully. By the end, he felt invincible.

When he finished, George and Letitia sat silently for a moment. George waited for Letitia to speak. Finally she did. "Oh, Tony, I love it!"

"Yeah," said George, "it's clever."

"And, just think, my little queen," said Farina gleefully, "you will be First Mistress … I mean, First Lady, of course."

"Either way, it sounds wonderful, darling. I can hardly wait."

"Well, we have an awful lot of work to accomplish tomorrow, and we'll have to get an early start," said Farina. "Suppose we amble on over to my quarters and get some sleep?"

There was a gleam in his eye.

"Are you sure you have enough room?" she asked, coyly.

CHAPTER TWENTY-THREE

The Mundane Ammunition Dump Command slept peacefully. The rest of the country threw up all over itself and never made it to bed.

By 11:00 p.m., the White House still hadn't responded to the Enemy communiqué of "thanks for the Lavager goodwill mission" or to the appearance of Dr. Lavager on national television. Bonfires were lit on sidewalks in front of Federal Buildings in major cities. Soap box orators from every walk of life spoke to the crowds attracted by the light of the fires. They demanded abolition of the harmful substance acts. They raged at the President for his handling of the Lavager disappearance. Some wanted Dr. Lavager to stay out of the country. Others wanted him back, to stand trial for unspecified crimes against "the pursuit of happiness," as if his life's work were unconstitutional. Many expressed the belief the Administration was hiding Dr. Lavager somewhere in the United States ("probably underground at some isolated Army base") in order to protect him from the justice the mobs were prepared to mete out.

There was scattered violence as opposing groups attempted to resolve their differences, which were usually over the degree to which they all opposed the Administration. There were threats of violence against Government property. Electric automobiles were overturned and short-circuited.

For the first few hours the police mostly stood by, acting only in cases of the most flagrant violations of laws and ordinances. Several hundred people were arrested for openly smoking cigarettes. At least one cigar smoker was fired upon, but escaped injury by scrambling into a storm sewer and tossing out his cigar in surrender.

The TV cameras recorded it all, and regular programming was interrupted every ten or fifteen minutes for special bulletins from various scenes of violence. Many viewers who had previously remained undecided on the popular controversial issues were so enraged by the interruptions that they, too, took to the streets to join one side or another.

During the 45-minute period between 11:15 and midnight, executives of the Logan Chemical Company, parent company of the nation's largest soap manufacturer, received a total of 879 telephone calls reporting that a bomb had been placed in a box of Bolderdash II detergent at an A & P in New Rochelle, New York, set to go off when the store opened the next morning.

There was no need for the Mundane Ammunition Dump Command to be put on alert, or even officially notified of the night's events. The police already had all the ammunition in the country, or so it was thought. The UP teletype in the empty Message Center chattered away all night long, taking down report after report of disturbances, announcements, political developments, weather conditions, and an occasional basketball score. When the paper roll was exhausted, the machine chattered on, though more softly, layering its information slavishly and illegibly on the rubber roller.

At midnight, the President's Press Secretary emerged bleary-eyed from the Oval Office and read a terse statement to the multitude of reporters gathered outside. "The President has asked me to announce that the alleged communiqué, allegedly from a source representing the Eastern Bloc and having as its subject matter the alleged presence of Dr. Gardiner Lavager in territory under the political control of the Eastern Bloc, is currently being examined by experts in the State Department who are attempting to determine the authenticity of the document, to study the language contained therein, and to render an interpretation to the President at the earliest possible moment. In addition, the President wishes it to be known that he is pleased that, as seen in news film released tonight, Dr. Lavager appears to be safe and in reasonably good health in spite of the ordeal of his circumstances, whatever those might be."

Pandemonium reigned, as the reporters dashed to telephones or extended walkie-talkie antennas to transmit the news to their editors. The networks interrupted for still another special bulletin. *The Washington Post* prepared its front page to proclaim, "LAVAGER MYSTERY DEEPENS." *The New York Times* got set to reveal, "PRESIDENT SAYS NOTHING ABOUT LAVAGER." And *The New York Daily News* set headline type for the morning edition: "PRES. IMPLIES IT'S COMMIE LIES!"

Shut-ins, unable to escape the special TV news bulletins by

joining the demonstrations outside, filled in the time between announcements by phoning thousands of false alarms to fire departments. At the A & P in New Rochelle, firemen responding to a false alarm discovered a police bomb detection squad inside the store. Mistaking them for robbers, the firemen called more police and then attacked the bomb detection squad with water from their pressure hoses to hold them at bay until the police arrived. With the floor six inches deep in water, the bomb exploded prematurely in a box of Bolderdash II, spreading huge quantities of detergent all over the store. The concussion triggered another bomb, which had lain unsuspected in a roll of white toilet paper. The A & P was awash in streamers of wet soapy toilet paper, and it was all the police and firemen could do to escape before they all turned into *papier-mâché*.

Similar scenes were repeated in scores of cities throughout the night.

At 1:00 A.M. the President summoned the ambassadors from Peru and Honduras.

"Gentlemen, thank you for coming," he said when they arrived, "especially at this hour."

"We are most honored that you would call for us yourself, *Señor Presidente*," said Peru, his gaze sweeping the room, "but we were rather expecting to see the Secretary of State here as well."

"Ah, well that is a problem, and I apologize. Secretary

Crenshaw has been embroiled in the Panama hat flap these past few weeks and is still in Panama City helping to sort things out."

"Indeed," said Honduras, "I do not think we have heard of that situation. Or at least your media have not 'got wind of it,' as you would say." He gave a wink at Peru which the President missed.

"Yes, well it seems the Commerce Department wanted to set the stage for importing large quantities of Panama hats because we expect a huge demand for them when the sun protection attire legislation is passed, so negotiations were initiated with Panama to get the best prices. However, it turns out Panama hats are actually made in Ecuador. Did you know that? Well yes, I suppose you would."

The two diplomats traded surreptitious grins as the President continued.

"Unfortunately, we didn't. So now the Ecuadorians are threatening to embargo the hats until we apologize, and Panama is raising prices of the hats they already have on hand at cruise ship ports and other tourist areas. Secretary Crenshaw has been shuttling between Panama City and Quito trying to straighten things out. We've been trying to keep it quiet. Anyway, sorry to burden you with that particular issue when there's an even bigger one to talk about."

"It is no problem, *Señor Presidente*," said Honduras with a shrug.

The two ambassadors nodded courteously and took seats

which the President offered them with a wave of his arm. Both sat on a long, white sofa, and the President sat across from them in a Boston rocker. Between the President and the ambassadors was a low cocktail table on which sat a silver coffee service.

"Coffee, gentlemen?" offered the President.

"Not from Brazil, I hope, *Señor Presidente*," said Peru.

The tone was jesting, but the President knew the diplomat was serious.

"No, no, I assure you," the President assured them both, "the White House kitchen uses nothing these days but a special blend of Peruvian and Honduran beans, and it's not decaffeinated. We still like to keep some of the hard stuff around for our good friends. It's the least we can do, after all."

This statement was pleasing to both ambassadors, and the President could sense a more relaxed atmosphere had been established. He poured them each a cup of coffee and indicated they could add their own sugar and skim milk, if desired. From a separate pot, the President poured hot water into his own cup, unscrewed the lid from a jar of Sanka, and spooned some out.

"You'll forgive me for this, I'm sure," he said apologetically. "As chief law enforcer of the country, I do have a certain obligation, even on occasions such as this ..."

They all sipped their respective beverages in polite silence for a moment, the ambassadors waiting for the President to start the real conversation, as was his prerogative.

"Gentlemen," he began finally, "tonight the United States of

America is threatened. Worse than that, she is threatened from within by divisive forces set in motion as the result of an extremely unfortunate set of circumstances over which the Administration has had little control. I'm sure you've been reading the newspapers this past week, and that you are aware of the crisis which has been approaching. Tonight that crisis is upon us."

"*Señor Presidente*," said Honduras, "not meaning to offend, but have you not brought this upon yourselves?"

"I suppose in a sense that is true," responded the President. "But it's ironic how things become twisted back upon themselves. Here we have set out to improve the quality of life for all our people by banning or restricting the very substances and practices which were about to destroy our civilization. We have vacated our previous warlike stance with regard to the rest of the world. We are realistic, however, and we have not abandoned the obvious need for defense against our enemies, but now we share that defense with the rest of the Hemisphere, as is the only sensible and appropriate approach to take to world peace. The nations which you gentlemen represent now have all the Free World's nuclear weapons, and the United States is, for all practical purposes, disarmed."

"And we do appreciate that, *Señor Presidente*," said Peru and Honduras, together.

"As do we," said the President. "But in spite of all of this, our people seem as determined as ever to destroy their own future.

They are enraged at the Harmful Substance Acts, but they haven't given them time to prove how valuable they will be once we've gotten through the inevitable period of transition and dislocation."

"All this is most unfortunate, to be sure, *Señor Presidente*," said Peru, "but why have you sent for us tonight? We have no treaties on the subject of aid in cases of internal strife."

"Oh, of course it's not that, gentlemen. It's true our police are running low on bullets, but I believe we can handle the situation, no matter how grave it becomes, as long as it does remain one of purely internal strife."

"Are you implying there may be Outside Agitators at work?" The two ambassadors looked at each other uncomfortably.

"I don't know for sure. I only know we must be on our guard. And now I must broaden my meaning of the words 'we' and 'our' to include your countries as well as all of our other allies. Here, I want you to look at this message which I received about an hour ago from the Soviet embassy."

The President went to his desk. It was a modest, if large, piece of furniture, made of weathered boards, some warped, and painted a glossy battleship gray. But it was one of the President's most treasured possessions, having been constructed of lumber from the platform on the beach at Atlantic City on which the young President-to-be had sat as a lifeguard for five summers before deciding to go into politics. Dismantled and re-constructed with loving care by New Jersey high school students, the desk was awarded to the President on the day of his Inauguration by the Atlantic City Chamber of Commerce.

He climbed the ladder to the top of the desk, about eight feet off the floor, found the sheet of paper he was looking for, and returned to the rocking chair. He handed the paper to the ambassadors. They read its short message in silence.

"But, *Señor Presidente*, this is a pledge of Enemy non-intervention in the current strife in the United States. What is the problem, then?"

"Ah, but that is, in fact, the problem, right there," said the President, grimly. "We would naturally expect the Enemy not to intervene, since it's none of their business. Why, then, do you suppose they have sent this gratuitous statement that they will not interfere in our affairs?"

The ambassadors let the President answer his own question.

"Gentlemen," he continued, "it can mean but one thing, especially when combined with the knowledge that the Russian ambassador does not always tell the truth."

"*Señor Presidente*," said Honduras, in shocked tones. "We cannot sit by without challenging such a statement."

"Okay, you've done your duty. You've challenged it. It is a fact, nevertheless, and this message can only mean the Enemy is planning to take over the government of the United States by taking advantage of our internal situation. I don't know how or when they will try to do it, but we must be ready for them. I have brought you here tonight to ask you to put your countries on alert for Enemy activity. The defense of the Free World rests with you, and I now call upon you to take whatever steps are necessary to help prevent an Enemy takeover of the United States."

"*Señor Presidente*," said Peru, standing up, "the history of the United States has shown it to be a great nation. It has been an example to all other nations of the free world and an inspiration to struggling new democracies everywhere. There was a time when such greatness would have been worth protecting at any cost."

"But where has that greatness gone, *Señor*?" asked Honduras, rising to join his companion. "Lately, the United States has seemed to go *loco*. Your foreign policy has become *laissez-faire*. You relinquish your own defense. You wash your hands of arms. You embark upon this mysterious quest for 'the quality of life' which your people cannot understand. What kind of an example do you present now, *Señor Presidente*, for all the peoples of the Free World to follow? Does a true representative democracy fly in the face of the will of the majority? It is no wonder your people are in revolt, your economy is in a shambles, your government buildings are being burned, and the Enemy awaits at your gates, ready to feed upon what will be left when events have taken their course."

"And now," took up Peru, "it seems you have even, however unwittingly perhaps, pitted your allies Panama and Ecuador against each other and your country as well."

"So we ask you, *Señor Presidente*, continued Honduras, "why should we help you? Why?"

"Gentlemen, unfortunately, we do not have time to debate such weighty philosophical issues," said the President. "The crisis is here, now."

"It is just as well we do not have the time," conceded Honduras, "because what I have already said is all that my government has authorized me to say."

"And mine as well," said Peru, "except for the business of the hats, of which you may presume I learned only a few moments ago."

"But, I can tell you this, personally, my friend," continued Honduras. "I think that you Americans have gone completely, ah, how you say … out of your minds. More than *loco*."

"Perhaps we have indeed, gentlemen. History will tell. But be that as it may, the facts of our situation tonight are not alterable. I'll give you one simple and compelling reason why you must honor the mutual defense treaties and the trusts which have been placed in you. The defeat of the United States, if it happens, will be the start of a chain of Enemy conquests which will not reach its conclusion until all the nations of the Free World are toppled. First the United States, then Canada, then Mexico, then … who knows who will be next to go? But the world's free nations will fall, gentlemen, one after another, inexorably, like the proverbial dominoes, Peru and Honduras among them, unless the Enemy is stopped right now and shown he cannot penetrate our defenses. All I ask is that you call an alert and become prepared to defend if necessary."

"Very well, *Señor Presidente*," said Peru. "I do not see how we can refuse, when you put it that way."

"Indeed," agreed Honduras, "but it is a shameful business. Nevertheless, we shall prepare ourselves as you have asked."

"The United States of America thanks you, gentlemen. You will not regret this decision. And now, it's late, and I'm sure you have many preparations to make before morning. Thank you again for coming."

The President rose, signaling the end of the meeting. The two ambassadors departed.

The President climbed up to his desk and turned on his TV for the latest news. None of it was good. The demonstrations had turned to riots in many cities. Fire-bombing and looting were reported everywhere. Shrill voices called for the President's impeachment. Saboteurs worked throughout the night, cutting telephone lines, blowing up railroad bridges, and flushing colored crepe paper down toilets all over the country.

Somehow, it didn't seem real. Sitting there, exhausted, watching it all on television, he felt as if he were just another citizen seeing pictures of events happening hundreds of miles away to other people, events which had no direct bearing on his own life, problems someone else would eventually solve while other problems came to take their place. Eventually, high atop the room in the chair behind his desk, with the TV still on, *Señor Presidente* fell asleep.

CHAPTER TWENTY-FOUR

At this same moment, in his castle nestled in a valley in the foothills of an obscure mountain range in the bowels of Eastern Europe, Emmett Karamazov, otherwise known to many as "Le Grand Malfaiteur" or to others as The Octopus, and to still others as both, was preparing to greet his breakfast guest. Adjusting his cummerbund, he regarded his massive frame and sculptured visage carefully in a long, antique mirror. He was pleased with what he saw: the image of the perfect master spy.

He took a few more seconds and practiced making his eyes look unmistakably cold and calculating.

This was to be the day of an exploit that could turn out to be the crowning achievement of a brilliant career of international intrigue. It would have to be. To arrange it, he had had to risk exposing his whole United States organization, and now there was too much at stake. If he mismanaged this one, it would spell his doom. Yet, if he were successful … he simply could not comprehend the lengths to which the Eastern governments would go to reward him. Emmett Karamazov, the 57-year-old son of a Russian railroad car wheel flange finisher, saw in the recent turn of world events an opportunity to perform a feat no less magnificent than that of taking over the United States of America itself, without a war.

It would be like a dream come true, the Revolution finally

reaching its ultimate goal. Like every other true child of the Revolution, Emmett had always wished for the destruction of imperialist America. From the time he was the school bully in his little home town of Mimsy in Borogovnia, it had been his personal goal. It was a goal he carried with him all through his days as a small-time arsonist, saving up enough extortion money to go to spy school, there to learn to speak English with an officious French accent, not a Russian one, and to spend years practicing self-discipline and working himself into the character whose very names now struck terror into the hearts of thousands. And now he and only he controlled the consolidated intelligence network of the Eastern Bloc, by dint of incredibly hard work, as well as an unfortunate fatal accident suffered by his predecessor. He moved and operated with almost complete autonomy, since, as it turned out, none of the Eastern governments was eager to criticize his actions for fear of offending one of the other governments which might have authorized them. It was a perfect setup, and now the unrest in the United States caused by the harmful substance controversy provided him the opportunity of a lifetime.

Indeed, it had been somewhat difficult at first for him to place his agents in sensitive positions in the U.S. where they could influence the outcome of scientific experiments so as to make innocuous substances appear to be harmful, and truly harmful ones even more so. But with the formation of the American Eco-Toxicology Association, that job became easier. It was no problem for his people to substitute cancerous rats for the healthy ones involved in starch research, for example. He had arranged for similar techniques to be used to disguise the true results of tests of dozens of other substances as well. In the growing hue and cry that ensued, with the weasel U.S. government losing its grip and with its defenses in the hands of weak third parties like Peru and Honduras, Emmett Karamazov prepared his final moves.

One of these moves was the relatively effortless kidnapping and use of Dr. Gardiner Lavager to confound the American people and the laughable U.S. Army chauvinists in MADCOM/DEATHCOM. Now Lavager was the key to the rest of the plan.

Le Grand Malfaiteur donned his shiny black suit coat, stroked his firm jaw before the mirror one last time, and walked out of the room. He descended the wide marble staircase, walked through the castle's cavernous main hall, and entered the library to greet his guest.

"Ah, my dear Doctor Lavager," he opened. "It is indeed a great pleasure to have you as my guest this morning."

The two men shook hands, Le Grand Malfaiteur exuberantly, Dr. Lavager as reluctantly as he felt he could without appearing rude.

"So you're Le Grand Malfaiteur," said Dr. Lavager, apprehensively. "Your man Andrei, who locked me in my room last night, told me that's what you're called."

"Yes, I am none other than Le Grand Malfaiteur, Chief of Espionage in the service of those noble powers to whom your weasel government refers as 'the Enemy.'"

"So you're Le Grand Malfaiteur," repeated Dr. Lavager slowly.

"That is correct, Monsieur. Often, I am also known as 'The Octopus.'"

"But I've never heard of you."

"And with good reason, I assure you. But welcome to my humble abode, *cher Monsieur le Docteur.* Do accept my apologies for your overnight confinement. It was unintentional on my part. My people can be a bit overzealous on occasion. Of course, you are free to go at any time. But for now, please, let us enjoy our breakfast, for we have much to discuss."

They walked across a hall to the dining room and sat down at opposite ends of a long, wide table set with sterling and crystal. Tuxedoed waiters slithered noiselessly in and out of the immense room, charting paths around its elegant furnishings. They carried samples of the many varieties of breakfast fare which the kitchen was capable of producing—a living menu brought before Dr. Lavager and his host in order that they might choose their pleasure with the luxury of perfect information.

"Isn't this a little wasteful?" inquired Lavager, raising his voice in order to be heard across the table's expanse.

"Not at all, Monsieur," said LGM with a shrug. "The servants are pleased to eat what you and I choose to leave. It is all consumed properly."

LGM stroked his neatly trimmed mustache with apparent amusement.

Lavager was now fully recovered from the drugs administered to him during and since his kidnapping, but psychologically he was still in something of a daze. The shock of awakening 6,000 miles from home and in the company of the Enemy had taken its toll, and he no longer fully comprehended what was going on at any given moment. He felt as if he were being tossed about like the toy of some impetuous child.

Yet, even though his life during the past week had been completely controlled, his hosts were friendly, and he had received the best of treatment and care. They had even gone so far as to provide him with a new wide-brimmed straw hat, a new pair of galoshes, a pair of expensive designer sunglasses, and three new muumuus, one of which he was wearing now. It was yellow. And paisley. There was never a word spoken about his outfit. Apparently, everyone simply assumed it was his normal dress. He was beginning to feel silly about the whole thing.

He stopped a waiter carrying a box of bran flakes on a silver tray. The waiter poured a heaping quantity into a small crystal bowl and provided a pitcher of skim milk. Le Grand Malfaiteur spread goose liver pâté on a croissant with a butter knife. After each bite, he sipped from a bone china demitasse of extremely strong coffee.

"Oh, do try the *pamplemousse*," suggested LGM. "I've had it flown in from Texas. It's the Ruby Red variety and very, how you would say, tasty."

"As much as I like grapefruit, I must decline, but thank you. I happen to know that kind was developed using radiation to trigger mutations, and of course I cannot support such a practice."

"I sincerely apologize. I was unaware."

Dismissively, Lavager ate a spoonful of bran flakes and then changed the subject.

"I suppose, or at least I hope, you have brought me here to tell me, at last, what I am doing in Europe, and for what purpose I am being used," he said, tentatively.

"Oh, my dear friend, you do us an injustice. You are our guest, here at our open invitation," said LGM grandly. "Ah, but I suppose you have forgotten. How unfortunate, too, that your President did not see fit to acknowledge our invitation. And then there was that regrettable misunderstanding associated with your transportation here, during which our agents received erroneous orders to drug and kidnap you, when you were on your way here all the time, acting on your own volition. We do indeed apologize for that, and I assure you the individuals responsible for the error have been dealt with most … appropriately."

"Well, I . . ."

"But, you are here. And that is what is the important thing, *n'est ce pas*? And most fortuitous, at that. By now my people have told you of the escalating turmoil that now exists within your own country. Believe me, *Monsieur le Docteur*, it is most lucky you came here when you did, as your very life would be in danger now if you were still at home."

"I suppose I should be thankful for that," said Dr. Lavager, "but I must admit things are a little confusing right now."

"Ah, do not worry. It is merely the time change, or what I believe you call the 'jet lag.' The same affliction befalls all international air travelers, you know. One of the minor drawbacks of this modern age. You will get used to it."

"When can I go home?"

"As soon as it is safe, my friend. And that is what I wished to speak with you about this morning."

The two men ate in silence for a moment before LGM continued.

"We have much in common, you and I. You see, we both crusade for the same thing: an end to harmful substances and the evil practices that are spelling the doom of mankind."

"I'd like to believe that," said Dr. Lavager. "But if that's so, why are you called 'Le Grand Malfaiteur?'"

"A political label, regretfully. Merely an unfortunate reference to methods I may have used in the past to accomplish certain … objectives … for my government but have since firmly renounced. How sad for a matter of such little importance to come between us now, when we must trust each other. But still you seem troubled. How can I alleviate your doubts?"

"Something about your name, I think. I'm not a linguist, but in proper French wouldn't it be 'Le Malfaiteur Grand,' with the adjective *after* the noun, the opposite of English?"

"Ah, an astute observation, Monsieur, but then I suppose I would expect nothing less from such a brilliant mind. Suffice to say the word order is tailored to the more typically less educated English speaker who would likely find the French syntax confusing. But now on to business."

The big man waved his hand, and the waiters disappeared, presumably into the kitchen. Now he and Lavager were alone.

"Your President has lost control. Even now the people are in revolt against him, and against what you and I hold so dear. Trouble has of course been mounting for some time, but the, how you would say, straw that broke the hump of the camel, seems to have been the threat of cancelling Thanksgiving."

"Hmm, yes, I thought maybe that could have been handled more delicately in the TV interview."

"And now chaos reigns, and as a result the fate of the world hangs in the balance."

As LGM spoke these words, Dr. Lavager listened attentively, a spoonful of bran flakes and skim milk poised at his lips.

"The powers I serve have decided that intervention is the only logical course of action at this time. If America goes, so will the rest of the world. We have decided to act to save America from itself in this, its hour of great need."

Dr. Lavager lowered his spoonful of cereal. His eyes

narrowed. He stood up and leaned forward with his hands on the table to support himself. He faced LGM squarely.

"Do you mean to tell me," he said, "that you, the Enemy, are going to take over the United States?"

"Please, please, do sit down, my dear Dr. Lavager. It is nothing to become alarmed about, I assure you. It is not, as you put it 'an Enemy takeover.' Merely call it an humanitarian gesture of aid to a confused but deserving people. Surely you realize the inevitable consequences of the strife in your country if no one does anything … if no friend steps forward to help in the fight for the quality of life."

"Yes, but … but what about our allies?" stammered Dr. Lavager. "What about Canada, Mexico, or … or Peru and Honduras? Have they been silent? I can't believe it."

"So far, that appears, sadly, to be the case. Perhaps they do not want to become 'involved.' Tsk, tsk, such a distressing commentary on our times, do you not think?"

"How do you know all this?" asked Lavager.

"Well there you see I suppose it is the octopus in me, my other nickname. I do have my unseen tentacles in a multitude of places, my invisible fingers in a thousand pies. It's blessing, and a curse."

"Well then, what are you planning to do?" Resignation in his voice, Lavager sat.

"That depends entirely upon how willing you will be to co-operate with us and to help in this most critical endeavor," soothed LGM. "Please keep two things in mind before you react too quickly…"

Lavager shuddered, but he listened.

"The first is the importance of this as an humanitarian gesture. That, I am sure you already understand. The second thing is that our intervention is to be only temporary. Naturally, as soon as public safety is assured and your government is once more in a position to maintain control of the domestic situation, we will withdraw. Of course, it is impossible to say at this time how long that might be. You understand."

"Of course…" Dr. Lavager was reeling. It was all so incredible. It was frightening. But it all made sense, somehow.

And it would mean he could continue his work. In the final analysis, nothing was more important than that, and now, if everything worked out as LGM seemed to be suggesting, Dr. Lavager's contributions could be enjoyed, not only by his fellow Americans, but also by most of the rest of the world.

Still, there was suspicion in the back of his mind. No boy who had grown to maturity in America in the 1940's and 1950's, as Dr. Lavager had, could have escaped it. Suspicion of the Enemy was a way of life. It was taught at Boy Scout troop meetings. It was preached from pulpits on Sunday mornings. It dripped from comic books. Newspapers, magazines, radio, television, high school civics courses—all were full of it. It was impossible to sweep it all under the rug, just like that.

Dr. Lavager decided to cooperate, but carefully, cautiously.

One false move by Le Grand Malfaiteur, one indication of bad faith, and he would blow the whistle. I may be politically naive, he thought, but I'm not stupid. This is the only way.

"What do you want me to do?" said Dr. Lavager in a voice so faint that LGM barely heard him.

"Ahh, Dr. Lavager, this is indeed a great day," enthused Le Grand Malfaiteur. "I am so pleased you have decided in favor of humanity. But then, I never believed for one second that you would choose otherwise."

LGM stood up and paced the room, gesturing expansively, and pointlessly, as he talked. Dr. Lavager followed him with his eyes.

"Your role will be simple, Monsieur Doctor. Very simple indeed. You will be our spokesman. You will explain our intentions, and you will enlist the help and cooperation of your government. The government will listen to you, even if the people will not."

"And what about the people, then?" asked Lavager.

"Among the people we are already beginning to gather support. Remember, first of all, the people are disaffected of your government at the moment. They are in the mood for someone to talk to them, to show them a different way. Our operatives are already beginning to suggest a different way … our way, of course. Subtly, but surely, Americans are being prepared for the moment when we can openly announce our intentions. At that moment, they will embrace us warmly. Then, and only then, can we begin the arduous task of re-educating

275

them to the dire effects of harmful substances. It will take time, Monsieur. But together, we can do it."

"And what of our defense forces? Do you think they will simply let you walk in and assume control of the country?" Lavager asked incredulously.

"But, my friend, if you have succeeded in convincing your government of our sincerity, it will be ... as you might say ... a slice of cake. Besides, your police are running low on bullets, and they will be glad to give up the fight. Also, do not forget your military is weaponless, and, frankly, I must express to you my grave doubts about whether nations like Peru and Honduras will rise to the defense of the United States when the, uh, how you say, 'chips' are down. Furthermore, the only remaining viable military force in your country, the Coast Guard ... well, what I am about to say will astound you."

"Nothing would astound me anymore," said Dr. Lavager quietly.

"Approximately one half of the Coast Guard are secret agents of the powers I represent. They joined us a couple of years ago, shortly after they were put on foot patrol of the Canadian and Mexican borders," said LGM.

"I admit it. I'm astounded," said Lavager.

"Putting the Coast Guard on foot patrol of land borders was, shall we say, not a wise move by your President."

"And to think, he did it on my advice," said Lavager, his hand on his forehead.

"Indeed? That, I had not known. But, regardless, it is really to your credit anyway, the way things have turned out, *n'est ce pas*?"

Lavager wasn't sure.

"But be that as it may," continued LGM, "on to the plan. Which is very simple as well. Deceptively so, I might add. First, we must get you back into the United States, quietly, so that you can contact the President. We will do this by releasing you off the coast of Virginia in an electric motor boat whose batteries have gone dead. You will be rescued by…"

"The Coast Guard, of course."

"*Naturellement*! Then, your next stop is Washington, and there…"

Le Grand Malfaiteur continued to talk. His guest listened intently, although the expression on his face betrayed doubt and discouragement. Absentmindedly, as if needing the therapy of something to fidget with while he concentrated, Dr. Lavager dipped his hands in a finger bowl and wiped them dry on his linen napkin.

Presently, LGM clapped his hands. The waiters reappeared and removed the breakfast dishes. Dr. Lavager and Le Grand Malfaiteur rose and walked out toward the garden. Although it was nearing 10:00 a.m., the sun was only now rising over the towering mountain peaks to the east. Le Grand Malfaiteur gazed in the direction of his Source, and he felt warm. Dr. Lavager looked away from his and felt cold.

CHAPTER TWENTY-FIVE

By noon the next day, tensions in the U.S. had mounted to emergency proportions. Although people were off the streets, many resting and recovering from the previous night of destructive goings-on, most were preparing to sally forth again under cover of the next night's darkness. Hundreds of fires burned out of control. Police abandoned their police stations and set up temporary headquarters in sporting goods stores, where there was easier access to the few remaining weapons they could use for crowd control. Shotguns and shells were issued, but there weren't enough to go around. Many patrolmen walked their beats carrying hunting bows, with quivers full of arrows strapped to their backs. Some of the arrows were tipped with rubber suction cups, but to the average citizen from a distance they looked deadly enough.

Practice ranges were set up in deserted Sears, Roebuck parking lots, and exercises in creative weaponry began. On at least one such range, a sergeant and eight patrolmen lined up, six feet apart. Each patrolman carried a golf club at right shoulder arms and a bag full of balls attached to his belt.

"Atten-hut!" commanded the sergeant. "Right face!"

The patrolmen executed the maneuver.

"Roll call!"

"Driver!"

"Brassie!"

"Spoon!"

"Daffy!"

"Baffing spoon!"

"Cleek!"

"Mashie!"

"Niblick!"

"All right, who said Daffy?" the sergeant yelled.

"Sorry, Sergeant," called one of the patrolmen, stifling a snicker. "I meant Baffy. I think."

"Well don't let it happen again!"

"No, Sergeant!"

"Present arms!" commanded the sergeant.

Eight club heads hit the ground in unison.

"One, two, three … Fore!"

At this command, a murderous barrage of eight golf balls was loosed toward a hypothetical crowd of wrongdoers.

The sergeant stood back and admired his work.

"Not half bad," he said to the patrolmen. "That ought to *slice* up a few longhairs, if you get my drift!"

At the White House in Washington, Major Farina, Letitia Lavager, and George Smith sat outside the Oval Office, awaiting an audience with the President—an audience arranged by the Secretary of Defense after a showdown phone call from Lieutenant General Victor Gotham, one of Farina's patrons.

Farina had spent the morning at the Pentagon, and, as

Captain Crockett had figured, it had been no trouble at all to convince the Gothams and the other generals to go along with him. A little patriotic pep talk, a few charts and graphs to demonstrate that everything was in readiness, lavish promises of power and influence, tempered with democratic restraint, of course, and suddenly they were converted.

Now the big moment was at hand.

Farina was resplendent in his green Class A uniform, with the black stripes of an officer down the outsides of the trouser legs and at the wrists of the jacket. His brass was polished as never before, and the "scrambled eggs" on his cap visor were brand new. His chest was festooned with ribbons and medals, several of which he was actually authorized to wear. His black leather low-quarter shoes gleamed in the light from the chandelier.

George had changed into civilian clothes for the occasion, as had Letitia. He was wearing his usual attire: Weejuns, white socks, black chinos, a Leland F. P. Mason Wesley, Jr., sweatshirt, and a brown tweed sport jacket with leather elbow patches. Letitia wore her usual form-fitting jump suit, and today it wasn't zipped all the way up.

A buzzer sounded. A moment later an aide approached the seated trio.

"The President will see you now," she pronounced in hushed, reverent tones.

They rose and strode through the white paneled door, Farina

striding in ahead of the other two. The door closed behind them, and they were in the sacred room, the Oval Office of the President of the United States. They didn't see the President at first, seated at his desk far above them. But then George caught sight of the tall gray structure.

"Look at that," he whispered. "What the heck is that thing?"

Letitia tugged on his elbow, and he closed his mouth, which had been agape.

"Ah, Major Farina," called the President, descending the ladder.

Farina snapped to attention and saluted the Commander-in-Chief.

"Oh, no need for that, Major Farina," exclaimed the President, crossing the room with his right hand outstretched. "May I call you, uh, Tony?"

"Please do, sir," said Farina, shaking hands.

"Letitia, my dear. How nice to see you again." The President took her hand when he had finished with Farina's and held it warmly. "And George. Good to see you, George."

George only nodded, speechless. The President offered them seats on the sofa and started for the rocker himself.

"If you don't mind, sir, I'd rather stand," said Farina.

"Very well, then, Tony," said the President. "I'd half suspected this might turn out to be more formal than a family reunion. Letitia, you and George please have a seat. I hope we have a chance to chat about your uncle, Dr. Lavager, in a few minutes.

You simply can't know how sorry I am about what has happened, in spite of the fact that I frankly do not know what has happened. Meanwhile, the major here seems to want to get down to business, and I must act accordingly."

The President climbed the ladder again and sat peering down on Farina, who was forced to crane his neck in order to address him. It was either that or move to the far end of the room, from which the angle of sight wasn't as difficult to hold. Farina strode to the far end of the room. He felt like a fool. But this was it; there was no backing out now.

"Mr. President, I'm afraid the only way to begin this is to make a small speech," he began.

"What are you afraid of about that, Major? People make speeches to me all the time. You know, you military people are all alike, aren't you? 'Sir, I'm afraid I have some rather bad news.' 'Mr. President, I'm afraid the Enemy has come up the Potomac in rowboats and captured the Kennedy Center.' 'Mr. President, I'm afraid I'm afraid.' Forgive me, Major, but it has been a rather difficult couple of weeks for me, as you may well know, and I didn't get much sleep last night. Why don't you just come right out and tell me you have something to say."

"All right then! Nuts! I have something to say!"

Farina couldn't believe such an outburst had come from his own lips, but it had. He felt like a child. For the first time in years, he wasn't in complete control of a situation. In the President he had met his match, and he hadn't even successfully started the conversation. There had to be a way to gain the upper hand, even from the bottom of a hole, which was about where he felt he was standing, so far below the President's lifeguard chair.

"Forgive me, too, sir," he started again, clearing his throat as he did so. "We've all been under a strain, with Dr. Lavager's disappearance and everything. Believe me, Letitia has been worried sick, and it's affected all of us."

"Yes, dear girl," said the President, "and I am so sorry, as I said."

"And I can well understand any impatience you may have with me, sir," Farina continued. "I realize this meeting was forced upon you…"

"Nothing is forced upon me, young man."

"I mean suggested to you, by the Secretary of Defense, and you're no doubt wondering what connection I have to Letitia, to Dr. Lavager, or to anything important to you."

"That, I am." The President was listening now.

"Officially, sir, I am the commanding officer of the Mundane Ammunition Dump Command, or MADCOM. For the past four years, my 'official' mission has been to protect empty ammunition dumps all over the country. Nobody's ever told me why."

"Are you questioning your orders, Major? Has it taken you a matter of years to get all the way up the chain of command to me? Is that what all this is about?"

Farina was unmoved by the ploy.

"I'm *afraid*, sir," he continued, "it has gone somewhat beyond that. No, in fact far beyond that. Oh, I've been taking care of those old empty dumps all right. And now they're not as empty as you might think."

"Now we're getting somewhere," said the President. "Please, go on."

He did. As the President listened more and more intently, Farina carefully revealed to him the secret mission of DEATHCOM, for which MADCOM was just a cover. Step by step, and with exhibits and statistics, he took the President through the history of the mission, from its inception by a group of fiercely patriotic generals who felt their hands were tied as a result of America's disarmament policies, to the underground development and buildup of harmful substance weaponry as a deterrent to Enemy aggression. He even explained the DEATHCOM role in Dr. Lavager's disappearance.

"Of course, it was never our intention that Dr. Lavager fall into Enemy hands," said Farina with true sincerity, "but we found out too late that one of our most trusted operatives was a double agent."

These reminders of the kidnapping scene caused Letitia to shudder noticeably.

"In a way," continued Major Farina, "I feel personally responsible for the violence and confusion which has resulted."

"But, Letitia, I don't understand," said the President, shifting his attention to her. "How do you fit into all this? What's your connection with Major Farina?"

Before she could answer, Farina spoke up. "Until the day of the kidnapping, she knew nothing about this at all. It wasn't until last night, when she and George infiltrated my headquarters at Camp Shafto looking for Dr. Lavager, that we met again after many years. You see, we were childhood … uh, friends … and had lost track of each other. When she learned the truth about her uncle, she graciously agreed to accompany me here today in hopes we might be able to help get the nation through this most difficult time."

"Why was I not informed of this MADCOM/DEATHCOM business? Why the secrecy?"

"We were going to come to you, sir, but at the proper time."

"Is there ever a proper time for such a deception? Major, this is a matter of national security. You have overstepped your authority."

"Please, sir. My superiors…"

"Your friends, the hawkish generals."

"Call them what you will, sir, but in a time when you and a namby-pamby Congress saw fit to give away this nation's very birthright, only this small group of stalwart men cared enough to risk their reputations—perhaps even their lives—to do the only rational thing left to preserve the greatness that has been America. Do you honestly believe our so-called 'allies' to the south will come to our defense when the chips are down?"

To himself, the President had to admit he had been having some doubts about that.

"I hardly think so, Mr. President. Nevertheless, as I was saying, my superiors felt that for you to know of our activities too early would have compromised you, made you more vulnerable to international pressures. Better to come to you—as we were about to do—as soon as some additional development work was completed, with Dr. Lavager's help. Better to come to you when we were in a full state of readiness, when there would be no question of the invincibility we could provide. Then, with an announcement by you to an unsuspecting Enemy, a lasting peace would have been assured."

"Major Farina," said the President in a low, over-controlled voice, "Major Farina, just what in blue blazes makes you think we were not in fact achieving a 'lasting peace,' as you put it, with the lawful, open and honest measures your elected leaders have already been taking?"

"That is not the point, sir."

"That is precisely and unalterably the only point, young man! Have you been to school? Have you forgotten your training as an officer? Have you read any of the multitude of political novels written during the past 20 years? Have you somehow missed out on the idea that this nation is governed 'by the people?' That's not just a poetic phrase, you know. That means the People, the civilians. The people elect their representatives who write laws. They also elect judges, or have their representatives appoint them, who review the laws and see to it that they are applied fairly. The people elect a President to carry out the provisions of those laws. The military is hired by the people for the people's defense. The military is not the people. You, Major Farina, are not the government. You are a hired hand. And that is the point."

A moment of silence passed before Farina answered, his own voice low and firm.

"Sir, that is not the point I have come here to discuss. The facts belie the relevance of that point."

The President sensed a threat about to be made, and he knew he had to keep control of his temper. For a moment, though, he toyed with the idea of sending a paperweight crashing into Farina's skull. But that wouldn't quiet the crowds in the streets, and it wouldn't get Dr. Lavager back. And it would probably not give him any satisfaction anyway.

"And what are those facts, Major Farina?" he asked.

"The facts are that you have lost control. Crowds are running wild, calling for your blood while fighting each other. The fabric of American society is being rent before your eyes. Your precious 'people,' as you put it, are telling you they have withdrawn the authority they gave you at Inauguration. They want it back, Mr. President, because they can't trust you, because when they did trust you, you did things they hated. Whether you realize it or not, 'harmful substances,' and religion of course, are what keep the majority of people in a civilized country from going crazy, either from the tremendous pressures of survival or from sheer boredom.

"Yes, it's true there have been excesses that require control," Farina continued. "That's been true since the discovery of alcohol. And it's possible to refine these substances and make weapons of them as I have done—weapons of peace, of course, never to be used unless absolutely necessary."

"You are making me very angry, Major."

"It's the 'people' who are angry, Mr. President. And their guard is down. And don't think the Enemy doesn't know it."

The President knew that fact all too well. He had spent half the night with it. That worried him. So did Peru and Honduras. He didn't know which worried him more.

And cancelling Thanksgiving had been, at best, premature.

"Sometimes, Mr. President," continued Farina, "I'll bet you wish you could just call out your 'hired hands.' But they're disarmed, and there you must sit. Yea, sir, with the police out of bullets, reduced to imbedding razor blades in Frisbees. With the Coast Guard wasting its time on wetbacks and Canadian bacon smugglers. With the Army, in droopy, wrinkled fatigues, sitting on its thumb. With your missile silos covered with graffiti written in Spanish. With…"

"Enough rhetoric, Major," interrupted the President. "What is your proposition? I assume you have one."

"It's an opportunity, Mr. President."

"Whatever you say, Major."

"All right, then, let me put it this way. It's the only way you're going to be able to get the country out of this mess before the Enemy closes in, and you're going to jump at the chance, whether you like it or not."

"Major, you truly are forgetting yourself."

"That's one thing I never do, sir," continued Farina, "and there's no point trying to talk down to me. Just sit up there and listen. I'm offering you the opportunity to patch the country back together. I've explained the DEATHCOM state of readiness to you. With the weapons at my command, I can stop the civil disorders within 24 hours, and just as easily I can prevent an Enemy invasion. I am prepared to do both."

"You have a condition, naturally?"

"Naturally, Mr. President. It's a simple one. I request only that you designate me President pro-tem, grant me full police emergency powers, and step down yourself."

"Bullcrap, Major! Forgive me, Letitia, but bullcrap and double bullcrap, Major! I ought to throw you out of here on your impudent rear end!"

"I wouldn't be so hasty, if I were you, Mr. President. Don't forget, my weapons are formidable. I've shown you the proof, right here in these exhibits. And don't forget, they can be used against you as easily as they can be used to support you."

"No one threatens the President of the United States…"

"Well, I'm doing it, old man, make no mistake about that. Why, come to think of it, this must be a history-making occasion. At least that ought to brighten your day. Now, as to my demand, I feel it's quite reasonable. I certainly don't want to have to act outside the law while I'm straightening out the country, so you'll have to give me the powers I need. Naturally, when things have settled a bit, and the country is more secure, I'll step down, and we'll hold free elections. That's fair, isn't it?"

"Well, of all the … I … I've never seen … never imagined such incredible gall!" The President stood up, almost bumping his head on the ceiling. "I think I *will* throw you out. I think I'll throw you in jail!"

"Not so fast there, Mr. Pres." Farina was fully into his stride now. His early nervousness had vanished. But he hadn't won yet. "Not so darn fast. You don't think I'd be stupid enough to walk in here with nothing more to back me up than a bunch of graphs and numbers, do you? Oh, no. Throw me out, and you'll see some action."

"What kind of action, you demented popinjay?"

"Call it a show of force. Call it anything you want. If you can't cooperate, you can cross off the little town of Knob Lick, Kentucky, by this time tomorrow night. Cross it right off the map, that's all, because there won't be anything left of it but a glob of sludge by the time my men have finished with it. And that's just for starters. If anything happens to me, you're going to have little towns disappearing all over the country. Then larger ones. What will the people do then? What will you tell them? What will they believe, coming from you?"

291

George and Letitia sat through the entire exchange without saying a word. Only part of it made sense to Letitia, but she was vaguely aware that the outcome of the discussion could have a bearing on the fate of her uncle, even though only passing references had been made to him so far. Once her initial awe of the President and his office had faded, she had become intent on observing the performance of Major Farina—Tony—the man she adored. He appeared to be holding his own quite well, and that's what was most important to her. For all she cared at this moment they could have been discussing ticket prices at Disneyland instead of the immediate fate of the country. Soon the meeting would be over and she and Tony would be alone with each other again. And George of course.

George was frightened. He sat on the sofa with his head bowed, determined not to let either of the two stronger men look him in the eye, lest they should somehow hold him accountable for all the trouble they were discussing. He felt like a child who cowers in the corner when its parents quarrel.

The President looked angry for a while. Then his expression changed to one of weariness, and finally to a forced boredom. In this pose, he descended the ladder and stood in the center of the room.

"Major Farina, please come here," he said with a sigh.

Farina, believing he had beaten the President, felt himself flush with excitement and experienced a rare moment of self-consciousness. His heart beating rapidly, he drew himself up into his best military posture, and strode toward the President. He was prepared to accept the Chief Executive's surrender gracefully. Major Henry A. Farina might take over the United States, but he would not bring dishonor to the Commander-in-Chief.

In spite of his own erect posture, Major Farina discovered the President was a good six inches taller than he.

"Major Farina, our interview is ended," said the President.

This unexpected blow had its effect. Farina's mind reeled. Fighting for control of his leg muscles as the adrenalin raced through his body, he looked up into the President's impassive face and started to speak. The President cut him off.

"I have other matters to attend to this afternoon. Meetings with legitimately important people who may yet be able to help solve some of America's grievous problems. I believe you are a crackpot. I'm sorry to have to say that in Letitia's presence, but it's best I be frank. Please believe me, Tony, I sympathize with you. I can well understand that you and your men have been under an unbearable strain, having to watch the country you all love so dearly undergo the agonies of the recent weeks and being unable to lend a protective hand in her defense. Your offer to help, although misguided, is sincerely appreciated. I choose to believe your threats to me are only your emotions getting the best of you in the heat of the moment. You do have courage, young man. It took guts to come here today. I hadn't realized the morale of the Army was so low as a result of the government's policies, and I intend to speak to the Joint Chiefs about it in the morning. Meanwhile, I suggest … no, I order you to report to the Pentagon dispensary for a thorough physical examination, followed by a couple of weeks of complete rest and relaxation. In fact, I'll phone your commanding officer as soon as you leave and clear it for you."

"Mr. President," said Farina, incredulously, "Mr. President, you haven't heard a word I've said."

Farina had backed away from the President and was going to try again, but this time his voice lacked its earlier confidence. Sensing a change in the situation, even George was now looking up, directly at the two men. Letitia began to bite her squared fingernails, discreetly.

"You don't seem to realize," Farina continued, "that I am my own commanding officer. For that matter, I am yours also. I hold in my power the immediate future of this nation, and of the world. There is no point in patting me on the head and shooing me away like a naughty boy, because I won't go."

"Good day, Major Farina. And thank you for coming."

"Very well, if that's how it's to be," retorted Major Farina angrily. "But by tomorrow night, if not before, we'll see if you're still so anxious to dismiss me."

The President impatiently waved him to the door. Letitia joined him, with George in tow.

"To the Pentagon with you now, Tony. You must promise me."

"Nuts to you, old man!"

The President slowed the door before it slammed, and he peeked out, watching his three visitors until they got all the way down the hall and were gone. Then he closed the door, climbed back up to his desk, and began making phone calls.

CHAPTER TWENTY-SIX

Back at their hotel, Major Farina was on the phone too, speaking to his Operations Officer, Captain Sims-Wellington, who was in a phone booth in the lobby of the Washington affiliate station of one of the leading television networks. The lobby was full of reporters, milling around and talking excitedly. They had received word a press conference of major importance was about to be held. As yet, they didn't know who had called it. Major Farina was almost shouting.

"I said, it didn't work the way we planned it, Tom!"

"Sorry, sir," said the voice on the telephone, "there's a lot of noise here. You say it didn't work?"

"That's right."

"Well, what happened? Did he threaten you? How much trouble are we in?"

"Never mind. Is the press conference set?"

"Yes, sir. For fourteen hundred hours ... I mean two o'clock."

"Good. We're going to go through with it. But instead of the President announcing my succession to power, we're going to shift to 'Plan B' and give it all we've got."

"My God, Major, does that mean we're going to do the deed?"

"You bet your rear end it does! Knob Lick, here we come! I'll show that ignorant old son of a nut cake what's what! Nobody talks to Colonel Tony Farina that way!"

"Can't quite understand you, sir! The noise!"

"Forget it! You just alert the rest of the staff, and get the ball rolling at all the dumps. We're on the move. I'll be at the TV station in twenty minutes, so get those reporters ready for the story of the century."

CHAPTER TWENTY-SEVEN

It was bright and sunny off the Virginia coast that afternoon, and the Atlantic was calm. The Enemy submarine slid silently beneath the gentle waves and departed, leaving Dr. Lavager alone in an inflatable rubber dinghy with an electric trolling motor and a dead battery. He was thankful for his protective costume, although the galoshes were uncomfortable in the heat. He smoothed the front of his yellow paisley muumuu and adjusted his hat and sunglasses against the glare from the water. Alone on the ocean, with the sound of the water lapping at the sides of his boat, Dr. Lavager felt a twinge of fear. But then he remembered with relief that he was on his way home at last.

To the west he could barely make out the low profile of the coastline through the light haze that still hung over the land in spite of two weeks without gas-burning cars, trucks and buses. No ships were in sight; he could discern no proud Coast Guard vessel making its way toward his rescue. Well, it would take time for anyone to notice him, he thought. At least he had a good supply of bran flakes and skim milk, and there was as yet no sign of sharks. Besides, he seemed to be drifting westward toward land anyway.

He was tired. It had been a long day, starting with a Learjet ride to Casablanca after breakfast. From there a smaller plane had taken him to an aircraft carrier. Two hours from the carrier to the waiting submarine by helicopter, followed by a depressing underwater ride to this spot within the twelve-mile limit, and Dr. Lavager was almost exhausted. But it shouldn't be long now at all. He leaned over the side of the dinghy and let his hands dangle in the cool ocean water for a moment. Then he took them out, shook the water off vigorously, and, after holding them up to his nose for a second, dried them carefully on the front of his muumuu.

CHAPTER TWENTY-EIGHT

The reporters were all in their seats in the Washington TV studio. No one had yet told them what the press conference was about, and there was much loud griping. Rumor had it this was to be something big, so it was going to be covered by all the major networks, pooling the cost. Speculation ran high. Most believed it was to be the President with some sort of announcement about the harmful substance crisis or about Dr. Lavager. If so, they were going to be prepared for him this time, with straight, off-the-cuff hip shooting hard ball questions.

The minute hand of the large electric clock on the wall edged ever closer to 2:00 p.m., and a man in the uniform of an Army captain stepped from the wings of the studio stage. As a hush fell over the crowd he strode to the lectern and its cluster of microphones. He was followed by a squad of twelve soldiers in droopy, wrinkled fatigues. They spread out across the stage, flanking the captain, six on each side, and facing the audience. Each man carried a can of Mace on his pistol belt. They stood silently, grimly, legs spread apart and hands clasped behind them in the position of parade rest. They all wore aviator-style sunglasses. The silvery, reflective, arrogant kind.

The reporters sat stock still, not knowing what to make of this setup. This was going to be big all right. And if not big, then certainly different. They were glad they had come.

At exactly two o'clock, the "On the Air" sign flashed, and the cameras went into action. The captain spoke into the microphones, too close at first, so the distortion prevented anyone from understanding him. Realizing his error, he backed off and continued.

"… on such short notice. Please do not be alarmed by my men. They are here primarily for decoration, as we are sure everyone in the room today will conduct him- or herself properly. Nevertheless, what our speaker has to say may be considered by some to be, uh, new and unusual, and, uh, we do want to make sure everyone has a fair chance to ask questions."

"Can we get on with it, then?" called a voice from the back of the room.

The soldiers tensed.

"Of course," said the Captain, with aplomb. "Ladies and gentlemen, Major Henry A. Farina."

"Who?" called the voice.

The captain, pretending not to hear the heckler, stepped back from the microphones and stood in a welcoming posture facing stage left. Major Farina entered from stage right, clearing his throat as he strode toward the lectern. The captain whirled, trying to act as if it had been planned that way all along, and he and Farina shook hands. The captain retired to a group of folding chairs behind the lectern and joined Letitia and George, who had followed Farina on to the stage. They sat down. Letitia's jump suit was zipped all the way up.

Without giving the reporters any time to speculate or react, Major Farina began to talk.

"Thank you, Captain Sims-Wellington. Ladies and gentlemen, I am Major Henry A. Farina, commanding officer of the Mundane Ammunition Dump Command, United States Army…"

There were a few snickers at this but they were quickly silenced as Farina continued in a firm voice.

"I appreciate your coming here today, and I assure you that you will not find your time wasted. I have just come from a meeting with the President."

A few scattered gasps went up. What could such a thing mean?

"The President is in good health," he said, gratuitously, aware of the disquieting effect it would have. "Unfortunately, it was not a mutually satisfactory meeting, in spite of the President's cordiality. But before going into that, I would like to tell you of the Mundane Ammunition Dump Command and of its mission. Difficult as it may be to believe, it affects every one of you, and it's about to affect the rest of the world as well."

Having established his authority and importance by alluding to recent dealings with the President, Farina now told the eager assemblage the story of DEATHCOM and the years of underground preparation for the day when a meaningful peacekeeping deterrent could be placed before the Enemy.

The reporters struggled to assimilate this information, but aside from some murmuring, they remained quiet.

Captain Sims-Wellington smiled. Not even Major Farina knew the true status of the "selective stockpiling" efforts or just how ready the Command was to carry out the orders that might be given today.

George sat as close as possible to Letitia but wished he were somewhere else. He leaned forward, with his elbows on his knees, so as to appear casual and nonchalant. It made him stand out from his two companions, who were leaning back, smiling with confidence. Beneath her facade, Letitia was worried. She still hadn't heard anybody say anything about getting her uncle back. Tony Farina seemed to be getting more and more carried away with himself these past few hours. But, she realized, the pressures on him must be intense. She would have to be patient.

"I know many of you will find this incredible," Major Farina continued, "but I assure you every word I have told you is the truth. While America has been sleeping, her forgotten men in olive drab have not forgotten her. Now, once again, this nation has a viable defense apparatus against a despicable Enemy, and your Army stands ready."

Now a louder murmuring rose from the audience. Several reporters were on their feet, waving their hands to be recognized for questions. The soldiers tensed again.

"Please, gentlemen, there will be time for questions in a moment, when I have finished.

"Now then, as I mentioned at the beginning, I have just come from the White House. The purpose of my meeting with the

President was to inform him of the successful completion of our secret mission. Yes, it was kept secret even from our Commander-in-Chief, in order that his position not be compromised in the event the Enemy learned of our plans prematurely.

"I carefully informed the President of our state of readiness. And, my friends, I can tell you we have reached this state of readiness in the nick of time. Our society is crumbling around us, even as I speak to you this afternoon. The people have taken to the streets to protest the anti-harmful-substance laws. They are confused over the Administration's handling of the Lavager affair. They no longer trust their elected leaders, and they are angry. Very angry. The Enemy sees this, too. And the Enemy waits hungrily at our gates because he knows his opportunity to devour our nation is near. My friends, America is ripe for a takeover. Even if such a takeover is delayed, our nation will rot from within if no one steps forward now to provide the leadership and protection America so desperately needs for survival.

"The President and I have talked of these things."

Now the reporters were silent again, hushed by the credibility Major Farina's tone and choice of words had lent to the fantastic story he was telling.

"Yes, we discussed these problems, and we discussed solutions. Ladies and gentlemen, it was my privilege to offer to the President one of these solutions … a solution so simple in concept as to be almost too easy for men of such vision as the President and myself to overlook ... a solution which deals, in one fell swoop, with the civil crisis and the Enemy threat. I offered the President the services of my command, DEATHCOM.

"I have already explained to you how DEATHCOM will function as a deterrent to Enemy aggression. Our arsenal of harmful substance weaponry is unique in all the world. As for the domestic turmoil, the solution is twofold: First, we restore law and order by means of these same weapons. And I hasten to add, not by using them. Rather, merely by having them, as a deterrent threat. Of course, the crisis is of such proportions it's possible we might have to use some of these weapons, carefully and very selectively, as a show of force, just to prove we are serious. But it would be for a brief transitional period, I assure you. And, once having restored calm to our great land, a moratorium would be declared on the harmful substance laws. We would see to it that, temporarily at least, limited amounts of the outlawed substances and practices would be dispensed. Just enough to keep everyone calm during recovery and reconstruction."

"Reconstruction from what?" It was the heckler again.

"Just a figure of speech," answered Farina.

"What about Dr. Lavager?" asked another reporter.

"Of course, of course," said Farina. "One of the first things we must do, obviously, is to get to the bottom of this Lavager mess. I wish I could tell you more about that, but that is one subject on which I am not yet well informed. It would definitely be one of our top priorities. Now, please, again, no questions yet."

Letitia was somewhat relieved. At least her uncle hadn't been forgotten. The reporters, though, were anything but relieved. In a moment there would be no containing them. Hands waved from all parts of the room. Voices shouted, "Major Farina!" Farina held up his arms and gestured for silence. Unnoticed in the clamor, Captain Sims-Wellington had moved from one soldier to the next, whispering instructions as he went. At some unspoken command, they slowly assumed the position of attention.

"Please, ladies and gentlemen," said Farina firmly above the din, "I am nearing the conclusion of my prepared remarks. There will be time for all your questions."

The crowd quieted, reluctantly.

"Thank you," said Farina. "Now, obviously, the first step in effecting such a solution is often the most difficult. At least the President found it so. Unfortunately, my friends, the President saw fit to decline my offer. It is now clear the people's distrust of our leader is well founded."

The reporters gasped.

"Yes. Yes, it seems the President places himself above the welfare of the people of the nation he was elected to serve. The first step in the simple solution I have described would have been for the President to step down in favor of a leader whom the people could trust. That leader would of course be the man who commands the forces of America's defense. And that man is Major Henry A. Farina!"

Pandemonium erupted. Chairs were overturned. People jumped up and down, shouting questions, shouting at each other, standing on chairs from which to see better without getting injured. Spotlights were broken, flashbulbs flashed, a TV camera fell to the floor with a resounding crash. Farina, too, began shouting, trying to maintain order and continue his talk. He grabbed one of the microphones in his right hand as his left hand waved futilely in the air. With the microphone practically in his throat, his distorted last words could barely be understood over the noise of the crowd.

"It would only be temporary! I told the President that, but he wouldn't listen to me!"

"Where did you come from, Farina?" shouted an angry voice in the crowd.

"Yeah, what rock did you crawl out from under?" yelled another.

"We'd hold free elections as soon as possible," countered Farina, desperately.

"Sure we would!!" came a chorus of voices. "You're a crackpot!"

"Go back where you came from, Farina!"

"Take your Army buddies with you!"

"Very well, you ingrates!" bellowed Farina, backing away from the lectern as he felt himself being showered with loose change and ball point pens thrown from the crowd, "I'll take this to the people!"

This was greeted with boos from all corners of the studio. The crowd began to advance toward the stage. The soldiers fingered their Mace cans nervously.

"Hear me! Hear me well!" continued Farina, backing farther away. "I'm giving the order for a show of force. You hear me, Captain Sims-Wellington?"

"Yes, sir!" shouted Sims.

"There, did you hear that, you idiots?" Farina was livid. "I've given the order! Now you'll see we mean business!"

Farina, Sims, Letitia, and George barely had time to escape through the back door of the studio before the reporters, joined by the TV technicians, bounded up on the stage, screaming for blood. The soldiers stood their ground bravely, spraying Mace in all directions until they were overpowered by the sheer numbers and ferocity of the angry mob. Farina and his party jumped aboard the steam bus Sims had rented to transport the soldiers to the studio. SP4 Jenkins drove, and they sped off toward a pre-arranged rendezvous with a communications platoon secreted in an out-of-the-way area of Washington's Rock Creek Park. They were not followed.

Farina muttered to himself during the whole trip, as Letitia tried to soothe him by rubbing his back gently.

George looked wide-eyed out the window, taking in the Washington sights.

"Nutty fools," muttered Farina. "Pitiful, stupid, ungrateful fools!"

"Tony…" cooed Letitia.

"We'll show them," said Farina. "We'll show them what's what. You hear that, Tom?"

"Yes, sir," said Sims.

"Forget about Knob Lick! We're going after the big stuff!"

"No choice, sir!" He grinned to himself. He knew what was really in the arsenal. The Major would be so pleased. Still a few months until his commanding officer's birthday, but it would be a great surprise present anyway.

"Right. When we get to the communications center I want you to put out the order. We're going to throw everything we've got into this. We're going to attack every major city in America tonight. Every single one. By this time tomorrow, those screw-offs back there will know who's boss, or I'm not Brigadier General Henry A. Farina!"

"Yes, sir!" shouted Captain Sims enthusiastically. That would make Sims at least a colonel.

"In the end, the people will be on our side. They're not so dumb."

Farina had unbuttoned his jacket and was perspiring profusely. Letitia continued her ministrations. Absentmindedly, she hummed the "Cloudburst" movement. It was a prophetic selection.

When the steam bus with Farina and his retinue arrived at

the secluded location of the communications platoon, he strode into the tent, followed by Sims, Letitia, and George. Soon after, the fateful order went out to all the ammunition dumps scattered throughout the country: The attack would be tonight. One by one, as Farina listened, the dumps reported in to Captain Sims.

All was in readiness. It would go as planned. Major Farina was pleased as he surveyed the scene around him. He took Letitia's hand, tenderly, and led her outside the tent, pausing to pick up two cans of C-Rations on the way. It was time to relax. Slowly, they strode into the woods together.

George stayed in the tent, fascinated by the complicated radio apparatus the soldiers were operating.

CHAPTER TWENTY-NINE

The President was not relaxing. Since his early afternoon meeting with Major Farina, he had been busy making arrangements of his own. Except for a hasty cup of Honduran coffee now and then, sometimes taken with a Danish slathered in butter from the dwindling supply in the White House kitchen, he had paused in his hectic affairs only long enough to watch Farina's press conference on TV. Since the press conference, the White House switchboard had been overloaded, and the President had had to use emergency circuits in order to complete his business. A large crowd had gathered outside on Pennsylvania Avenue, and reporters were practically tearing down the wrought iron fence around the Executive Mansion in their efforts to speak to the President.

But there would be no statement from the White House tonight. Anything but silence might tip the President's hand and jeopardize his plans to counteract whatever Farina's people tried to do. By Presidential order, authorities were now preparing to close in on each and every Army ammunition dump in the country. The President had brought into action every law enforcement agency under his direct or indirect authority for the task. After some arm-twisting of state governors, National Guard units were called up. State and local police were ordered to report to staging areas near each dump. Near Omaha, after countless nights of lying in the fields surrounding Camp Shafto, avoiding contact, the FBI and CIA were mobilized.

The Teamsters, the AFL-CIO, UAW, IBEW, and other observers, including the homeless, were not mobilized, only mystified.

Almost everyone was ready now for the President's order to advance upon the dumps. The only disappointing performance so far, the President noted, was that of the Coast Guard, half of whose personnel had unprecedentedly called in sick when notified of the maneuvers.

Since the President had no way of knowing when, where, and how Farina would strike, and since the President's forces had no weapons or ammunition to speak of, the success of his defense would be nip and tuck. He could only hope the Enemy wasn't in a position to take advantage of the situation. As for Peru and Honduras, he wasn't counting on them except in the event of an overt Enemy attack. Even then, he wasn't sure how much help they would be.

The Farina press conference was seen by almost everyone in the country. In the absence of any information from the White House, 200 million Americans old enough to read and watch television— those not directly involved in the President's defense plans or under Farina's command—were in a complete panic. This time, all rhetoric notwithstanding, the very life of the United States of America, and possibly of the free world, hung in the balance. Neither Major Farina nor the President knew of the other's precise plans. The odds would be on the side of whoever acted first.

CHAPTER THIRTY

At seven minutes past 11:00 p.m., Eastern Time, it happened.

Dr. Lavager was washing his hands in the ocean again when he looked up, startled, thinking at first it was lightning from an approaching storm. He cursed his luck, to be caught out in the middle of the ocean in a small boat in the path of a storm with no more rain gear than a pair of galoshes and no Coast Guard rescue vessel in sight. As he hastily dried his hands on his muumuu, he saw the flashing light again … only this time there could be no mistake. It was most certainly not lightning. Lightning is yellowish. The lights Lavager saw were red, white, and blue. Their greatest intensity seemed to be in the area where he guessed Washington, D.C., to be, over the coast a few miles west of his position. Fainter red, white, and blue glimmerings could also be seen to the north of the brightest lights, perhaps over Philadelphia. He thought he could also discern the same kind of lights to the south, where Norfolk might be. Then the sounds reached him too. It was the noise of bombs bursting in the distance. There were hundreds of dull concussions, like those at a fireworks display.

By now, he was completely bewildered. Stroking his goatee did not help. There was no conceivable explanation for what he was witnessing. However, two things were clear. The phenomenon was not a natural one. It was manmade. As such,

315

it was probably harmful. He sat back and thought about what he was going to tell the President as soon as he got ashore. Something simply had to be done about this shameful deterioration of environmental conditions.

CHAPTER THIRTY-ONE

Back in Rock Creek Park, protected from the effects, if not the sights and sounds of the mayhem around him, Major Farina sat in his rented steam bus and stared out the windows, viewing his handiwork. Although it was almost midnight, it seemed more like noon … a hellish, surrealistic noon.

Strains of "The Star Spangled Banner" ran through Farina's head. Bombs bursting in air, the rockets' red (and white and blue) glare as o'er the ramparts we watched. He didn't know exactly what a rampart was, but as a vantage point, the bus was good enough. Outside, soldiers whose duties required them to be in the open dashed about in crouched, head-down postures. The rapid staccato of the bomb blasts and the intermittent flashes of brilliant light had a stroboscopic effect so that the men seemed like so many tripped-out disco dancers as they ran in and out of the communications tent. Once in a while, a particularly loud concussion could be felt as a bomb exploded nearby, rocking the bus on its pneumatic springs. Farina's lips formed unuttered expletives when this occurred, but he sat still.

SP4 Jenkins cowered in the on-board restroom with the door closed.

Letitia was also on the bus, and she was frightened. She huddled on the floor in the aisle next to Farina's seat, looking up at him beseechingly. He made no move to comfort her, so wrapped up was he in his own thoughts. George sat transfixed and wide-eyed in the back of the bus. His expression was that of a child scared stiff by his first ride through the fun house at an amusement park.

Major Farina had to admit that logistically his attack was extremely successful. Working with the efficiency that comes from dedication to duty, intense loyalty to their commanding officer, and years of preparation and training, the men of the Mundane Ammunition Dump Command were carrying out their orders to perfection. From Maine to Miami, Philadelphia to San Francisco, and Chicago to San Diego, the dumps were unleashing the full fury of their harmful substance arsenal on every American city of any consequence. Farina's decision to bypass the show of force approach and go straight for the President's jugular was being carried out with a vengeance matched in spirit by what was in Farina's own heart when the fateful order was given but unmatched in sheer physical intensity by any manmade cataclysm since Hiroshima.

Impressive as the pyrotechnics were, surprised and debilitated as the President's forces must be at this moment, it was still a hollow victory for Farina. As he stared out the bus window, his expression now a mixture of disbelief and dejection, the loneliness of command became much more than a Hollywood cliché. No one could help him now as he sat watching, powerless to reverse events, while his hand was being played out, everywhere, all at once. Not even his loyal staff could rectify this situation, one that they themselves, in their overzealous love for their commander, had created. "Selective stockpiling," they had called it.

But they had lied.

Tonight there were no nicotine bombs, no polluting gasoline additives, no insecticides, no cardilinis artichokes, no harmful rays, no concentrated doses of hexachlorophene, and no deadly microorganisms in the water supply. In fact, there was no variety or diversity of harmful substances at all. Only one. One harmful substance secretly stockpiled by the DEATHCOM staff—stockpiled as a birthday tribute to Major Farina, and chosen for its special historical military significance.

Where had he gone wrong? Where had he lost control? And how long ago? Yes, he thought ruefully, he should have tried to overcome his fear of caves at the very beginning. He should have made personal inspections of the underground development labs and storage centers back at Camp Shafto and at other dumps. If only he'd had some idea it was this substance they were stockpiling to the exclusion of almost all others.

Some birthday surprise. And with his thirtieth birthday still months away. But there it was. As long as he lived, Farina wouldn't forget the almost worshipful expression on Captain Sims-Wellington's face as the eager operations officer announced to his commander what weapon had been chosen for their private birthday Armageddon, what harmful substance of immense symbolic significance now rained down on most of the 3.7 million contiguous square miles of the continental United States of America. Thousands of rockets launched from underground silos carried the substance aloft, exploded it in multicolored patterns, and broadcast it in the air to sift down slowly and cover all it touched. Countless formations of borrowed Air Force bombers blotted out the moonlight in their flight as they dropped their payloads, in torpedo-shaped plastic bags with explosive devices set to go off at low altitude. Hundreds of crack DEATHCOM saboteurs stacked crates of the substance on the roofs of the largest buildings in the smaller towns, and then set off charges under them. DEATHCOM frogmen placed giant gelatin bags of it in rivers, bays, and harbors.

Now a tear, the first he had felt on his own face since childhood, trickled down Tony Farina's right cheek. It was finished. The hopes and dreams of a lifetime dashed. The only perfectly executed *coup d'état* ever to be attempted in the history of the United States, thwarted. And all of it done in by good intentions. The years of training, the development work, the delicate espionage, the stockpiling, the status reports, the tremendous personal sacrifice and risk for all involved. And now, when the ultimate order was given, when the might and right that was MADCOM/DEATHCOM rose up to consummate its mission, while opposing forces were closing in all around, Major Farina's men, with bravery and courage to the fore and no thoughts of personal safety, proudly released their arsenal:

Five hundred million tons of red, white and blue starch bombs.

CHAPTER THIRTY-TWO

"It's good to see you again, Gardy," said Dr. Baldwin warmly.

"Thanks, Ted. I can hardly believe I'm back."

The two men shook hands and started walking toward the remains of Dr. Lavager's laboratory building.

"Cigarette?" asked Dr. Baldwin, extending a pack.

"Don't mind if I do."

They paused and lit up.

"I must say, you're not looking too much the worse for wear, considering what you've been through," remarked Dr. Baldwin.

"Nice of you to say so, but truthfully I'd probably look better if I hadn't had those four Bloody Marys on the plane," said Lavager. "You're looking good yourself."

This was a white lie, and Dr. Baldwin knew it, but it made him feel good anyway. The older man had aged in the past few months. He guessed it had started the day Dr. Lavager disappeared. His world seemed to fall apart after that. Between his worry about the safety of the university, his concern over the whereabouts and welfare of his friend, and the vague feeling he was systematically being left out of things, it had been rough on him. Now, at least, most of those worries had been resolved. True, the university had been partially destroyed by angry mobs during the anti-Administration demonstrations that followed Lavager's disappearance. Yes, he had indeed been excluded from the President's confidence during the last climactic weeks leading up to the starch bomb attack and the subsequent takeover of the United States by troops from Peru and Honduras. These events were hard on him, to be sure, but at least he didn't have to worry about them anymore. And Lavager was back safely, apparently unharmed.

In contrast to the aging administrator's conservative, five-years-out-of-style business suit, Lavager's dress was casual. He wore a blue knit golf shirt with an alligator logo and peach-colored slacks that flared at the bottom. Designer sunglasses hung from the open neck of his shirt, a souvenir of his encounter with Le Grand Malfaiteur. His black goatee, now salted with a touch of gray, was unkempt, and he needed a haircut. But he still wore his galoshes. "I never wore shoes in them," he had explained with some embarrassment when Dr. Baldwin met his taxi in front of the Struthers Memorial Bell Tower, "and they messed my feet up so bad that now I can't find a pair of shoes that fit."

The campus of Leland F. P. Mason Wesley, Jr., University seemed almost deserted. A few classes were in session in the least-damaged buildings, and here and there an instructor could be seen conducting an outdoor seminar. A few of them stroked goatees absently as they taught. The aroma of marijuana was everywhere. Once in a while a car went by, belching fumes, and just as the two men reached the crumbling wall surrounding the laboratory building a motorcycle gang roared up, their highly polished Nazi-style helmets reflecting the hazy sunlight. A Peruvian soldier on the corner waved cheerily at the bikers. The bikers waved back and continued on their way.

Like many other buildings on the campus, the lab was a shambles. The broken garden wall was overgrown with poison ivy. Although the dense concrete walls of the building itself had withstood the fury of the mobs and their incendiaries, they were covered with obscene graffiti. The bushes and trees were trampled and dying, the lawn was cratered and plowed up, and the front door was off its hinges. Wordlessly, the two men entered the building. The dark corridor echoed with the sound of broken glass being crushed underfoot.

The room that had been Dr. Lavager's office had no door at all, and the inside was black from the fire that had destroyed its contents. Dr. Lavager saw the charred remains of his desk and the filing cabinets. The records and memorabilia of a brilliant career in eco-toxicology had gone up in smoke. Lavager paused briefly at this pyre, sighed, and moved on.

Miraculously, the mob had turned back for some reason before it got to the laboratory itself. With a thin smile, Dr. Baldwin opened the door and made an "after you" gesture. Lavager took a last look back down the empty corridor and then stepped into the lab.

George saw them come in but didn't get up. Instead, he continued to stare at a newspaper that was open in front of him on the big composition-top table.

"He's like a zombie," whispered Dr. Baldwin. "He hardly ever speaks. I don't know how he managed to make his way back here from Washington in that condition, but he just showed up one day."

"Is he dangerous or anything?" asked Lavager, also in a low voice.

"I don't think so, poor fellow. He sits there, day after day, poring over the newspapers, once in a while clipping out an article on harmful substances for me to read, as if he were trying to relive the old days before you left."

"Is anyone treating him? A psychiatrist?"

"I'm afraid not. Those guys are booked solid into the next decade right now, and I can't claim George is an emergency case. I do think he's getting worse, though. Lately, when he's finished going through the paper, I've seen him chewing on parts of the sports pages."

"Ugh!" said Lavager compassionately.

"I suppose it has something to do with Letitia being taken out of his life so abruptly," said Dr. Baldwin softly, not looking directly at his friend.

"You're probably right, Ted. The President ... I mean the ex-President ... filled me in on a lot of things while I was in Washington. He told me all about this Major Farina fellow and how afterwards he and ... he and Letitia ... escaped to some small town in Kentucky and then vanished altogether for a while."

"I'm very sorry, Gardy," whispered Dr. Baldwin. "This must be awfully hard on you."

"No, it's all right, Ted. I've had time to … adjust. I guess you know by now Farina surfaced in Tegucigalpa a few days ago, along with Letitia. He's a national hero in Honduras and literally the poster boy for their military recruiting."

"Really?"

"Yes, and the ex-President even showed me the poster. It shows Farina striking a defiant pose in a black leather flight jacket covered in medals with the wind in his hair and a silk flying scarf streaming behind him like he was the Red Baron or something and shouting the word '*Nueces!*' to an adoring crowd."

"'*Nueces*'?"

"Yeah. It means 'nuts' in Spanish."

"What do you suppose that's about?"

"I have no idea," said Lavager with a shrug. "For all I know it's a subconscious self-diagnosis."

"That would make sense. There's a screw loose somewhere for sure."

"Anyway, Lima is reportedly not a little upset, but the papers say Farina has promised to spend equal time in Peru."

"So at least you know Letitia's okay. That must be some comfort."

"Yes," Lavager admitted, "and I must say, I don't miss 'The Grand Canyon Suite' very much."

Oblivious, Baldwin moved on. "But you know, Gardy, I'll never understand why, with all those logistics and weapons going for him, not to mention the element of surprise, why Major Farina's coup didn't succeed."

"Oh, everybody was plenty surprised, all right, including the President, although he says he knew there was going to be an attack of some kind," Lavager explained. "In fact, technically Farina did succeed even if he didn't become king of the world as he'd apparently hoped. It's just that with all that starch everybody was stiff as a board and hardly noticed when Farina tried to announce he was taking over. Nobody could move for about a week, and that gave Peru and Honduras time to make good on their mutual defense agreement, although it was in a way the President hadn't counted on."

"I remember the stiffness all right," said Dr. Baldwin, "and then those soldiers appearing out of nowhere one day, wearing strange uniforms and giving orders in Spanish. I hear Lima and Tegucigalpa have signed a mutual defense treaty with the Eastern Bloc now, too."

"That's right, but I'm optimistic."

"No choice, really."

"Don't you just love saying that?" asked Lavager

"Saying what?"

"You know … 'Tegucigalpa.'"

"I really hadn't thought about it."

"Tegucigalpa."

"Stop it."

"Okay. Say, it's dark in here. Tomorrow let's get rid of these ridiculous ultraviolet filters."

"Which reminds me," said Baldwin, "the darter snail thing turned out to be a hoax."

"I wondered about that."

"It was just a student applying for a government grant, intending to use the money to get a Ph.D. in philosophy. He leaked it to an overzealous reporter who made up the landfill story, and the media ran with it."

"I assume he got the grant," said Lavager.

"Oh yes. Now he's teaching a class on situational ethics right here at the university."

"He's obviously an expert."

"I can't fire him; the class is quite popular."

Lavager stubbed his cigarette out in one of the sinks and crossed over to his old armchair, the point from which his errant journey had begun so many weeks before. There was a small package on it, addressed to Letitia. "Well, what do you know?" he mused.

"What is it?" asked Dr. Baldwin.

"It's from Chock Full o' Nuts," said Lavager as he unwrapped the package and held up a handful of skimpy dull white paper napkins.

"Better not let George see those," warned Dr. Baldwin.

Lavager tossed the package into the storage closet where it

broke open, scattering napkins across the floor. "Oops! Oh well, I can clean it up later."

"What about the rest of Farina's henchmen?" asked Baldwin. "Have they all been rounded up?"

"They didn't have to be, according to the ex-President," said Dr. Lavager.

"You mean they turned themselves in?"

"No, it seems Farina, right before he took off for Kentucky and while everybody was still starched up, acted like he'd won a great victory. He threw a big pizza party for his staff. Everybody ate too much and got drunk as skunks, and by the next morning they were all sick as dogs, except Farina, Letitia, and George. It turned out to be poisonous mushrooms on the pizzas. Fortunately, they all got aggressive medical treatment and recovered in a few days, but it was very suspicious, the whole business. It looked like Farina had planned it as a diversion to cover his tracks while he escaped with Letitia. The President was going to have his whole staff arrested, but then he figured what was the point? Nobody knew what to charge them with, and they'd all been acting under Farina's orders anyway. And Farina's patron generals apparently slunk off to their homes in McLean, Virginia, and haven't been heard from."

"How was your trip in from the airport? Much traffic?"

"It was horrendous. Just like the old days. And the smog. But I have to admit I kind of missed it."

"So all the harmless substance laws have been repealed, then?" asked Baldwin.

"Well, no, Congress has been in recess since the attack. The Attorney General just quietly put the word out that the laws wouldn't be enforced. Saved the President from having to issue an Executive Order. Not that anybody was observing them anyway, apparently."

"Apparently."

"And all those Peruvian and Honduran soldiers? Well, technically they're illegal aliens, but the ex-President says we're going to ignore that too because someday they'll all be voters."

"Seems only fair."

As Lavager prepared to sit down, he noticed two more pieces of mail on his chair. The package of napkins had covered them.

"And what do you suppose these are?" he asked Dr. Baldwin.

"They were addressed to George," explained Dr. Baldwin. "I took the liberty of opening them. One's a BankAmericard bill for expenses George and Letitia ran up on their trip to Farina's Army base. We all thought that's where you were, and they went off to rescue you. The other is a bill for two bicycles George and Letitia rented and never returned. I don't know what I'm going to do with bills like that. University funds are already exhausted. Alumni contributions have fallen way off, as you can imagine. And the FBI claims they never heard of the Lavager kidnap case, so I can't expect any help from the government."

"I'll take care of it somehow," said Lavager with a sigh.

"Speaking of Farina's Army base, I heard Wong Lee took a pretty bad beating from Letitia back there when she found out he'd been helping my kidnappers."

"Yes, she almost killed him, but I called the hospital in Omaha the other day and they told me he's out of his coma and will survive, although maybe not as the Wong Lee we knew. The doctors say he's taking solid food and talking, asking for a harmonica of all things, and that he now speaks perfect English. He recites random lines from 'Jabberwocky' to the nurses. They can't explain it. I still feel sorry for him, but I can't afford to give him his old job back."

"Well, let's hope he finds something."

George continued to scan the newspaper. Lavager reached into his shirt pocket and took out a fat cigar which he unwrapped and lit, momentarily obscuring his upper body and head from Dr. Baldwin's view in a cloud of dense, blue-gray smoke.

"Gardy, you still haven't told me how you got back into the country."

"Ha, well, that's a story in itself. I told you on the phone about Le Grand Malfaiteur and about getting into the crippled boat from the submarine and being left for the Coast Guard…"

"Right."

"Well, I never saw the Coast Guard, that's for sure. I watched the Great Starch Bomb War on my first night at sea, and then nothing happened for about a week. If I never see bran flakes and skim milk again, it'll be too soon, believe me!"

"What finally happened?"

"There I was, off the coast of Virginia waiting for the Coast Guard, and then suddenly I was captured by a Cuban patrol boat and detained on charges of fishing within Cuban territorial waters. With my little dinghy in tow, the Cuban boat chugged around in circles for a few hours while the captain talked to Havana about me on his radio. Havana must have remembered my connection to Le Grand Malfaiteur because after that it was all smiles and apologies, but just as they were about to let me go, this big gunboat full of Peruvian sailors steamed up, and we were all arrested for fishing in Peruvian territorial waters. The Peruvians took us to Norfolk, and I was escorted to Washington after a week of interrogation, all in Spanish, of course, which I don't speak."

"Funny, I thought you spoke a little Spanish," said Baldwin. "I mean, besides *nueces* and Tegucigalpa."

"Well, I did pick up a few words while I was in Havana after the hijacking, but before that it was pretty much limited to *Si, Cómo estás?*, and *¿Es una mala sustancia?*"

"That's a lot better than I could do. But anyway, how is the ex-President, Gardy? He never calls, you know."

"Still the dedicated public servant. I've got a lot of respect for that man. He told me how he faced Farina down when the major attempted to blackmail him. He had the law enforcement agencies and the Coast Guard poised and ready to apprehend Farina's people at the first sign of an attack. They were prepared for almost any kind of weapon except starch, I guess. You know the rest. I understand the Peruvians and Hondurans have taken over the White House, and they're paying the ex-President to stay on as an advisor until, as they put it, 'the country is ready to hold free elections again.' He and the ex-First Lady have a room at the Howard Johnson in Georgetown, which they're also paying for."

"Such a pity."

"Hmm." Silently, idly, Lavager wondered what Le Grand Malfaiteur thought of the way things had turned out. A sort of Pyrrhic victory for his cause, probably, but one he may or may not have survived.

They sat in silence for a few moments, having temporarily run out of things to talk about. George turned a page of the newspaper. He made a low sound which might have been a belch, but said nothing.

CHAPTER THIRTY-THREE

There were other loose ends to tie up, of course, but somehow most of them didn't seem to matter much after all that had happened. Dr. Lavager and Dr. Baldwin found themselves in a world gone mad, leaving both of the academics feeling rudderless and adrift.

Their institutions had been demolished. Their country had rejected their services. Events were no longer within their control. Worst of all, they were unemployed, or the next thing to it. For Lavager there was only the memory of a defunct American Eco-Toxicology Association, all of whose members had quietly renounced their affiliation with it. For Dr. Baldwin there was only a bankrupt university he would probably have to try to sell to the State of California on behalf of the trustees, most of whom now behaved as if they had never heard of it. Worse than that, the former statesman would no longer be an advisor to governments and a confidant of powerful political leaders.

Yet, for the living, it is said, there is always hope. As the two men sat brooding, each lost in his own thoughts, with an occasional rustling of newsprint heard from George's table, a forgotten, but familiar, sound began to fill the room. Loud, yet delicate, clear and pure, it penetrated the concrete walls of the lab building. Its vibrations filled the corridor and spilled in waves into the lab, reverberating between the greenboard and the cinderblock walls. It was an inspiring sound, an oasis of clarity in a wasted atmosphere of smog.

Lavager was the first to react. He stood up and went to the door. He filled his lungs and looked down the corridor, allowing himself to be enveloped by the wonderful sound. Even George looked up.

"It's the bells, Ted!" exclaimed Lavager, still looking down the hall. "The old chimes in the Struthers Memorial Bell Tower!"

"Yes," said Dr. Baldwin, also standing now. "The rioters climbed up and knocked the glass out of the belfry."

"I'd forgotten how beautiful and moving that sound could be," said Lavager softly.

"The suicides are back, of course, but..." Dr. Baldwin shrugged his shoulders.

Together, Dr. Lavager and Dr. Baldwin walked slowly through the corridor and out the door into the yellowish daylight. They stood facing the direction of the chimes, although the bell tower itself couldn't be seen through the haze.

"You know, Ted," said Lavager, turning to his friend, "when I was in Washington I had a chance to talk to the leaders of the junta. They said they were very impressed with my work."

"That's nice. But are you sure they weren't just talking about what Major Farina had done with it? That's really about all they saw, I would imagine."

"Yes, but I don't think it matters much. The point is, I think if I play my cards right and come up with a research project that will interest them, they'll give me a grant. I hope so anyway."

"Congratulations."

"Well, I haven't received it yet, but I've been working on the idea," said Lavager.

"What areas do you think will interest them?" asked Dr. Baldwin.

"Hard to say for sure, of course. But I did notice they all seemed appalled by the relatively small amount of coffee the average American drinks as compared to their countrymen, and also by how much of our coffee comes from Brazil and Colombia. That's not good for their pocketbooks in Peru and Honduras, you know. I think I can help them rectify that situation."

Dr. Baldwin said nothing. After another moment, the two men started walking slowly in the general direction of the bell tower. Lavager's sunglasses remained in his shirt. The chimes continued their sonorous concert in the still afternoon air.

"Naturally, that's not the only idea I've been working on," confided Lavager as they strolled along. "Of course, I realize I'll be starting from the beginning on a whole new career, and it'll be hard work. But I think it'll be worth it."

"Well, there's one thing I've observed over the years, Gardy," said Dr. Baldwin, "and that is there's money to be made by a man who's not afraid to get his hands dirty."

"Right. Now, whaddaya say we go find a bar!"

"That sounds good to me, although I hope you won't mind if I stick to cranberry juice."

"Whatever floats your boat, Ted. You only live once."

"Okay then how about this?"

"How about what?"

"Tegucigalpa."

Back in the laboratory, George wandered into the storage closet.

He noticed the paper napkins and bent over to pick one up.

The End
* * *

If you have enjoyed this book, please consider leaving a review for Walt on Amazon, Goodreads or at the Fantastic Books Store to let him know what you thought of his work.

You can find out more about Walt below and on his author page on the Fantastic Books Store. While you're there, why not browse Walt's other works and the rest of our literary offering?

www.FantasticBooksStore.com

Also by Walt Pilcher

On Shallowed Ground, including Dr. Barker's Scientific Metamorphical Prostate Health Formula® and other Stories, Poems, Comedy and Dark Matter from the Center of the Universe (Fantastic Books Publishing)

The Fivefold-Effect: Unlocking Power Leadership for Amazing Results in Your Organization (WestBow Press)

About the Author

 **Walt Pilcher's** comedy writing career coincides with a business writing career of over 30 years, during which it was often impossible to tell them apart. He retired from the latter as a former CEO of two major apparel companies in the U.S. and one in Japan, although not at the same time, having lived in Tokyo for 14 months during which two comedians were elected as governors of Japan's biggest cities. He holds a BA from Wesleyan University and an MBA from Stanford University, is a former Regent University trustee, currently serves on the boards of two Christian non-profit organizations, and enjoys an occasional adult harmful substance.

He is the author of *On Shallowed Ground, including Dr. Barker's Scientific Metamorphical Prostate Health Formula* and *other Stories, Poems, Comedy and Dark Matter from the Center of the Universe*, published by Fantastic Books Publishing. His writing CV includes the first issue of *Galileo*; *The Worm Runner's Digest*; the *Fire & Chocolate* poetry anthology of Writers' Group of the Triad; *Fresh, Ancient Paths*, and *O.Henry* magazines; and the *Fusion* and *Ours* sci-fi and poetry anthologies from Fantastic Books. His business leadership book, *The Five-fold Effect: Unlocking Power Leadership for Amazing Results in Your Organization* (WestBow Press), was a First Horizon Award finalist in the 2015 Eric Hoffer Book competition.

Walt lives in Greensboro, NC (USA), with his wife, Carol, a darn good artist.

CPSIA information can be obtained
at www.ICGtesting.com
Printed in the USA
BVOW09s0839201217
503310BV00014B/343/P